THE

ORDER

BIRDY BROWNE

Published 2023

ISBN Number: 979-8-9890055-1-2

THE
ORDER

1

Walking into class, the minute my foot crossed the threshold of the door, I knew something was off. My eyes lined up with the second column of desks from the wall, third row seat.

A boy with shaggy hair, dyed an obscenely teal color, sat at my desk, idly drawing in a notebook.

I stood there a second, considering what to do. That was my seat, I'd picked it out the first day of classes. This was college, not elementary school. People didn't steal seats. It was an unspoken college rule—the seat you sit in the first day, that's your seat for the rest of the semester, unless you miss the first day of classes.

Realizing I was blocking the doorway, I shuffled over to the only seat I knew wasn't taken, the one against the wall in the last row. I set my notebook on my desk and my backpack on the floor beside my chair, then settled my chin in my hand to stare at the seat stealer.

He kept his head low. Not like he knew I was staring at him, but like he didn't want anyone in the room to notice him.

That's when I realized it. I should have realized it the minute I saw him, with that obscene hair. This kid was new, or at least new in the class. Two months into the fall semester, and he'd just now shown up.

He couldn't have just transferred in. But he also couldn't have missed a Tuesday-Thursday class for two months.

My eyes shifted as the professor dimmed the lights to start her PowerPoint on some new part of biology.

Joy.

After an hour and fifteen minutes listening to yet another dry lecture, I was more than ready to get out of the classroom. The minute our professor gave us the okay to leave, I swept up my belongings, not even bothering to put them in my backpack. It wasn't until I was already out the building, on my way to a section of tables outside to sit and do some homework, that I remembered the blue-haired boy.

I groaned internally. It was way too late to turn around and hope to find him. Of course, what was I going to do? Walk up to him and ask him why he'd just now started coming to class? Or better yet just follow him around campus and hope to find some clues about him?

It didn't even matter that much, how or why he was just starting. I could just get to class earlier and reclaim my seat.

I sat down at an empty table and opened my textbook. The sooner I could finish this homework, the sooner I'd be truly free from the class, at least for today.

After ten minutes of diligently working, my phone lit up with a text. I'd already read the name before I could decide to ignore it. My best friend, Meg, asking for my location. I gave it to her, and within three minutes, she was sliding into the chair opposite me. The sunshine on my book shifted colors, now filtering through her reddish curls.

"Hello hello girlie," she said brightly.

"Hey," I muttered without looking up.

"Oh," Meg said as she laid her books out in front of her. "What's that attitude about?"

I looked up at her, rolling my eyes. "Remind me why I'm taking biology as a history major."

"I couldn't tell you. You should have taken Chem 1 with me." She poked her thumb into her mouth as she flipped through her notes.

"No thank you," I said, looking back down at my textbook.

"It's not as bad as you think," Meg said.

Surely a subject I'd barely passed in high school was just as bad, if not worse, in college. I was two problems away from finishing my assignment when Meg silently squealed, "Oh my gosh."

"What?" I asked, not bothering to look up. I just needed to finish these two questions and I could yabber all I wanted to.

"Don't look, but he's staring at you."

"Who is he?" I asked. One and a half questions.

"Mark Sanders. The guy from the party."

The second night of my college career, homeschooled, sheltered Margaret Stephens had convinced me to go to one of the biggest frat parties of the year. Three months later, the dress I'd worn still smelled like cigarettes, marijuana, and tequila. In a house filled with upward of a hundred students, I'd talked to one person. His name was Mark Sanders, one of the brothers living in the house. In addition to him being a genuinely nice person, he was also one of the only boys not black-out drunk. Plus, he was cute. I'd found myself thinking about him in the days following the party. My mistake, telling Meg. She'd made it her mission to get us dating in time for me to bring him home to my parents for Thanksgiving dinner.

"Why aren't you looking?" Meg hissed.

"You said not to," I replied, but I looked up now anyway.

He stood in a blue t-shirt and jeans talking to some other obvious frat brothers. As if someone tapped him on the shoulder, he turned, and our eyes met.

"He's looking over here," Meg breathed.

"I know," I whispered, flashing him a small smile. He probably didn't even remember me.

Mark smiled back, but only for a second before one of his brothers slapped him on the back and pointed to something on his phone for Mark to look at.

I turned back to my textbook, where one and a half problems were still unfinished. Unfortunately, that little distraction had been enough to completely shift my focus. "You know what happened today in my bio class?" I asked.

"Oh my gosh, you're talking about this now with your future husband standing a few feet away?" Meg asked, her eyes still on the frat boys.

I rolled my eyes. "Not all of us are destined for each other like you and Ben."

"A little faith, Cori," Meg said, finally pulling her eyes away. "What happened in bio?"

"This guy took my seat."

Meg blinked at me, like I'd told the most underrated story ever. "And?"

"Well, you don't do that. This is college. First day seat is your seat for life," I replied. "But also, I'm pretty sure the kid is new."

"Just because you've never seen him doesn't make him new. It's a small school, but there's still a good number of students."

"Meg, this was his first day in the class. It's been two months." I shook my head as I closed my textbook. My biology would just have to go unfinished for now. "It's just odd to me."

"Maybe you're just bitter about your seat?"

"Yes, that's it." Standing up, I tossed my book into my backpack and shoved my highlighter into one of the pockets.

"Leaving already?" Meg asked.

I nodded. "I have English, and he locks the door one minute before class starts."

"What a stickler," Meg said. "Okay, bye."

I waved to her as I headed toward the English building. Truthfully, I didn't mind heading to English early since it was my second major.

The class passed by too quickly, and I stayed at my desk an extra five minutes just scribbling notes. My professor didn't even give us any homework, which only made me extremely unmotivated to do my other homework when I got back to my dorm. At least English homework was enjoyable. It took me a good thirty minutes to get myself focused on my homework, and after that I was able to power through.

I was just finishing my economics homework when someone knocked on my door. I woke the screen on my phone just to make sure I hadn't missed a message about someone coming over. Seeing none, I went over to the door and pulled it open.

Outside the door, looking indescribably handsome, stood Mark Sanders. His attention was down the hallway, but he must have heard me breathing or something because he quickly turned his face to look at me.

My jaw slacked.

"Hey, Cori. Sorry to just show up like this. Your friend Meg told me this is where I could find you."

I forced my jaw to work, though the only words I could get out were, "Yes, I live here."

Mark nodded, a smile across his face. "Good, that's what I assumed."

I wanted to shut the door and start over, but that would make me seem more socially awkward than I already did. "Did you need something?"

"Yeah, um," Mark rubbed the back of his head, pushing those strands upward. "I wanted to know... Or to ask really... If you had plans tomorrow night? I thought maybe, well if you wanted to, we could go to a movie."

"I would love to," I said, pressing my feet into the floor to keep me from jumping on him in a hug.

"Really? Great. I can pick you up here tomorrow. Meg said you already have my phone number?"

I did not, I wanted it now, but I also didn't want to make the impression that Meg and I were two friends who lied to make the other look better. Apparently, we were. "Yes, I do. But how about I put my number in your phone so you have it?"

Mark seemed more than happy to hand over his sleek phone.

I cherished every second holding his phone, typing my name and number in. I handed it back with a smile. "See you tomorrow."

"Have a good night," he said as he walked down the hall.

My heart was bursting, but I kept it together until I saw him disappear around the hall. Granted, I could have closed my door way before he made it to the corner, but I couldn't pull my eyes away from the curves of his back muscles, the sharp lines of his legs. His butt.

Finally closing the door, I leaned against the inside for a few minutes, processing what had just happened.

Mark Sanders asked me on a date. No, he asked me to the movies. Did that mean a date though? Would we get married after college? Where would we live in our 30s, a hip young people city or a sleepy town in the Northwest?

I took a deep breath to calm my absolutely erratic, irrational thoughts.

It was just a friendly outing at the movies. Mark and I. Mark, the most attractive man on campus.

Hopefully my future husband.

✶✶

I found Meg the next morning in the dining hall, sitting alone waiting for me to join her for breakfast. Not bothering to hide my frustration with her, I stomped over to the table and plopped down in the seat. "You said something to Mark."

"Mark who?" she asked coyly.

"Mark Sanders," I replied. "He came to my room last night to ask me on a date."

Meg blinked her eyes. "And you're upset about that?"

Of course, I wasn't upset about that, I could kiss Meg for that really. But still, she hadn't said a word to me about it.

"Why did you tell him I had his number when I didn't?" I asked.

"Makes you seem cool."

"How?"

"That you've had his number all this time and never used it." Meg shrugged. "I don't know. It's mysterious."

I didn't respond to her as I ate—I just didn't have a response to something so illogical. I didn't notice how quickly I was tearing through my French toast.

"Are you nervous?" Meg asked, and I noticed she'd only finished hers a quarter of the way versus my three quarters.

"A little," I replied, setting my toast down so the bread was actually detached from my hand, and therefore from my mouth. "But still excited. Would you and Ben want to come with us?"

Meg's eyes bugged out of their sockets, and she grinned from ear to ear. "A double date with my best friend? Cori, I've been waiting for this day!"

I rolled my eyes, although it was surprising in the nine years we'd known each other we'd never gone on a double date. She'd been dating Ben for two years, and I'd dated in that time period.

"This is going to be so great! I'm so excited!" Meg gripped my wrists. "For you, of course."

A grimace crossed my face. "Of course."

✴ ✴

For someone who claimed she was excited for me, Meg took full control over the date. Somehow in the time between when we talked and when the date was supposed to happen, Meg convinced Mark to let Ben drive all of us to the theater. So instead of Mark picking me up, Meg picked me up an hour before the date to redo the preparation I'd already done to be seen by Mark Sanders.

When Ben did come to get us, Meg forced Mark to sit in the passenger seat beside Ben so her and I could 'intrigue Mark with our hushed conversation.' I didn't believe for one second that Mark was intrigued by our conversations—we weren't even talking about anything, just class assignments—and Mark seemed invested in his conversation with Ben.

When we parked at the theater, that was the first time since the previous night that I stood beside Mark.

"I like that shirt," he commented with a smile. "Third Eye Blind. Pretty nostalgic."

I nodded, glancing down at my basic band t-shirt. "Yeah, they're my favorite."

"They're a good band. My dad and I listen to them a lot."

"Really?" I asked, feeling a wider smile trying to creep onto my face. "My dad and I do too. We would spend afternoons just listening to album after album."

"That sounds awesome," Mark said. He looked like he had more to say, but his attention was pulled away by Ben tapping his shoulder and pointing at a movie poster on the outside wall of the theater. The two of them went over to check it out while Meg and I went ahead inside.

We managed to make it one person from the front of the line before the boys came inside.

Meg tapped her foot and glowered at her boyfriend. "Were you going to make me pay for the movie?"

Ben chuckled and patted her head. "I wouldn't dream of such a crime." As the person in front of us finished, he stepped forward to purchase the tickets.

It was my turn next, so I turned to Mark. "I can get my own ticket."

"No way," he said with a smile. "It's polite, and I can't let Ben upstage me."

His smile made me smile, even as he walked past me up to the ticket booth to buy our tickets.

Meg and I scooted out of line to wait, and she gave me the biggest and slyest grins. "I think you love him."

"What?"

Her grin grew. "You love him."

I rolled my eyes, glancing over to make sure neither of the boys were approaching. "I've known him a grand total of twenty-five minutes."

"So? I knew Ben only five minutes before I knew he was the one."

That was true. But I didn't want to think about love or anything close to that now, if anything to keep me from blushing every time I stood next to Mark.

When both boys had bought the tickets, we entered the main theater, stopping once again because Ben decided he wanted the overpriced movie snacks.

"It'll just be a minute, we have time," he said as he got in line.

The three of us waited off to the side, content on not selling an arm and a leg for a bag of popcorn.

Meg and Mark chatted about a teacher they were both suffering through, while I let myself stare into space at nothing in particular. I began to fall inside myself, recessing so deep inside my own head that Meg and Mark's conversation—and all other conversations—sounded miles away.

And somehow, in the depths of my absentmindedness, I still noticed him.

I spotted him out of the very corner of my eye first, then turned my head to look directly at him.

He stood over six feet, closer to seven, wearing a brown robe I'd only seen in pictures worn by friars. Blond hair poked out from his hood. He had a harsh face with unmoving bright brown eyes as he watched the theater crowd. He was peculiar, that was for sure.

"Do you see that guy?" I asked the others.

"What guy?"

"That man. He's standing right there. By the sign."

Meg looked in the direction I was. "Cori, I don't see anyone."

"What are you talking about? He's right there." As the words left my mouth, the man's eyes shifted, and he looked directly at me.

Caught completely off guard, I stared back. His face didn't become any less strict, and his eyes pierced me. I was frozen, locked in our stare.

"Cori," Meg asked, putting her hand on my shoulder, "what are you looking at?"

"That man," I replied, and immediately he broke off the stare. Feeling Meg's hand on my shoulder gave me some attachment to where I was standing with my friends, but I couldn't take my attention off the strange man. He had broken our stare to look around and started walking toward the exit. I knew Meg still hadn't seen him because she would have said something, as well as not continued to squeeze my shoulder. "He's moving, he's walking over there," I instructed. "Toward the exit."

"He's probably gone now," Meg said. Before I could respond, Ben came back over, carrying a bag of popcorn in either arm.

"Ready?" he asked.

"Why'd you get two?" Meg asked.

"It's going to be a good movie," Ben, who had already started toward theater 8, called to her over his shoulder.

I didn't think about what happened in the lobby during the entire movie. In fact, as I sat in the theater between Mark and Ben, my stomach kept doing backflips as I tried to figure out if Mark would try and make a move. Ben and Meg had been on plenty of movie dates so by then, they were satisfied with Ben simply putting his arm around her shoulders. I didn't know what Mark's movie date style was. Every time he moved, I flinched.

He didn't make a move, and by the halfway point I managed to forget my anxiety and focus on the movie. Ben was right, it was a good movie—he even finished both bags of popcorn.

I'd forgotten about my strange encounter until we reentered the theater lobby. It wasn't some hooded stranger that caught my attention this time, but a boy with blue hair.

I pulled Meg's arm and whispered, "Do you see that guy over there? With the blue hair?"

She looked behind her and nodded. "What about him?"

"That's the new kid in my bio class," I said.

"So what, Cori? He stole your seat, are you afraid he's going to steal your date?" She didn't bother to hear my answer and turned back around to listen to the boys' conversation.

I couldn't take my eyes off the boy. Something was especially strange about the way he stood, his hands shoved in his pocket, constantly looking over his shoulder. "I'm going to go introduce myself," I said to no one in particular, and without waiting for a response, I started to cross the room to him. I was so focused on the boy that I had to stop short as a little girl ran across my path. That finally broke my stare, as I watched the little girl toddle to the other side of the lobby back toward the theaters. My blood chilled at what I saw standing just inside the door.

The same hooded man from before. And again, he was staring at me.

I blinked, and his gaze had shifted to the right. I followed his line of sight to figure out what he was staring at now.

The boy with the blue hair.

I looked back at the man, and in the same instant, he started toward him, taking large strides.

I knew nothing about either of them, but in that moment, I felt like blue-haired boy was in danger. I sprinted forward toward him. "Hey!" I yelled, waving my arms at him.

The boy looked up, a bewildered expression across his face. He turned to look behind him and saw the hooded man heading in his direction as well. The second he saw the man, he bolted for the set of doors on the opposite wall.

I didn't stop, picking up my speed to get to him. "Wait!"

The boy didn't wait, dashing out the doors. I made it out just seconds behind him, but the boy was nowhere in sight. I looked over toward the other set of doors to see if his stalker had maybe come out through there. I didn't see the hooded man anywhere.

2

I wouldn't say that I ruined my chances with Mark Sanders. But they'd all seen me run out of the theater lobby, my only explanation that the boy from my bio class seemed to be in danger from a hooded stranger. At best, he thought I was weird.

Naturally, I also didn't get any messages from Mark that night or the next two days after. By then, it was safe to say I'd ruined my chances.

Which was fine, I accepted my fate as someone who could only mess up opportunities with the opposite gender and decided to refocus on my studies. A week went by without any thoughts of Mark or the theater.

I sat in the dining hall, waiting to meet Meg for a late breakfast. We hadn't seen each other much since the theater, but at least I knew she didn't think I was any weirder than she already knew me to be.

Her red head bobbed into the hall, her eyes scanning and landing on me in seconds. She jogged over to the table, grasping it once she reached and looking at me with excited eyes. "I have something to tell you," she sang.

I raised my eyebrow as I ate a spoonful of cheese grits. "Oh?"

"I'll be right back, let me just grab some yogurt," she said, practically hopping in her shoes. When she came back five minutes later with a cup of yogurt and spoon, I looked down at my own plate where there'd once been two waffles, bacon, and my grits.

"That's all you're going to eat?" I asked her.

"On a diet," she replied, waving her spoon in the air. "Anyway! Guess who still thinks you're cute?"

I looked up at her through my eyelashes. "My mother?"

"No silly," she said. "Mark!"

The week of woe fell off me like a cloak. My posture instantly straightened. "Why do you say that?"

"I ran into him today—"

"By accident or on purpose?"

"Doesn't matter. Anyway, I spoke to him, and he said he had a good time. He'd like to hang out again."

"Well, that's nice," I said, slouching out again. "Glad he doesn't think I'm a total weirdo."

Meg nodded. "And that's why I suggested all four of us go up to my mountain house this weekend."

I choked on air, nearly throwing up the grits. "What?"

"It'll be fun! The important thing of course is you and Mark, because Ben and I have been there lots of times."

I shook my head. "I can't just go to your mountain house with you and two boys."

"Of course you can. We're in college, we can do anything."

"Not anything," I said, leaning my cheek against the palm of my hand. College kids could, in theory, do anything. No parents and barely any rules. But I, Cori Andrea Lewis, could not do just anything. My make-up as a person simply did not allow me to just step on past the bolded boundary that made up my comfort zone.

"Okay not anything, but this is definitely something we can do," Meg said.

"I don't know."

"Come on, Cori. Please. You know you want to," Meg said, gently shaking my arm. "And Mark really likes you. He thinks it's pretty cool you tried to save that guy from whatever weird man was chasing him."

Without the cloak I'd worn all week, it was easy for me to travel back to that moment in the theater. "You didn't see that man at all?"

Meg rolled her eyes. "Cori, please focus. The mountain house."

I chewed on my lip. "I don't know. That's not really my style. I know you and Ben go up there all the time—"

"Think about it," she interrupted. "I know if you think about it, you'll come to the right answer."

It would only be the right answer if it was her answer. But I nodded that I would think about it. And unfortunately, I did think about it. Not in the way Meg wanted me to, but in a dreamy way of what it would be like if I were to do such a thing. Mark and I going for a hike or cuddling by a fire. Mark kissing me. Mark asking me to be his girlfriend.

I dreamed about it all the way up until my bio class, where instinctively, I dropped the delusion at the door to the science building.

Since I'd lost my cloak earlier, when I walked into class, the first thing I noticed was the absence of Blue Hair. I always arrived early and for the little time I'd seen him in class he always arrived late. But that particular day I held a hollow feeling in my stomach as the minutes ticked by and other kids arrived, but not him. Something felt different. At exactly one fifteen, the professor walked in, closing the door behind her.

I stiffened. He still wasn't here.

As the professor sat down, she started calling out the role. With every name, my eyes jumped to the student who raised their hand in turn. I barely squeaked out a 'here' when she called me.

"Chance Mathews?"

No one raised their hand or called here, and I knew that was the blue-haired boy. As the professor began her lecture, her voice settled into background noise and my gaze rested on where the blue-haired boy—Chance—would sit. Was it a coincidence that he wasn't there, after what I'd seen at the theater? Maybe that hooded man had appeared later and kidnapped him, or worse.

My pen dragged against my paper, but only produced a mix of scribbles and random words. I didn't know the boy at all, he'd just started coming to class, but yet I wanted to see him bumbling in through the door, sweat dripping from his brow from the sprint he'd had to do across campus just to make it before class ended. An hour passed and the lecture ended, and he never came.

I looked around at the other students as they scurried to leave the class. No one else seemed to give one notice that one of their classmates had missed the lecture. And why would they? This was college, people skipped all the time. I guess if one of them had seen that same classmate being followed by a weird, hooded figure, maybe then they'd care.

Meg found me that evening in the dining hall, sliding into the seat opposite me with her large plate of salad.

"It's dinner time you know," I said before taking a bite of my own slice of veggie pizza.

"Have to look good for the mountain," she said.

She wanted an answer, she could fish all dinner for it. But my mind was still on other things. "Chance wasn't in class today," I said.

"Who is Chance?"

"The boy with the blue hair. The one who stole my seat."

Meg shrugged. "Maybe he went back to not showing up for class."

He'd just started showing up to class. It was hard to curve a bad habit—or start a good one—but that conclusion didn't sit well with me. "I don't know."

"Do you think he's cute or something?"

"No. Something just feels really weird."

She sighed. "Maybe he's sick or is having issues at home. Maybe a family member died. It could be a whole list of things."

Rationally, yes, there was a long list of possibilities as to why Chance hadn't been in class. But in my gut, there was only one reason, and it had to do with the hooded man from the theater.

What had he looked like again? I squinted my eyes as I thought, like I was trying to see him better. His hood hid the majority of his face, but I was sure I'd seen blond hair. Had I seen his eyes? I couldn't remember, the only image coming to mind were black beads, but I couldn't recall exactly if he'd looked that menacing.

"Did you decide?" Meg asked, cutting into my thoughts.

I looked back up at her. "On?"

She rolled her eyes, and with the number of times she'd done that at me recently, her eyes might just roll on out their sockets. "The mountains."

She wouldn't let it go. Even if I didn't go, she wouldn't let it go. She would constantly remind me of the time I let possible love pass me by, an instance she'd add to her long list of instances I'd let pass.

"Come on, Cori," she whined. "It's Wednesday, and we'd head up there Friday, right after my last class. Make a decision."

"You're rushing me to make a decision, but you're only going to accept one answer."

"There should only be one answer," she said. She hit the bottom of her fork against the table. "Do you want to find love or not? You have to start taking more chances on you."

I rolled my eyes like my mom was lecturing me. She was right. Not about 'finding love,' but it was true, I wasn't a risk taker, especially on things that didn't have clear outcomes. "Love is very dramatic," I said, but I noticed the smile already breaking out across her face. "But I will go. Consider this a favor."

"And on your wedding, consider my debt repaid," Meg said.

For a debt she owed, I spent the next few days feeling I owed something to her. I meticulously contemplated each piece of clothing and jewelry to go in my travel bag, made lists of conversational topics, and even studied a couple sports terms. I was making too much of this, I knew it, but at the same time, a part of me wanted this opportunity with Mark to be perfect. Maybe love was waiting for Cori Lewis.

I received a break from my thoughts for a few hours on Friday. Meg and I rode in her car while Ben and Mark drove in another. With my worries about Mark subsiding, that made room for one lingering question.

I turned down the volume on the song, gaining me a quick glare from Meg. "I have a question," I said before she could comment.

"Fine, but we're putting that song back on after, from the beginning."

I twiddled my fingers, hesitating. It was about to be a silly question, especially to her, but I had to ask it. "So, you see a lot of people around campus ..."

Meg groaned. "You are not talking about that kid with blue hair again."

"I'm just curious if you've seen him around since Tuesday."

"I wasn't looking for him," she said. "He's probably sitting in his dorm room or someone else's dorm room playing video games and blowing off his classes. It's not a murder mystery, Sherlock. Let it go."

I actually had been letting it go, the past few hours my concern was waning. She was right, and I wasn't a detective, nor was it my job to be. My eyes had probably been playing tricks on me or, worst case scenario, that kid owed somebody a lump sum of money. Either way, there was no point stressing myself out about it. Not at the same time I was stressing about creating the perfect weekend.

"Promise me you will not mention him the rest of the weekend," Meg said.

"I promise," I mumbled. And I intended to keep my promise, at least verbally. I couldn't control the questions that pecked at my brain.

It only took us three hours to get to the mountain house. Although I knew not to expect a real woodsy cabin, I was still surprised when I saw the Stephens' lodging in person. It almost looked out of place within the tall trees, built more like a two-story beach house than a rustic cabin. The boys pulled in right after us and did most of the legwork bringing in all the bags.

Once everything was inside and the drivers had about five minutes to rest their tired eyes, Meg stood up, pumping her fist into the air. "Alright, who's ready to get this party started?"

"What did you have in mind?" Mark asked. He looked around the fashionably decorated living room and added, "Doesn't look like this place has seen a lot of parties."

Meg rolled her eyes. "It's new, and rarely used. We'll christen it."

"I thought you and Ben come up here a lot," I pointed out.

The blush almost took over Ben's entire face. "We usually spend most of our time upstairs." Meg punched his arm, and the red disappeared from his face. He picked up his backpack and waved it in front of Mark and me. "If it's a party you want, then that's what you'll get. I've got the goods."

"The goods?"

Ben unzipped his backpack and took out two bottles of Vodka and then a small baggie with an eraser size bush of marijuana.

"Yes!" Meg exclaimed, picking up the two bottles, inspecting them.

I couldn't pull my eyes from the marijuana. "Ben, I get the alcohol. But why the weed? None of us smoke."

Ben flashed a look at Meg, and she couldn't keep the grin off her face. She picked up the bag, then smiled at me. "College is for trying new things."

I nodded, but my body felt like it was curling inside itself like a wilting piece of spinach. I'd stepped outside my comfort zone coming up here with a boy I barely knew. Now I was so far away I couldn't even see my comfort zone. And we still had two whole days left.

Mark laid his hand on my shoulder, and the warmth alone almost caused me to jump out of my skin. "If you're not into it, that's cool too. College isn't for peer pressure, that's what high school was for."

I smiled, my organs practically melting inside from his touch. He didn't know me well enough to know peer pressure wasn't even a concept I acknowledged. But in my desire to make up for the last time we'd hung out, I wanted to seem as liberal as possible. It was nice to know I wouldn't be pushed—by him at least—to do things I really didn't want to.

It took Meg and Ben, professional partiers since high school, no time to set out the cups and drinks. We started with shots, then moved to mixed drinks and conversation.

Two hours in, I was convinced Meg made my drinks stronger than normal. I'd been to a couple parties, but to that day, I'd never been as drunk as I was then. I skipped the stages of buzzed and tipsy, falling right into sloshed. Every joke and every story Meg told was hilarious, even though in the back of my head I knew I'd heard them all a hundred times.

Between us we finished a bottle and a fourth in two hours, including Ben and Meg intermittently pausing their drinking to smoke. Mark didn't smoke, and I figured it was because I didn't, as I saw him eyeing the bowl a few times.

Meg, whose eyes could barely open past the middle of her irises, dragged me into the kitchen to pour some chips in a bowl. "Isn't this fun? This is so fun. Isn't this so fun?"

"This is really fun," I slurred.

She spilled a few chips onto the counter, which she without hesitation picked up to eat herself, swaying the entire time. "I think Mark really likes you."

"You think?" I asked, feeling my pupils widen. "He's really sweet and really fun."

She nodded, beginning to full on dance with her handful of spilled chips. "He seems really attentive to you. And I think he's only not smoking because you're not."

My insides were mush, mostly because of the alcohol, but also because I really liked Mark. As much as I liked him, and as much as all my thoughts swam across my mind, I had to address the elephant in the room. "Have you given any thought to, uh, sleeping?"

"What are you asking?"

"You and I are sharing a room, right?"

"Um ..."

"Meg."

"Cori, I love you, but I want to sleep with my boyfriend."

"I don't want to sleep with Mark. This is my second time hanging out with him."

"Third," she added. "The frat party counts."

"Okay, third. I still don't want to sleep with him."

She exhaled loudly, closing her eyes. "Fine. Since one of us can't just be an adult, I'll sleep with you."

I smiled at her as she opened her eyes. "Thank you."

"Now let's go back. I don't want them to finish all the vodka." We made it to the door before Meg turned around so fast her curls whipped her in the face. "But Cori, I really want to sleep with Ben."

"You've been sleeping with Ben since you met him. Can you please do me this favor?"

"Fine, we'll just all sleep together in the living room. It'll be like a giant slumber party."

I let out a sigh of relief, mainly because she was so drunk and stoned. Sober Meg would have argued me down to the tooth and nail and I would have ended up uncomfortably sleeping with Mark.

When we finally finished all the alcohol and weed, and the conversation was tapering off, Meg popped in a movie. An hour in the alcohol started to wear off. With its warmth dissipating, a shiver ran down my spine.

"It's pretty cold in here," I said. "Meg, how about turning up the heat?"

She sucked in her cheeks with a little laugh. "Yeah, working the thermostat here has never been my strong point. Plus, I think it's like password protected because my dad doesn't want us just changing it whenever. To save money or something."

I rolled my eyes. Typical Meg, always half listening to instructions.

Mark held his burgundy hoodie out to me. "Would you like my hoodie?"

"Really?"

"Of course."

"Thanks," I said as I slid it over my head. "I really appreciate that."

He turned his eyes back to the screen, but a smile sat on his lips. Thank God Meg convinced me to come, I was having the best time.

By the time the movie ended, Meg had already fallen asleep on Ben's shoulder.

"I don't know about you guys," he said, stretching as best he could with his girlfriend's head on his shoulder. "But I'm ready to turn in."

"You won't get any opposition from me," Mark said. He turned to me. "Cori?"

"Yeah, I'm exhausted." Not wanting the boys to know I was the prude, I added, "Meg said she wanted us all to sleep in the living room. Something about not wanting to mess up the bedrooms, I can't really remember."

"That sounds like her," Ben said as he maneuvered his way off the couch to not wake Meg up as he laid her out. "Password protected thermostat, I doubt it."

Mark and I stood up off our couch at the same time. "Cori, you should take this couch," Mark said.

"Are you sure? I don't mind sleeping on the floor."

"I don't mind sleeping on the floor," he insisted, even taking a step back to give me room to set up.

A warm blush came to my cheeks, and thankfully in the dark room he couldn't see. We each got out our pillows and blankets, Ben and Mark creating makeshift beds on the floor. I only pulled my blanket up to mid-chest since I was still wearing Mark's hoodie.

Ben clicked off the tv and the room immediately fell into darkness. Slivers of moonlight made it through the blinds. I quickly became aware of all of our breathing patterns, mainly my own. It sounded louder than Mark and Ben's, faster too, and for the next few moments I concentrated on trying to make it sound normal.

Theirs tapered off, and soon they were asleep. I was just beginning to doze off when the sound of a tree branch snapping caused my eyes to shoot open. I stayed there in place for milliseconds, listening for any more sounds, then sat up. "Did you guys hear that?"

"What?" Mark asked.

"It sounded like a branch snap."

"Branches snap," Meg mumbled.

"It sounded really close, like right outside."

Ben sat up now. "Are you sure you heard something?"

"I'm sure."

"Like, really sure?"

I glared at Ben, regardless of if he could see me in the dark. "Yes."

"Alright, I'll go check it out." I could just make out his silhouette as he got up and headed for the back door.

Meg exhaled loudly. "You better have heard something."

We sat there for a full minute, the only sound our breathing. The next minute, we heard a loud crash followed by a thud from the kitchen.

Meg shot up. "Ben?"

Mark and I stood up, and I immediately turned on the lamp. Meg was already out of the room.

Mark put his hand up to shield me from anything that could come flying into the room. "Ben? Margaret?"

Neither responded, and a deathly silence settled on the house.

"I'm going to go check—"

I yelped and jumped back as a man descended the stairs. He wore a long brown robe, but the hood rested on the back of his shoulders. I could see his face. His skin was an unnatural olive color, with a black undertone like ink swirling right under the surface, and his hair rolled down from the top of his head to just above his waist. He was easily over six foot.

"What? What is it?" Mark asked me, his head swiveling around the room.

"Don't you see him? Right there on the stairs," I replied, backing up toward the window the farther the man got down the stairs.

Mark looked toward the stairs, blinking rapidly. "Cori, I don't see anything."

A loud whooshing filled my ears, pounding like air was hitting them. I couldn't take my eyes off the man. He'd reached the bottom stair now and was heading toward us. Mark stood right in front of me, but I felt helpless. He couldn't see him! Why couldn't he see him?

"Cori, please tell me what you see."

"He's right in front of us, he's heading for us," I said, my voice just above a scared whisper.

Mark turned so he was staring right at the approaching man.

I couldn't stand there anymore. I turned to bolt for the front door, and jumped backwards again, this time knocking into Mark.

Outside, glaring in through the window, was another man, wearing the same robes, with the same length hair, only his goldish blond. What got me were his eyes. Two brown gems with something like glitter or stars inside them. Looking into them, I weakened, numbed, but I couldn't pull my gaze away. I didn't hear Mark behind me anymore. I didn't hear anything. Silence wrapped around me, smothering me. Blackness crept from the ends of my vision, working its way to the center. The world fell into darkness, and the last thing I saw, those eyes.

3

I woke up in the middle of a gasp for air. My chest ached and my entire head felt fuzzy. Stretching out my jaw, my face tingled with numbness, and my nostrils burned. I attempted to take a calming breath, but the air came out shaky.

I was staring up at the bottom of a bunk bed. To my left was a concrete wall, I could feel its presence without even looking. I turned my head to the right. I was in a room similar to a bomb shelter, filled with bunk beds. Some of the beds were occupied, but not all.

My body ached as I forced myself into a sitting position. Looking down at my clothes, I still wore my tank top, torn blue athletic shorts, and Mark's hoodie. My memories were hazy, I could barely remember how I got here. I remembered leaving the university or Meg's mountain house. I slightly remembered alcohol bottles. But nothing beyond that point.

My body went rigid as a woman somewhere over the six-foot height walked through the maze of beds. She stopped at mine upon noticing I was sitting upright. She had black hair separated into two thick braids hanging in front of her. Countering her size was a bright face with a kind smile, though her skin color unnaturally olive, like it was painted on.

The skin color. Bits and pieces started to assemble in my mind. I'd seen that skin color before, in fact I felt like I'd seen it several times. And something was very familiar about the length of her hair.

"I see you're finally awake," she said, and her voice reminded me of how your teacher talked to you after just waking up from naptime.

I couldn't get my brain to pause trying to piece together memories to form a response.

The woman pointed to where the bunk beds formed a corner. "Just follow the pathway out. When you leave the room, you should see a line of kids. Stand in it until it's your turn to be checked out by Phaenna."

I was still weary of my new surroundings, but she seemed nice enough to at least follow her instructions. As I walked through the maze, I began to remember more. Going to bed all together in the living room. Waking up because I heard something. Something happening to Ben and Meg. Seeing a man come down the stairs. Seeing—

My thoughts halted as I made it to the line. I was now in an open hallway, much like the grand halls of one of those prestigious colleges, and in front of the four kids waiting in line, a woman sat at a table covered with a black tablecloth.

The boy in front stepped up to the table, she spoke to him with a scowl, and then the boy took off his outer clothes. The woman looked him over, scribbling down notes, then pointed to two piles of clothing, one a mix of clothes and one completely gray. The boy went over, dropped his clothes into the left pile, then took some clothes from the gray pile.

This happened to the three people in front of me, and as every one of them stripped down to their underwear, I found myself more and more appalled. Then I stepped up to the black table.

The woman had black hair like the first woman, only hers was in a tight, low ponytail behind her head. Lines sprouted from her eyes and mouth. The scowl was definitely her permanent face. She had a little name plate at the corner of the table that read Phaenna. I wouldn't be bothering to try and pronounce it.

"Cori Lewis?"

"Yes."

"Your number is five hundred and seven, don't forget it. You will be called by your number here. Names are not important."

I glanced over at the nameplate. "You have your name right there."

Phaenna's eyes flashed up at me. "Our names matter. How else would you address us?"

"I thought names weren't important."

"Our names are important." I heard the annoyance in her voice. She scribbled a few notes, then flashed her eyes back up at me. "Well?"

"Well, what?"

She put down her clipboard and gave me an exasperated look. "This is a health screening. I have to screen you. Take off your clothes."

"Excuse me?" I asked. "I am not taking off my clothes."

She set her pen down, glaring directly into my eyes. "Don't make me have to ask you three times. Take your clothes off."

"Make me," I hissed.

"You impotent little ..." She didn't finish her sentence as she stood up from the table, looming at somewhere close to seven feet. "I'll strip those clothes right off you, along with your skin."

By now the others waiting in line were all paying attention to what was happening with me. I stood my ground however, but the whooshing was slowly returning to my ears.

Phaenna clenched her teeth as she spoke, "Take off your damn clothes, Number Five Hundred and Seven."

I mimicked her clenched teeth and indignant expression as I replied, "No."

The second the word left my mouth, Phaenna came from around the table, and I backed up to keep at least her top half fully in my visual field. She looked like she would strike me, but I wasn't going to back down.

She opened her mouth to say something vile, but another voice stopped her.

"Phaenna, what is the matter?"

She whipped around, and I looked around her to see another one of them approaching, this one a male.

The whooshing suddenly stopped, and a shiver racked my body.

The male approaching us was the hooded man from the theater, and the last one I'd seen before passing out.

His eyes stayed on the two of us—which was good because I didn't think I could solely take his gaze—and his hair caught the air from the movement of his walking.

"This girl is refusing to comply with the health screening," Phaenna snapped. "I don't have time for this."

The man looked at me, and I felt myself shrinking. He looked back at his counterpart. "I'll take care of it." Then back at me. "Come with me."

Him defusing the situation didn't take the glare off Phaenna's face, but I ignored her as I followed him out of the big hall and into a smaller hall filled with rooms. All of the doors were shut except for one, and that was the room he turned into.

He went straight over to the counter and started writing on a clipboard.

I felt like I was getting my yearly check-up, although I was here against my will. "Why did you bring me in here?" I asked him.

"You were being difficult about Phaenna doing your screening. Now I'm going to do it."

I crossed my arms, attitude pouring out of me. "And who the hell are you?"

He didn't look the slightest bit fazed by my swearing. "My name is Kanyn."

"Cannon?"

He gave me a look like I was the dumbest person on the planet. "Ka-Nyn."

I nodded, but the correct pronunciation of his name really didn't matter. "Where am I? What is this place?"

He completely ignored my question, pointing to a poster of letters on the wall. "Read that from here."

I was standing maybe ten feet from the poster, and my vision was average, so I could read the normal amount.

"We'll do your hearing now," Kanyn said after writing something about my results. "Can you hear me?"

"Of course," I replied.

He dropped his voice a decibel. "Can you hear me?"

"Yes."

He continued to do this until his voice was just below an audible whisper. It wasn't the standard hearing test, but it satisfied him. He jotted down my results.

"What is your weight?"

"One hundred and fifteen pounds," I replied, flatly.

He wrote that down. "All that's left is for you to take off your clothes so I can examine you. When I'm finished you will put those clothes on."

Clearly no matter who I was with, I wasn't going to get out of stripping to my underwear. "What will happen to the clothes I have on now?"

"They'll be discarded."

I blinked. "Discarded?"

"Yes."

I looked down at my attire. Nothing I was particularly attached to, but I didn't want them thrown away, that was for sure.

Kanyn turned around in his chair and began writing something on the paper in front of him. "You may take your clothes off now."

My lips were set in a hard frown, and I glared at his broad back. Reluctantly, I removed the hoodie and my shirt, then untied the string on my shorts, and slid them off. I kept my glare at his back the entire time I undressed, until I stood there, cold in my underwear.

Kanyn didn't turn around, still jotting down his notes.

I crossed my arms in a futile attempt to keep myself warm and glanced around the sterile room. Completely white walls that bounced the fluorescent lights off them. Unlike a doctor's office, the walls were void of any type of posters or over-dramatic paintings. When I got bored looking at the room, I looked back at Kanyn. He hadn't put his pencil down.

Loudly, I cleared my throat, and said, "I'm undressed."

He still didn't stop writing. "You may put the other clothes on."

"You didn't even look at me."

He turned his head a fraction of an inch to the right. "You may put the other clothes on."

My glare returned, but I didn't say anything else. I should have been grateful that he wasn't going to look at me in my underwear. Quickly, I shrugged on the gray slacks and shirt, and pulled on the gray socks and Keds-like sneakers. The second I stood up straight, Kanyn stood up and turned to me.

"I know I said that was the last thing, but I just remembered one more thing."

"What?" My voice sounded as dry as sandpaper.

He opened one of the drawers and took out what I recognized as a Breathalyzer. He held it to my lips and instructed, "Blow on this."

My fighting spirit was lessening, and I blew without questioning.

Kanyn looked at the number on the screen, then sat back down at the desk to scribble more notes. "Down from your 0.13 BAC level," he said.

"How do you know that?"

"Your blood sample."

I narrowed my eyes. "I didn't give a blood sample."

He ignored my comment. "Aren't you a little young to be drinking?" he asked.

"You're going to tell me about what I've been doing wrong?" I snapped. "You kidnapped my friends and me. Where the hell even are we? What the hell are you supposed to be?"

He didn't answer me, but looked at me. No, he looked into me.

I began to feel the same wooziness I had back at the cabin when he'd looked at me. I didn't want to back down, but my legs felt like they'd give way any second, so I sat down in the chair.

"You need to rest," he said. "Well, you need to eat first because it's been hours since your last meal. But then you need to sleep off the rest of the effects of the chloroform."

"So that's how you did it," I muttered.

Kanyn flashed me a look I couldn't read. "That's how we got you here."

Whoever they were, they certainly weren't above using whatever means necessary to get what they wanted.

"You may go," he said. "When you leave, Phaenna will direct you on where to go next, but really you could just follow the others."

I crossed my arms and as I turned to leave the room, my eyes fell on Mark's hoodie. They could burn my clothes for all I cared, but I didn't want to lose that. I turned back to Kanyn and asked, "Can I keep the hoodie?"

"No," he replied without turning around.

I was growing tired of his indifference, but trying to keep a level head, I decided I'd just use the same tactic that had worked before. "I'd like to keep my hoodie," I repeated with an added firmness in my voice.

"You may go." He didn't turn to face me, but even still, I could hear the conclusiveness in his voice. I'd used up all my chances with him.

I felt the tears start to sting my eyes from having to part with the hoodie, and I quickly stalked out of the room. When I came back to the big hall, Phaenna was still there checking kids. A girl stood there in her underwear, clutching her arms to herself like they would hide her entire body, as Phaenna wrote down notes about her. Before Phaenna could look up and see me, I quickly followed a boy walking away from the table.

I figured we were going in the right direction when I noticed another one of them standing in the hallway, seemingly just watching to make sure people went the right way.

This one looked like he could be a few inches taller than Kanyn, and there was certainly more to him, with beefy shoulders and thick arms. He was looking at his left arm, inspecting some kind of deep gash, but I felt he was still keeping track of my movement past him.

The boy and I came to a large room and inside I could see a bunch of other people my age standing around the room. Some looked downright horrified while others had made nervous groups to converse with. The boy knew another boy, and he quickly joined that circle.

I made my way to the other side of the room, standing a few feet from the wall by myself. Looking around I immediately noticed three more of them. All of them had the same long hair. What were they? They could be humans with irregular tanned skin, or maybe just a rare race of people.

Their height however was the most daunting. Six feet seemed to be the minimum for them.

My eyes started darting around looking for exits. Who cared who they were or what they were. I didn't need to stick around to find out.

The room had one way in, the doors I'd just come through. There were windows close to where I stood, but the bottom sill started above my head, I'd have to climb on something to reach it. If enough of us gathered together maybe we could just bum-rush the guards, but I didn't know if I alone could mobilize such a coup.

"So." The voice startled me out of my thoughts, and I looked to see who was talking. At first glance, I didn't recognize the brown-haired boy, but after a few milliseconds I recognized his face. Chance, but without the blue hair. "They caught you too."

"Who is 'they?' What's going on?"

"Hell if I know," he said, glancing around.

"Why are you here?"

He shrugged. "I don't know. I assume I saw something I wasn't supposed to."

"What did you see?"

Chance looked at me, and I couldn't read the expression on his face. "This guy—one of these guys—he cornered this kid from my school in an alley. I was just passing by and happened to see. I didn't stick around, I probably should have." He shook his head, moving some hair off his forehead. "Anyway, after that I kept seeing these guys. It wasn't even the same one. They always wore those robes, sometimes they'd even have the hoods up. I escaped them maybe three times before I packed up and switched colleges."

"That's why that was the first time I saw you in bio," I said.

He nodded, smiling a little. "With that god awful blue hair. I thought my disguise would work, that and being at a new school. But they found me."

"So what, because I stopped that guy from attacking you at the movies, they came after me?"

"I assume so," he replied. He looked around, but I still couldn't tell his thoughts simply from the look on his face. I thought I was just doing a good deed stepping in, but somehow that had cost me. I just didn't know what exactly it had cost me.

"Do you remember how you got here?" he asked.

I shook my head. "I just remember waking up in a room, almost like a bomb shelter. There were other people in the room, but they were all still asleep. As soon as the woman in the room noticed I was awake, she sent me out to a health screening."

Chance nodded. "Yeah, I remember the screening."

"Did they make you take your clothes off?"

He raised his eyebrow. "Yes. Didn't they make you?"

Suddenly self-conscious of my seemingly special treatment, I crossed my arms and lowered my eyes. "Yes."

"Ridiculous," he said. "Hope that woman got a good look. And anyone behind me. What were they even checking for like that? This isn't a doctor's office—"

"Did you get a number?" I asked to change the subject.

"Four hundred and ninety-eight," he replied. "You?"

"Five hundred and seven."

Chance's eyes were still circling the room. "I doubt there's going to be any calling of our numbers for prizes."

I looked at one of them, the one standing closest to us. He looked older than the first woman, Kanyn, or the one I'd seen in the hallway, but much younger than Phaenna. He had very dark hair that was still obviously brown which he wore in a thick ponytail. His eyes scanned the room. From his jaw alone, anyone could see the strength in him—if they needed more proof, muscle rippled in the part of his arm that could be seen where the sleeves of his robe pulled up from his arms being crossed.

"Do you know anyone here?" I asked Chance.

He shook his head. "No, though I've tried looking for that boy I saw before. You?"

"Maybe," I replied. "I was with three friends when we were—"

"Cori!"

I turned my head to see Meg running across the room to me, her hair flying behind her. She almost tackled me with her hug. As I struggled to get out of her grip, out of the corner of my eye, I noticed the guy with the braid watching our interaction. "Calm down," I said quietly. "You're drawing attention."

"Sorry, I'm just relieved to see you," she said. She did a quick glance around, though obviously still not noticing the one particular stare she was getting. "Where are we? What is this place? What happened?"

"Yeah, I really don't have any of those answers," I replied. "I was hoping you would."

She shook her head.

"What about Ben and Mark? Where are they?" I asked.

"I haven't seen them. I was hoping they were with you."

I shook my head, but then added, "I'm sure they just haven't woken up yet. Ben has always been a heavy sleeper."

Meg nodded. "Yeah, that's probably it. I can't believe they actually knocked us out for that long."

"They used chloroform," I said.

"How do you know that?" Chance asked. "I thought you said you didn't remember anything."

"I don't," I said. "One of them told me."

He raised his eyebrow. "Really? One of them actually talked to you like that?"

I remembered I hadn't told him about my contrasting experience, and quickly added, "Briefly. I was being kind of difficult, so they said a few more words to me than the others."

He slowly nodded, but I couldn't tell if he actually believed me.

Changing the subject, I decided to introduce the only two people I knew here. "Meg, this is Chance," I introduced. "Chance, Meg."

"Hey," he nodded to her.

"You look familiar," she said.

"He used to have blue hair," I said.

She snapped her fingers. "That's it! You're the kid from the movie theater."

"Yes, that's me," he said.

Meg narrowed her eyes. "Cori said you were running from someone then. Do you know why we're here?"

Chance shook his head. "Nope, I'm just as confused as you are. And apparently as equally recovering from the effects of chloroform."

Meg flashed me a look, and I knew she didn't fully believe him. "Well, I'm going to need some answers pretty soon before I—" She was cut off as our attention turned to the sound of the doors to the room closing.

"Great, this is probably where they slaughter us like animals," Chance muttered.

I didn't really think they were going to go through everything they had just to trap us in a room and kill us, but being that none of us had absolutely any reference, my heartbeat did speed up a bit.

Since we were near the wall, we had to follow the direction of the attention of the people more toward the center. Everyone in the room clustered in a semicircle facing the doors. We moved closer so we could see too.

One of them stood in front of the door, this one undoubtedly the oldest of all. Although his brown hair hung below his shoulders like the others, gray peppered his roots. Wrinkle lines cracked his face like an old sidewalk. The rest of him was hidden inside his robe. He clapped his hands together, his signal for everyone to quiet down.

When the murmurs quieted to whispers, he began to speak. "I'm sure you all have questions, and I assure you they will be answered in due time. In the meantime, the less questions you ask, the better. The answers will only confuse you, and therefore interfere with your time here."

By now the room was pin-drop silent. "You have no reason to be afraid. This is a special place for you. Think of it like a boarding school. You'll take classes, exercise, and work. We'll be watching you all, assessing you."

Almost automatically my eyes shifted to the one of them stationed nearest to us.

He looked like he was paying attention to what the front man was saying, but still very closely watching the crowd.

"The rules are simple," the speaker continued. "Follow the schedules that will be given to you. No causing trouble, especially fighting. No disrespecting any of us. If you try in any way to make contact with the outside world, you will be punished. And if you even think of trying to escape, you'll be severely punished."

A wave of nerves washed through me. As harmless as he tried to make things seem, they still clearly had every intention of keeping us here.

"This is a place for all of you to learn and to grow on your own. As I said, there's absolutely nothing to fear. None of us mean any harm to you."

I glanced at the mass of people. Not one of them looked convinced they weren't in any danger.

"Does anyone have anything to say?"

A skinny boy with freckled arms raised his hand, and the speaker acknowledged him. "I know we aren't supposed to ask questions but ... What is this place?"

"This place and all of us here are The Order."

A low murmur worked its way through the crowd, but no one raised their hand for another question, nor did they let their murmurs get above the volume of a whisper.

"If there are no more questions or concerns," the speaker said, "you'll be shown to your rooms."

Two of them—Order members I guess I'd call them—escorted us out of the big room. They introduced themselves as Tolison and Provos. As was the fashion among Order members, they both wore their long hair down. Tolison's was jet black, the same color as the woman's from the room I'd woken up in. Provos's fell somewhere between a dull yellow and brown. Of the two, Tolison was the taller, standing a whole head above Provos. But also of the two, Provos looked more approachable. His face didn't look set in as tight a frown as everyone else's. They said they were taking us to our rooms, and along the way they pointed out places we should know, like the dining hall and the library.

As we were walking around, one kid with braces and a chubby face said aloud, "This place is like Hogwarts."

If I remembered correctly, the kids there hadn't been kidnapped and held there against their will.

They showed us the sleeping halls. Bathrooms were located at the end of each hall. On the outside of each bedroom door was a black chalkboard with two numbers scribbled on it. I assumed they were our numbers, which I was proved right as Tolison instructed those with matching numbers to get acquainted with their rooms. I was relieved to see my number was paired with Meg's.

"Breakfast is at eight tomorrow morning," Provos said to us before he went with the remainder of the group down the hall.

Meg and I exchanged glances before she turned the knob and pushed open the door. The room was no bigger than a dorm room and set up in the same style. Two beds on either side of the room, a dresser in the middle with a clock and a lamp on top, and a mirror on the right side of the room at the end of the bed. Our eyes landed on the extras in the room at the same time. Two duffle bags, one on each bed.

Meg and I exchanged a look.

"Maybe they gave us our stuff back," she said, going over to the left bed. I watched her unzip her bag, and a deep frown grew on her face.

"What's in it?" I asked.

She glanced at me, grimly, and pulled out a fresh packet of underwear, like the value pack you'd buy at the store. "Just the essentials."

I went over the bed on the right and opened my own bag. Toothbrush, toothpaste, soap, vials of shampoo and conditioner, two more sets of the gray outfits, and a pack of underwear and bras. Inspecting the packs, I realized they weren't sealed. They'd been repackaged. I took one of the briefs out and a sick feeling settled in my stomach looking into it. It was definitely brand new, never worn. But in the backside a little tag was sown in with my assigned number.

I looked over at Meg, who was sitting cross-legged on her bed holding up the bras to her busts. "You don't seem too worried," I commented.

She looked over at me, resting the bra on her lap. "I could say the same about you."

That was true. For someone who had been kidnaped, I probably should have been having a panic attack or actively trying to escape. But somehow, I felt strangely calm about the situation. That of course could have been a side effect of the chloroform.

She continued, "I guess I don't see a point in freaking out just yet. I mean I really want to know where Ben and Mark are, but I'm sure we'll see them tomorrow. Then we can logically figure all this out. Besides, this is probably just some hidden camera game show or psychological experiment."

"Maybe," I said, but I could feel my eyes closing. Crawling under the covers, I turned my face to the wall to get some sleep.

"You're not going to go through your stuff?" Meg asked.

I shook my head. "I'll do it later. I need some sleep."

"Good night then," she said.

I fell asleep quickly, like my pillow itself knocked me out. When I awoke, the first thing I did was roll over and look at the clock. Two in the morning.

I didn't have an immediate sense to go back to sleep, so I figured I could go through my bag as Meg had earlier. She was fast asleep, and I knew turning on the bedside lamp wouldn't wake her.

I hadn't even moved the bag off the bed before going to sleep, and I pulled it closer to me by the straps. The same items I'd seen before were still inside, including the personalized underwear. As I took out the bulkiest items, our outfits, I realized there was something else at the very bottom of the bag.

I had to blink away the sleep to see it more clearly without taking it out.

The hoodie.

4

When we woke the next morning, we found schedules posted on the outside of our door, one for Meg and one for me.

There were only five classes: science, math, philosophy, physical training, and something called expressive learning; and then a block for free period and another for lunch. Out of those, the only thing we had together was free period.

"Laundry duty?"

I scanned my schedule and noticed that block in the nine to ten slot. "They did say we would have work. I guess that's what we got assigned."

"I wonder what the other options were," Meg muttered.

"I bet kitchen duty was one," I said. "I wouldn't have wanted that."

She groaned. "Ugh, I have philosophy first? At nine in the morning? For fifty minutes? Are they serious?"

It was better than math at nine in the morning.

She groaned again, putting an ounce more disgust into it. "They're actually treating this like school."

"Which they kidnapped us for, don't forget."

"I'm honestly not really concerned about that."

I looked at her.

"Yeah, I mean who kidnaps people to put them in a classroom setting? You torture them or rape them, something horrible," she explained. "I'm resolute thinking this is all some kind of study on young adults. How we handle new environments, how we cope, stuff like that."

A sensible idea, but for me there were other things that forced me not to accept that. For instance, if this was a study, what was with the Order members? They didn't even look like they were from this world. They could all have been actors, but still. Things were just off.

Meg and I did our best to get ready like we were getting ready for a normal day of college. Using the shared bathroom, putting on our designated clothes, and then heading to the dining hall for breakfast.

For a kidnapping or a scientific study, they had pretty generous options for breakfast, including fruit, cereal, oatmeal, pancakes, and bacon. And it was set up more like the cafeterias in high school, with Order members behind the line preparing and overseeing the food. As Meg and I were looking for seats, we came across Chance sitting by himself and joined him.

We ate in silence for the first few minutes, and I kept my mind occupied watching the many people around our age file in and out of the dining hall.

Chance finally spoke, breaking the silence. "You've noticed it, right?"

"Noticed what?" Meg asked.

"The others. Our group that had that weird orientation yesterday, we're not the only ones. There are many others who were here before we got here." He looked around the room, then nodded to a boy with purple hair spiked into a Mohawk. "That kid, he wasn't there yesterday. I would definitely have remembered him."

"Great, more weirdos," Meg mumbled before slurping the last bit of juice from her juice pack.

"I've been trying to figure it out," Chance said. "Is this place like a Nazi camp? Is it a terrorist base? Maybe it is Hogwarts."

"It's not," I said, dryly. "Or else where's my magic?"

He at least chuckled.

"So do you think they're only kidnapping college students?" Meg asked. "Everyone here seems about that age."

"I actually talked to a boy who was sixteen," Chance said. "He's really scared. He said in ten years, last night was the first time he'd wet his bed."

"He's that scared?" Meg asked.

"Are you not?" Chance asked.

"She's convinced this is just some kind of study for young adults," I replied.

Chance looked at her, and it seemed that a comment was sitting on his lips, but he didn't say anything.

"They don't want us asking questions," I said. "And they're expecting us not to."

"Hell, I don't need to ask questions to find my answers," Chance said, looking around the room.

I wished I could be that confident. Not a single person I'd seen looked like they could give me answers.

"You haven't seen Ben or Mark come in here?" I asked.

Meg shook her head. "I'm really worried. I haven't seen them anywhere, and I'm sure they'd be looking for us."

"They're fine, I'm sure," I said, doing my best to console her before she entered into a panic attack. "This seems like a big place, they probably just haven't found us yet."

"I hope," she said, tapping her finger on the table. "Or maybe there's more of these simulation schools. Maybe we're not at the same one."

I didn't want to entertain the idea of multiple holding camps like this one. Or even more of those Order members. Every single one of them was six foot or taller, with long hair. Their ability to look so similar was just bizarre.

A soft bell, one low tone, rang for about five seconds. The other kids in the dining hall began getting up, throwing away their breakfasts and gathering their books.

"I guess that's the bell," I said, standing up myself.

"Not a simulation of college," Meg said, standing up as well. "No bells there." She pulled me into a quick hug. "Good luck. But don't get too invested. We're getting out of this crazy study as soon as possible."

I nodded, but my breath came out unsteady. She was still much more convinced than me that this was a study.

I mainly followed the flow of the crowd to find the classrooms, which were all grouped close together in two halls. Each room had a sign beside the door with the subject. It didn't take me long to find the math classroom, even though besides the sign, they all looked the same. I found a seat in the middle but at the very last column from the door. Other kids milled in after me. It felt so much like my first day of college, I was almost comfortable. But my anxiety itched, crawling up and down my spine. This wasn't college.

The Order member teaching the class stiffly introduced himself as Brunhild. I noted the German in his name, meaning that was a place we could potentially be. Those of us who were "new" were given a notebook and writing utensils, but other than that, nothing was said to get us introduced into the system. Brunhild started with his lesson, which consisted of basic math I'd taken in my senior year of high school.

For the beginning of the class, I couldn't concentrate, hardly writing any notes. My eyes kept jumping around the classroom. Some kids acted like it was just another day in class, diligently taking notes and paying attention. Only a few kids looked around nervously, some of them the new ones who'd come in with me.

It wasn't until the bell rang that I realized I'd been holding my breath for the majority of the class. As I exited, putting myself safely in the middle of the mass trying to get through the door at the same time, I looked over at the Order. They all appeared so physically unhuman-like, but yet were so impervious to the surrounding nervous energy. Brunhild didn't even look up as we exited, focused on scribbling notes.

I had science as my second period, which went by as excruciatingly as the first period. And in that period, even less people looked like their nerves were getting the best of them. It was like I'd stumbled into the twilight zone, and I was one of maybe four people who realized it.

By the time I got to my third class, physical training, my nerves had started to numb. The more the day went on, the more it did feel like the first day of school. Everyone just going from class to class, the only goal to finish the day. I noticed a few kids here and there with wide eyes or white knuckles as they walked through the halls, but for the most part, everyone slugged through like a normal school.

I was almost certain physical training would be inside as well, so when I found that 'across from Room H' actually led to the outdoors, I was quite shocked. The hallway opened up on the right side with several large archways that led out to a large grassy area. In the distance was a tall brick wall, obviously built to keep anyone on either sides from seeing over it.

The instructor, whose name was Trainus, did the same as Brunhild and Isolde in my first two classes, asking for any newcomers. Myself and another girl raised our hand to that.

Glancing at the other newcomer, I tried to find any hint of a debilitating alarm on her face, but to no avail.

The first thing Trainus had us do was stretches. As I bent toward the ground, I mentally went back over the beginning of my freshman year. Had I signed up for some weird psychological study and not remembered? It was possible, everyone bombards you for the first two weeks. But an international study? This was clearly not something for my college alone.

From stretching we transitioned into short laps across the grass. As I waited my turn, a round headed boy with a sharp nose and dark crew cut brown hair sidled up next to me.

"New. How nice," he said, shielding his eyes from the sun.

"I guess," I replied more as a mumble. His comment wasn't much of an introduction, but I figured if I had any chance of figuring this out, I needed to start somewhere. "I'm Five Hundred and Seven."

The boy laughed. "I don't even remember my number. The name's Gianni."

"Cori." I glanced around the yard. "I guess you see new people pretty often."

"Not really," he said, bouncing up and down on his feet. He was ready to run. "I don't really notice 'em anymore. Too many people, you know?"

Another question began forming in my mind, interrupted by me noticing a sparkling band on Gianni's left arm. "I like your bracelet," I said.

He said a word in another language, which sounded almost Russian. "It was my mother's, and she gave it to me before she left Nikopol."

"Nikopol? Where is that?"

"Ukraine," he said with a proud smile. "My mother left my brother and I for some job in Paris."

Even though he hadn't said anything frightening, my heart dropped down to my knees. Just the idea of someone being here from somewhere as far away as the Ukraine unsettled me more than anything in the past few hours.

"Did you come here yourself?" I asked. "All the way from Nikopol?"

Trainus called Gianni's number, and a wide smile donned on Gianni's face. "Of course not. No one came here by choice." He left me with that, jogging forward to run his laps as soon as the current running person finished.

✳✳

Thankfully Chance had the same lunch period as me. When I sat down at the table next to him, I realized he was sitting with two other girls.

"Wow, you're really popular with the ladies," said the girl wearing a backwards black hat atop crimson colored hair.

"This is Cori," Chance introduced me. "We were at the same college." To me he said, "This is Shauna and Airi. Met them both in my physical training class."

"I think 'met' is a loose term," Shauna said. She turned her attention to me to tell the story. "Airi here has asthma, among a bunch of other ailments. They had us running laps and she almost passed out on the third lap. So Chance helped her run the other two laps, stayed by her the entire time."

"Wow," I said, glancing at Chance who pridefully beamed.

"Thanks again," Airi said softly. She was clearly of Asian descent, with dark chestnut colored hair and soft brown eyes that pointed at either ends. She wore thick black wire rimmed glasses. Her gray clothes swallowed her small body.

At the tone of her voice, the pride left Chance's face, replaced by a gentle smile. "You just looked like you needed some help. No need fainting."

"Are you new too?" Shauna asked me.

I nodded.

"What do you think?"

"I mean it's ... Like school," I replied. I didn't know quite what to say. It was like school, but with a sinister edge that I couldn't put my finger on.

Shauna nodded. "Like a prep school, uniform and everything."

"They let you wear the hat?" I asked her.

She nodded. "It's only the clothes they care about. Otherwise, they encourage that we 'express' ourselves."

I didn't feel very expressive wearing essentially lounge clothing—that on top of not having a clue as to what I was doing here. "How long have you been here?" I asked.

She closed her eyes as she thought. "Almost two months now, I think. Seems about right. You're so isolated from the outside world, you can't even tell how long it's been."

I almost choked on my food. Two months? I certainly didn't want to be here for two months. I swallowed a lump trying to form in my throat. "And what do you think of it here?"

Shauna shrugged. "When I first got here, I had no idea. Like, I thought these people were terrorists or some shit. But, turns out they're pretty okay. Still don't know why I'm here but I figure I'll find out one day, right?"

"Yeah, I guess." It threw me how laid-back she was about the situation. It threw me how calm everyone was. But at the same time, she'd been here almost two months, while I'd been here less than a day. I was still fresh and scared. After two months here with no answers, a sort of apathetic acceptance settled over the anxiety.

"What do you think, Chance?" I asked, hoping I'd get a response somewhere along the same thought process as me. He was still new.

He shrugged, picking at the salad in front of him. "I mean, Shauna's right. It's like school, so it's probably some kind of study or something. Or maybe something cooler, like a secret agent training. Two months is kind of a long time."

"But you're okay?" I asked, my stomach seemingly unzipping inside the more he talked. "You're not worried?"

"Not yet."

I stayed quiet for most of lunch, letting the three of them do the talking. Their conversation made the hairs on my arms stand up. They talked so casually, like we were in a normal situation. I couldn't allow myself to be so offhand yet.

When the bell rang to change classes, I didn't bother hurrying to my next class. It'd been a good few months since I left high school, and going back to the constant changing of classes left me beat.

When I walked into the classroom for the class called Expressive Learning, I expected it to be like every other class I'd had up until then. The first difference were the desks, or rather the lack thereof. In place of individual desks were long wood tables, long enough for five people per table to sit on the same side.

Also, unlike in my other classes, the teacher wasn't in the room early. In fact, two minutes after the second bell rang, the teacher still hadn't arrived.

Looking around, it seemed—of course—that no one was worried, so I returned to doodling in my notebook.

Finally, five minutes later, the teacher walked in, and my jaw dropped open. The Order who'd been in the room when I'd woken up.

As though she wasn't late, she sat at her desk, resting her chin in one hand, her eyes drifting around the room inspecting each of us. Her eyes seemed brighter than the other Order members, almost dancing around the room, and a hint of a smile rested on her lips.

Despite her not calling us to attention, the class automatically quieted down. We watched her watch us.

Finally, she spoke, and the airiness of her voice caught me off guard. "Hello. I see some new faces in here. For them, welcome to expressive learning. My name is Kat." She pushed herself off the desk, stretching as she stood on her feet. "I'm always glad that you all are here. This is a very special class. This class is for creating. You can do whatever you want, as long as you're creating something. There are many items in this room, from paper to fabric to pieces of wood. If there's something you need that's not here, just let me know, and I'll be sure to get it for you."

Her friendliness felt completely out of place, but by no means ingenuine. If we were being brainwashed, she had to be an integral part.

"The mind is a powerful thing. From it can come anything." She left us with those words, turning her eyes down to a journal in front of her.

This was nothing like the other classes I'd been in, full of structure and work. The class compared to an elective in college, but even then, I hadn't found any electives where I could just work on anything. I also didn't have anything to work on, and with my constant anxiety from the situation, I couldn't conjure up any ideas of what to work on. For an hour I let myself switch between doodling and watching my other classmates.

Sometimes I looked up at Kat, but I didn't want her to ever notice my glances, so I only looked for a few seconds at a time. She was so different, it was almost alluring. The way she held herself looked so different than the other Orders I'd met. I didn't get a sense of rigidity, she seemed cheerful. She never asked for newcomers. She barely ever looked up, working in her journal, pen to paper, for the entire period. I wondered what she could be writing so relentlessly. A novel? A sonnet? Maybe I was being fooled by her strokes and she was actually drawing a masterpiece. This was Expressive Learning, whatever that meant.

Just before the hour was up, I checked my schedule again, unable to remember my next class. Free period, a class I could finally appreciate, and my only class I shared with Meg. I made it to the room first, dawdling outside until I saw any signs of her red hair in the crowd. Free period was held inside a large room, the only furniture being a few tables and chairs against the wall. I watched kids filter in, and for the most part, it seemed kids stood or sat around on the floor and talked.

Meg ambled up a few moments after me, clutching her notebook to her chest, her knuckles so white it made the color on her nails pop. Finally, someone who seemed as jittery as me, though I didn't expect it to be her.

"Hey," I said, trying to greet her with as little apprehension as I could, even though my nerves were bouncing to greet hers.

Her eyes doubled in size as we proceeded to enter the room. "Hey?" she hissed, keeping her voice at a whisper. "How can you be so casual?"

"I can't say 'hey?'" I asked. Honestly, just being beside my best friend eased my spirit. As for her, when I'd left this morning, she'd been the confident one.

Meg's eyes jumped around. She stared so intently I almost expected the kids around us to burst into flames when her gaze landed on them. "I haven't seen Ben or Mark. Have you?"

I shook my head, biting my lip because I'd honestly forgotten to even keep an eye out for them.

"God, where are they?" We'd stopped in the middle of the room, standing facing each other. Meg's arms were tightly crossed in front of her chest, her foot beating against the floor.

"Chance did say this is a big place," I said, purely to keep her in a sane place. Anything to do with Ben set her off, and neither of us knew what that would get us in a place like this. "Is it just them that's bothering you? What happened to the Meg from this morning? You said this was just a study."

"Yeah, I did say that," she snapped. "And this entire day I haven't seen one recording device, one external note taker, nothing." She covered her eyes with her hands. "This is a hostage situation, some kind of awful hostage situation, and I don't even know where Ben is."

"It might not be," I said, although none of me believed the words I was saying. "Just be patient. We'll figure out what's going on, then we'll do something about it."

"Be patient?" Meg asked, slapping the air. It may have been meant for me, but physically we were too far apart. "We don't even know where we are. And everyone here seems to just be okay. I'm not okay with being clueless about where I am or my boyfriend."

I didn't have to come up with something else to comfort her because Chance walked up to us. "We're seeing each other a lot today," he said.

"You're rather calm," Meg grumbled.

He raised his eyebrow and looked at me. "What am I supposed to be?"

"She's upset she hasn't seen Ben yet," I said.

"He's probably around," he said to Meg. "He just hasn't found you yet. Or maybe they release us out into this simulation a few at a time. Maybe he's in the next wave."

Meg's arms were so tightly crossed, I didn't know if blood was even circulating through them. "We should have been released together."

"What, because you're dating?" Chance asked, the cynicism thick in his voice.

My ears slowly closed to their conversation as I started looking around the room. Meg could huff and puff on about her boyfriend for days, she was obsessed with him. And while I really did hope he was safe, I didn't believe talking about him would make him suddenly appear.

Among the mix of chatting and studying kids scattered around the room, three of the Order members stood like pillars at opposite walls. One of them was the one who'd given me my entrance examination.

He didn't notice me looking at him, seemingly watching everything but my area of the room. It was amazing how still he stood, not even his lips twitched. Even still, he didn't look as menacing as the other two. One, the other male, had long dark hair and a scar down the left side of his face to match. His eyes were so dark they could have been black, and maybe they were. The other, the woman, had light brown hair that also flowed down her back and, if possible, wore the exact same expression on her face, save for the scar. At least I could see her green eyes. All three of them wore the same brown robes that hid their feet.

Chance and Meg were still enveloped in their conversation over the metrics of why and how Ben hadn't been found yet, and I used that opportunity to slip away, easing myself through the crowd of kids. Although he still wasn't looking at me, I tried to make my path random, like I was wandering around the room instead of blatantly heading closer to him.

Something inside me made me stand beside him, mirroring his stance, like I was watching the others instead of trying to have a direct conversation. He didn't acknowledge my presence, but I spoke anyway, making my words clear and gentle. "Thank you."

Kanyn didn't take his eyes off the room. For a minute I thought he hadn't heard me, but then he spoke in a low placid voice, "For what?"

"The hoodie," I replied.

Another lengthy pause, then he said, "You're welcome."

Obviously I wasn't going to get a conversation out of him—which was probably for the best, I didn't need to be fraternizing with them—so I headed back over to Meg and Chance.

"You actually talked to one of them?"

"Yeah, what was that about?"

I still felt self-conscious saying anything about the hoodie. "I was just asking where the nearest bathroom was."

"It's down the hall. You didn't notice it on your way?"

I shook my head. "Wasn't paying attention. Just trying to find this room."

Chance chuckled. "I said this place is big, but it's not that big. Pay attention, Cori."

"Not even for that," Meg added. "Pay attention so we can find where they're watching us from."

"Back to the idea that this is all one big study?" I asked.

She nodded. "I'll admit, I panicked a bit there. Especially being away from you. But this is definitely some kind of study. Just look at the sample, there are people from a variety of ethnicities. They're just trying to figure out something, probably in time for some big scientific discovery that's about to come out."

I tapped my foot as I mulled over her theory. She was the one who'd been panicking only five minutes ago. Although I was used to her brief breakdowns, this one didn't feel like the others. Her concerns were more believable than her rationale. At least she seemed to be in a better mood. "You ready for laundry duty this evening?" I asked.

She groaned. "I really don't want to. Any chance they'll reassign if I ask nicely?"

"Doubt it," Chance said. "I haven't even seen one of these weirdos crack a smile. Well, except that one Kat. She's really cool."

"I like her," Meg said. "And her hair is really gorgeous. Would love to ask her what she does for it."

The thought of having normal conversation seemed far from possible, especially after the encounter I'd just had with Kanyn. But if Meg's theory turned out to be right—that this was all just one big ploy for science—maybe new friendships could be a silver lining.

✳ ✳

Before Meg and I had even arrived at the laundry room, laundry duty was already a pain. First, we got lost trying to find the room, which led to us having to approach one of the Order members to ask for directions. As if that wasn't stressful enough, after receiving the new directions, we got lost a second time. By the time we arrived at the laundry room, we were both mentally exhausted and very not ready to do laundry.

A girl with brown hair and squinty eyes stopped us when we walked in. "Are you two on laundry duty?"

We nodded.

"We're new," Meg said.

"Oh okay," the girl said. "Well, I'm Ella, and as you can see, this is the laundry room. Your job is easy. You go to your section, you sort, you wash, you dry. Don't mix clothes between sections because they're separated so that people get the same sizes back. Gloves are provided."

Meg and I nodded, and Ella showed us our pile of gray clothing to wash. The washers and dryers alternated in a line, forming an L shape. Our spot was in the back of the room around the corner where we couldn't be seen from the door. If we wanted to, we could spend the whole night goofing off.

Meg must have been thinking the same thing because as soon as Ella rounded the corner, she said to me, "We got a good spot."

I chuckled as I put on a pair of gloves and started loading clothes into the washer. "I don't think this will be that bad. We're waiting for most of the time."

"This will get old real fast," Meg said as she began helping me.

I paused with the clothes halfway to the washer and looked at her. "Do you really think we'll be here long enough for this to get old?"

She gazed at me, and I saw a twinge of apprehension flicker through her eyes. "It'll be old by tomorrow."

I nodded and continued loading the clothes into the washer. We worked in silence getting all the clothes loaded. Once the washer was going, we stood back and looked around. Others, who I assumed were all used to this, chatted amongst themselves or read books. I wondered what was the longest any of them had been here.

My attention sparked when I heard Meg whispering, but not to me. I turned to see who she was talking to.

A boy, maybe a year older than us. He was tall, tan, and thin, and he leaned against the table talking to Meg. I couldn't hear his words, but his whisper was rushed and excited.

Meg glanced back at me, then turned back to him and nodded.

I didn't have to wait long, Meg motioned me to join their conversation.

"What's up?" My eyes darted to the boy, then back to Meg.

"You two wanna get out of here?" he asked, and I could hear a thick Greek accent in his words.

"What do you mean?" I asked.

"I'm breaking out tonight," the boy replied. "I've been here long enough to have this place down to a science. If you want to get out of here, I'm your way."

"Who are you?" I asked, but my eyes stayed on Meg because what in the hell was she getting us into?

"Names aren't important," the boy replied. "Look, do you girls want out or not? I've got a whole schedule and I'm already running behind by offering myself to you."

At the same time I opened my mouth to decline his offer, Meg beat me to it with a confident yes.

"Alright," the boy said, rubbing his hands together. "We'll leave in about five minutes, when people start to unload."

Looking at my arm, I saw goosebumps that hadn't been there before. In five minutes, the clothes spinning inside each washer dulled to a rumble. I looked over at Meg a few times, but she kept her eyes on the clock.

Just as I was about to suggest we wait to make a better plan, the boy hopped up away from the table, gave us a quick motion with his hand, and headed toward the exit. Without hesitation, Meg followed, and I did too.

As the others in the room worked to unload washers and load dryers, no one batted an eye toward us. We left behind the room full of motors, and suddenly we were the loudest things in the building. Even though we were tiptoeing, every step down the hallway echoed. The shadows from the dim hall lights against the black night wrapped around us, perhaps covering us, but they were suffocating.

The echoing amplified, and I realized I was speeding up, trying to match our guide's increasing pace.

He was steps in front of Meg and I, and as he turned a corner, both of us jogged to catch up. To our dismay, when we looked around the corner, we were met with a short cut-through perpendicular between two hallways.

"Shit, which way did he go?" I breathed, my skin so cold my shirt scratched against it.

"I think he went this way," Meg replied, jogging down the short hallway. "Come on."

I hurried after her, although my confidence in escape waned. She waited for me just at the end, letting me go first. Just as I was about to step around the corner, out of the edge of my vision I spotted someone else in the hall with our escapee. Immediately I flattened myself against the wall, and Meg stopped next to me. I was closer to the corner, so I peeked out, just enough so that I had a view of the hall.

An Order stood in front of the boy—towered over him really—and just like the rest, a scowl was etched into his face. The Order leaned his face close to the boy's. "Where do you think you're going?"

"I was just going to get some water, I swear!"

"Do I look like a fool to you?"

"N-N-No, of course not."

"Clearly you think I am, to dare say you were just getting some water." The Order grabbed the boy by his collar, forcefully jerking him even closer to his blazing eyes. "Look me in the eyes boy and tell me you were just going to get water."

"I was just going to get water."

The Order's eyes narrowed and his voice came out just above a cruel whisper. "You're bold to lie." In one motion, he slammed the boy against the wall. "Try again."

The boy would not let his lie go. "Just water, I swear."

The Order slammed him into the wall again, this time so hard his head smacked against the cement. "Try again."

I couldn't watch this Order kill that boy. I pulled my head back from around the corner and pressed my back up against the wall. Meg had crouched to the floor and was holding her head against her knees. I wished we had stayed in the laundry room.

"Amaris, what is the issue here?"

I recognized the voice immediately, causing me to peek back around the corner.

Just as I'd thought, Kanyn had walked into the hallway, and not that he ever looked pleased with anything, he looked less than pleased with the one called Amaris. Next to Amaris, Kanyn's hair didn't seem as golden, but more of a butter scotch blond. Amaris's hair was golden, as if someone had poured the molten liquid right atop his head.

Amaris sneered at Kanyn, but loosened his grip on the boy. "This kid was trying to run away. Then had the nerve to claim he just wanted water."

"I'm sorry!" the boy managed to gurgle out. "I won't do it again."

Kanyn's gaze stayed on the boy for a few seconds, and I thought he might actually let him die. Then he spoke, "Amaris, let him go."

Without hesitating, Amaris shoved the guy backwards into the wall, but stepped back from him. "You got lucky, kid. Better not try that again."

The boy rubbed his throat, tears brimming in his eyes. "I won't, I won't."

"Where are you supposed to be right now?" Kanyn asked him.

"I-I'm on laundry duty right now."

"And you left without permission?"

The boy nodded.

"That's a shot."

A shot. Provos had briefly touched on that while he was showing us to our rooms. Shots were like points on a license. He didn't tell us what consequences the points equaled to, he only told us we wanted as little as possible, none being the best option.

"Yes, of course, that's fine. I deserve that."

Kanyn tipped his head. "Alright, let's get you back to the laundry room."

I looked at Meg but the same thought had already entered her head. Not looking behind us once, we scurried back the way we came to the laundry room. I took a cursory glance around as we rushed into the room, and sighed with relief seeing we'd beat them back.

I'd just opened a dryer when the door to the laundry room swung open. Even being in the back around the corner, I knew they'd arrived.

Everyone stopped what they were doing and looked in their direction. The only sound as they walked through was the sounds of the machines and their footsteps.

Before they reached the corner, Meg shot me a worried look.

I made my face as neutral as possible. There was no way they could know we'd left, they hadn't taken the same path back.

But what if they did know? What would they do to us? Amaris had almost killed that boy.

The more those thoughts rushed through my head, the faster my breathing became. I had to work twice as hard to maintain a normal speed.

By the time they turned the corner, my face was extremely hot, but my blood ran icy throughout the rest of my body.

This was it, they knew. That boy had probably told them on the way back that he hadn't left the laundry room alone. They were going to take us and punish us for trying to run away.

The boy went back to his post a few washers down. Kanyn and Amaris stayed in the room for a few minutes, their eyes washing over everyone, before they finally left.

Heaving a huge sigh, I sat down on the floor. We didn't make eye contact with the boy for the rest of the shift.

5

Last night was too close for comfort. Going to bed, my frayed nerves still popped, echoing in my head like our footsteps had in the hall. That night, I didn't sleep. I waited. Any moment Amaris would burst into our room in the middle of the night to punish us. He'd hold us by our collars and shake us until the life left through our eyes.

Amaris—or any member of the Order—never came. I awoke in my bunk, my sheets fitted tightly against me like a shield.

I was numb during my first two classes. The worry of Amaris coming to get me sat heavily on my shoulder like a hawk.

Amaris looked like he was going to kill that boy if Kanyn hadn't stepped in. He probably would have done the same to Meg and I. And how many had he treated like that before?

To that point, did they all treat people like that? Yes, that boy had broken the rule, and if anything, these Order members seemed to care deeply about the rules. But the deadly look on Amaris's face was burned into my brain. That was the face of a killer.

Making my way to my next class I was a droplet of water flowing through the sea of students. I barely noticed them, and they barely noticed me.

My thoughts ate at me all day. I barely spoke to Meg during our free period, which visibly crushed her. She liked to talk things out, to verbalize her thoughts. I didn't. I barely let out three words at dinner, but at least then Meg had Chance, Shaun, and Airi to talk to. Since I didn't have laundry duty that evening, after dinner I went to the library to look around, and most importantly to be by myself.

As I walked through the doorway, a wave of comfort washed over me, flushing my thoughts out through the back of my head. They'd set the library up like the academic ones so familiar to me. I didn't even have to bother the female Order sitting at the front desk. I wandered directly to the section I was looking for. Not that I was looking for anything particular, just anything to take my mind off last night. I ended up consuming myself in a book I came across at random.

I reached the middle of the book before finally looking up at the clock. After ten already. I put the book back, disinterested in bringing any of their items into my personal space, and left the library.

Leaving such a safe space, my thoughts began to run wild again. The attempted escapee, Amaris, them, this place. Going straight back to my room to try and go to bed would only give my anxieties the opportunity to fester. Instead, I decided to roam a little. I came to the area where we had physical training, finding another boy leaning against one of the archways, a cigarette between his fingers.

My plan was to just walk past him, but when I was within his earshot, he spoke up. "Already having trouble sleeping?"

I nodded, slightly hesitating in my step.

"I've been here a few weeks, maybe a month now. It doesn't get easier." The boy blew smoke out the side of his mouth, considerately in the opposite direction of me. "My name is Yannis. You?"

"Cori."

An expression of recognition crossed his face. "Laundry duty?"

"Yeah," I replied, curious as to how he knew.

He chuckled. "It only took you a few hours to try and get out of here."

I looked at him. He obviously knew something, but I wasn't about to give anything away.

"The guy who convinced you he could get you out of here. He's my friend, Ermis."

"If you guys are friends, why wasn't he taking you with him?"

Yannis took a long drag from his cigarette, then let the smoke escape through the hole in his lips. "Because he is *ilíthios*. Stupid."

"Yeah, he didn't do such a great job getting us out. We barely made it down the hallway."

He shook his head. "Not that. Where did he think he was going to go? You see there's a giant wall that encircles this place. He didn't have a plan to get over that wall. And even if he did, what would he do then? Where would he go? How would he get there?"

"You don't have a lot of faith in your friend."

He took another drag. "I've seen people try and escape here. None of them have succeeded. No one thinks past getting out these walls." He tipped his cigarette toward the wall in the distance. "It's that wall that's the obstacle, the first obstacle. Next is getting past what's beyond it."

"And no one knows what's beyond it?" I asked.

"Not for sure. I've heard guesses. The majority of people think we're on an island, so they assume there's some kind of plane or boat waiting beyond the wall. That has to be how people get here." Yannis shrugged. "Then again, we could be in the middle of the city, and just beyond the wall is a bustling town." He looked at me and his lips parted to a small toothy smile. "My money is on the island theory."

I nodded. "It seems more likely."

"Outside the air smells like Greece," he said. "But I'm from Patmos. I'd hate to find out all this time I was so close to home."

So close to home. These people here—these kids—has been taken from all over the world.

"You said you've been here a month," I said.

"About."

"And others? Do you know what the longest is?"

Yannis rubbed his chin as he thought. "I know a couple people who have been here two months. Maybe one that's been here three months. There aren't many that have been here past that. And people have left."

"They send people home?"

"They've left," he replied.

I furrowed my brow at him. "So, they went home?"

"Maybe."

"What do you mean maybe? Where did they go then?"

"I don't know," he replied. "You'll start to see. There isn't an announcement or anything. Just one day, this person isn't in your class anymore—isn't in your room anymore. You never see them again."

"Sounds like they went home."

"Maybe."

We turned our attention to the hallway at the sound of footsteps approaching. It was Trainus, and he flashed us a curt look when he noticed us.

"Curfew is at eleven."

"Yes sir," Yannis said. He held up his cigarette. "Smoke?"

Trainus narrowed his eyes. "No." He kept walking.

As the Order member walked away, Yannis tilted the cigarette back to his lips, but his expression had darkened. "Something's not right here," he said.

"Of course," I said, flashing a look at Trainus's back.

"No. I don't know how to explain it. But something is really off about this whole thing. I just can't figure out what it is."

I looked at him. "Something beyond the fact that we've been kidnapped and brought to a boarding school?"

He nodded. "Yes. Something beyond that."

✳ ✳

I wanted to talk to Yannis again the next morning during breakfast, but he didn't show in the cafeteria. He was the first person I'd met that seemed like he'd be able to tell me about this place, and with the same amount of suspicion I had. I didn't see him in the halls either between my first few classes.

As I entered the courtyard for physical training, my stomach flipflopped. Cones were placed in pairs at different lengths apart. I knew immediately what the activity for the day would be. Long jumps.

I wasn't a runner, and I wasn't a jumper, nor was I really too concerned about those flaws. But I also didn't want to do either of those things at the moment.

Trainus unfortunately wasted no time getting us into stretches and then lining us up to start the humiliation.

I did better than I expected on the first two, but the third I only landed a foot or so away from the starting cone. I attempted it two more times, each with the same result.

Standing off the side, I watched some of the other students go. Some were good, some weren't at all. It was just like P.E. Except I was eighteen, and some of the others were too, if not older. We were past the need for a class like this. What was the point, just to repeat our academic experience?

I looked over just in time to see Gianni landing his jump, a big smile across his face. He really was good at them, but it seemed he was good at everything.

I wasn't the only one who noticed. Trainus walked over to him. "You really are doing well at these," he said to Gianni.

The smile on Gianni's face brightened. "Of course. These are nothing."

"You were quite the athlete in school?"

"The athlete?" Gianni asked. "Try the best athlete. I'm on every team. Basketball, rugby, football, track. Number fourteen for all of them."

"Fourteen, huh?"

Gianni nodded. "Picked the number myself. You know, it came to me one day like in a dream or something. Figured it must mean something."

I couldn't listen to the rest of their conversation, partially because I felt like I was going to throw up. Breakfast was revolting from being thrown around so much.

I spent more time sitting out for the rest of the class than jumping, but at least I wasn't the only one. At least five other people also gave up on jumping, or at least had no desire to improve on what they could already do.

It was a sigh of relief when the bell finally rang.

As I made my way towards my next class, I noticed two Order members down the hallway, standing against the wall a few feet from one another on opposite sides. They weren't members I'd seen before.

The way they stood made the hairs on the back of my neck stand. They were rigid like stone pillars, and there was nothing in their eyes, as if they weren't looking at anything. But I knew, of course, they were.

"They're telepathic."

I spun on my feet, startled. Glancing at the blonde girl now standing beside me, I asked, "What?"

"You can tell," she said, "just watch them interact."

I looked back at the two Order members.

They were still watching opposite sides of the hall. Then, the one with darker hair turned so he was looking directly at the one with lighter hair. The lighter haired Order didn't return his gaze, but then he nodded, and walked away. The one with the darker hair went back to watching.

"Did you see that?" the girl asked.

I nodded, unsure if I really had seen it. Maybe he'd just mouthed something to the other across the hall. But I hadn't seen his lips move, and the one with lighter hair hadn't even looked in his direction.

"My name is Kaisa," the girl said. "Or as they call me, Number Four Hundred and Sixty-Seven."

"I'm Cori," I said. "Five Hundred and Seven."

"The numbers are supposed to take away our identity."

"I figured, but I tell anyone I meet my name," I said.

"Me too," she said with a small smile. "Guess they didn't plan for individual thinkers."

I nodded, but I was still stuck on the first part of our conversation. "Do you really think they're telepathic?"

"What do you think of them?"

I looked back at the remaining Order member. "I don't know what to think of them. They can't be human, right? They just don't seem it. They're so tall and their skin color, it's so unnatural."

"I agree," she said. "But it's not like I would ever ask one of them what they are."

"Because they told us not to ask questions."

She arched her eyebrow. "No."

"Then why?"

"Because by asking, that lets them know that I've noticed. It gives them an insight as to what I'm thinking. I'd prefer them to believe my thoughts align with everyone else's. More importantly, align with what they want my thoughts to be."

She seemed like someone I could talk to honestly. "Do you find it weird that more people aren't, well, deathly afraid of being here?"

Kaisa paused before shaking her head. "Not really. They've normalized the situation, so it doesn't seem as threatening. And it's impossible to live every moment in fear, the brain can't handle it. Everyone is just coping the best they can." She eyed me. "You?"

"I guess you're right. I don't really feel that scared."

She grinned. "Good. Then when the time comes. whenever that may be, you'll outsmart them. They want you to be scared, that's all they have." She glanced at the clock on the wall. "I better get to my next class. See you around."

I nodded as she walked off, needing to get to my next class as well. I took my time, however, mulling over what Kaisa had brought to my attention.

Telepathy. If they were capable of using telepathy, then they certainly weren't human. So, what were they?

❋ ❋

I didn't run into Yannis or Kaisa again the rest of the day. I wanted to ask both of them questions. They'd been here longer than me, and they seemed to know a few things.

I had no idea where to find Kaisa at this time of night, not even to where her room could be located. But it was coming up on the time I'd come upon Yannis before.

Meg fell asleep, curled up at the edge of her bed. At a quarter past ten, I tiptoed out the room, making my way back to the spot I'd found Yannis before. To my disappointment, he wasn't there, not even a lingering trace of a cigarette.

I leaned against the inside of one of the archways, the same way Yannis had been, but I directed my attention to the outside. To the wall.

I hadn't had much time to really study the structure. I'd been trying to lay low for the most part, go to class and back to my room. But now I could really look at it. A tall brick wall, tall enough that no matter how far back you stood you couldn't see even a hint over it. And it was smooth, nothing to even dream of climbing.

Yannis's words came tumbling in, the idea that a bustling city could be right outside. I doubted it. We should've been able to hear something of a city. Even if there were no cars, we should hear a shout or some kind of communication at least once.

"Curfew is at eleven."

I turned around to see Kanyn walking up to me. He wasn't scowling like Trainus had been, but he wasn't smiling either. "I'm sorry, I guess I lost track of time."

Kanyn's eyes left me for a moment to look up at the sky. "Stargazing?"

"Yeah. It's very clear skies here, not like in the city."

He stared up at the sky a moment longer, then looked back at me. "The best place to stargaze is in the far side of the north wing." He turned and headed back inside.

I couldn't help but watch him walk away. I'd expected him to hurry me off to my room, maybe even lead me there himself. But he hadn't. I didn't want to believe it, but I couldn't help but consider, something about him was different.

I waited as long as I could for Yannis, but he never came, and I didn't want to risk getting a shot for being out so late.

✳ ✳

The next day I searched again for both Yannis and Kaisa, though admittedly not very far. The hair on my body rose at even the thought of going somewhere I wasn't allowed to. I only looked for them on my way from our room to breakfast, and from breakfast to the library. They had quite the vanishing act. Even on a campus with more people, I saw the same people frequently. And they weren't the only ones.

I dragged through my first three classes, especially physical training. I was exhausted. I'd kept myself awake making lists of what could be on the other side of the wall, and then going through those lists item by item on how plausible each item was. Somewhere in all that I fell asleep, but my dreams were filled of things outside the wall, things I used to be doing.

It wasn't until I was slogging across the field on my way to my next class that I realized who else was missing from my day.

Gianni.

Though my eyelids were barely open and much of Trainus's instructions were garble—that was normal—there hadn't been a constant pompous chatter in the background. Nor had my eyes had to roll from an unnecessary athletic feat.

I couldn't say I missed his presence, and clearly not if I hadn't even realized it until after class. Lucky him, he'd probably sneaked his way out of class. Or maybe even out of this place altogether, just as Yannis had said. I added him to my list, three long now, of people to look out for during the day.

My heart actually fluttered when it finally came time for free period. I could sit in one place, maybe even close my eyes for a little bit.

Meg and Chance waited for me at the doors.

"I need this today," Chance commented.

"Same," I mumbled, my eyes suddenly becoming so heavy I could barely lift them from the floor as we started walking in. I looked up for just a moment and my eyes met Kanyn's. As quick as they met, I pulled mine away. But as I trailed behind Meg and Chance farther into the room, I felt him still watching. We sat down near the back wall, and I dared to glance at him again, but his gaze was on the front half of the room.

I thought back to our interaction in the hallway last night. He could have easily barked at me the same way Trainus and every other Order did.

But he hadn't, in fact he'd almost been gentle with his words. Reserved, but gentle.

"I can't do this," Meg said, cutting into my thoughts.

"What? Not posting on social media?" Chance asked.

She reached over and slapped his shoulder. "This, Chance. All of this. What even is this? School?"

"I know just as much as you do," he said. "In fact, I should know less. It was you two that tried to fast track it out of here."

I threw a look at Meg. "You told him?"

She shrugged. "It slipped out. Besides that was days ago. Or was it? I'm losing track of time already."

"I think it's kind of nice," Chance said. "Not having my phone or laptop. Just pen and paper and books. Have you walked around a little? It's nice outside."

"You mean besides the wall," I said.

"Well yes," he replied. "The wall is pretty obtrusive. But still nice."

"You sound like a crazy person. Thinking this is nice," Meg said. "What's on the other side of the wall? It's obviously there to keep us in here. Why?"

"Maybe it's actually keeping something out," Chance said. "You know walls can have many purposes."

Their debate fell into the background noise as I glanced over at Kanyn again. Something was different about him. He'd given me my hoodie back and told me where best to see the stars, things I'd never expect from any of the others.

I needed answers about this place, and he might just be my best option. Just as I had before, I ambled through the room until I positioned myself right next to him. I thought I felt him slightly shudder at my proximity.

"I didn't get a chance to make it to the north wing," I said in the same clear and gentle voice I'd used before.

His same pause, and then he said, "Probably for the better. You shouldn't be wandering around."

"I wouldn't call it wandering," I said. "It seemed like an invitation."

Another pause. "If that's how you chose to hear it."

My brow furrowed. I had to concentrate hard to hear his words above the noise but also to hear how he said things. He kept the briefest of an edge in his voice, but other than that he was gentle.

"It must suck that the rest of the Orders get to teach and you have to be babysitter for twenty or so kids."

Another pause, this one shorter. "I don't mind. I'm not much of a teacher. More of an observer."

"How do you focus with so much going on?"

"Selective attention."

"What are you watching for?"

"Everything."

"Everything," I repeated with an impulsive smirk. "You're only focusing on selective things but yet you're watching for everything."

I thought I saw his lips attempt to mirror my smirk. "I hear how that sounds. Let's say I'm focusing on everything then."

I watched him for a few more seconds out of the corner of my eye. If he was attempting to smirk, he never allowed it to fully form. I asked, "Does anything ever happen?"

"Sometimes."

"Like?"

"I wouldn't concern myself with that, if I were you," he replied.

I felt my eyebrows sliding into a scowl. Maybe thinking I could have an actual conversation with him had been a mistake.

"You don't want something to happen," he added, his tone sharper.

My blood chilled. He said it like a threat, like it would be the worst thing if 'something' happened for any of us. I nodded once. "Well," I said almost hoarsely. "Thanks for that. Good talking to you."

He didn't respond and I didn't linger. I made my way back over to Meg and Chance, who were even deeper in their argument than when I'd left them.

Meg sighed and crossed her arms. "Couldn't they at least give us a laptop here? It would be so much easier to look things up."

"I've seen like two desktops in the library I'm pretty sure," Chance said.

"They're crap, I've already tried them," Meg said. "They're dinosaurs, they can barely access the internet. And I think they've got so many blocks on them, no results can even get through."

"They really want us blocked from the outside world," I said. I thought about the wall around us. They had us completely cut off. Watching us like hawks inside a facility unknown to the rest of the world.

We made small talk the rest of the hour, revisiting some events from our time in college.

By the time I was walking to my last class, all I wanted to do was to curl up for a nap right after. I propped the side of my face up on my fist, but immediately felt my eyelids droop. Shaking my head, I repositioned with my chin resting on my arms.

Viscount walked in, but another Order trailed behind him. Just as the others, this Order had long brown hair and a humorless face, though it was hard to see since he kept his eyes pointed at the ground. Better that way. He diverted from Viscount, walking along the perimeter of the classroom until he reached the very middle. Propping himself up against the wall, he looked up and I shuddered. From my seat, his eyes were piercing. He carried every ounce of rigidness in his jaw.

As the kids finally stopped milling in and the bell rang, Viscount cleared his throat, causing the class to drop into silence. His eyes swept the room before he started speaking. "I see we have some new faces."

I glanced around. Not that I knew my classmates well enough to know who was new and who wasn't, it seemed like the girl in the back room hugging herself could have been a newbie. Everyone else looked a little more relaxed.

"I am Viscount and that, over there, is Hunter," Viscount said. "Don't mind him, he just wanted to hear some things from class."

I had to stop myself from constantly looking over at Hunter. He was so still it was unnerving, and his eyes looked like black holes in his head. I could feel whenever his gaze swept over my section of the room.

The class crawled by, and although the presence of the other Order created a tense air around my classmates, their attention still faltered. Eyes closing then quickly reopening, pens twirling.

My own eyelids threatened to close, Viscount's voice becoming a dull hum in the background of my mind.

A new sound suddenly scraped through my ear drums. My eyes fully open, I looked behind me to see a girl standing up at her desk, her eyebrows knitted into deeply slanted slits.

"I'm tired of this shit," she said, her hand in a fist at her side. "This is ridiculous. I'm a senior in college, I graduate in December. I have a life to get back to."

"Number Four Hundred and One, please sit down."

"No, this is bullshit." Four Hundred and One looked at all of us. "What is wrong with all of you? Just going along with all of this. Don't you get it? This is basic psychology, it's Milgram's study of obedience. They've got nothing. We only feel scared because they portray authority figures." She turned back to Viscount. "I'm not afraid to stand up to your 'authority.' It's all fake anyway, I bet there's a car waiting for us right outside the wall or something. We're probably in the middle of the city."

Viscount's gaze had turned icy. "Sit down."

"I don't need this." Four Hundred and One picked up her notebook and pencil, and strode toward the front of the classroom. "This is bullshit, you're all full of bullshit, and I don't need—"

The next moment happened so fast, I blinked and missed most of it.

Four Hundred and One was one row from the front of the classroom when Hunter jumped—he had to have jumped from his position on the wall—in front of her. The scariest part was the knife he held at her throat. And the eeriest part was that he wasn't actually holding it. It floated a few centimeters in front of his outstretched hand, pointed directly at her neck.

Hunter didn't take his eyes off her, but even after jumping to action like that, he wore the same expression.

Four Hundred and One on the other hand looked like she was about to cry, her eyes jumping from the knife to the rest of us, pleading for help.

"Now, Number Four Hundred and One," Viscount said, "if you would please take your seat." He didn't look a single bit fazed by what was happening.

Hunter straightened up, lowering his hand, and subsequently the knife, as he did.

Four Hundred and One hurried back to her seat, lowering her head.

I then realized I'd dropped the pencil I was holding while watching everything. I wasn't the only one frozen in shock.

What in the world had just happened? Had we really seen that? Had Hunter used some sort of telekinesis to hold a knife at her?

I didn't know what to do. I didn't know what to think! I hadn't decided if the members of the Order were humans. After that, I definitely did not believe they were.

✳ ✳

If I thought I couldn't sleep before, now it was really bad. I even went straight to my room after class to nap, but my eyes refused to shut as I lay pin straight in my bed. My mind exhausted itself replaying the scene over and over in my head, so much so that I couldn't even focus on reviewing any of my notes. I grabbed a box of cereal from the dining hall but opted to nibble away at it on a bench in one of the more secluded hallways. I didn't even want to return to my room just thinking about the challenge it was going to be to keep my eyes closed again.

My attention turned away from my sleep troubles as I heard voices around the corner. Getting up from my bench, I tiptoed over to I could hear better. Too curious, I peeked my head around.

A little way down the hall stood Amaris, Hunter, and Kanyn.

"Heard about what happened," Amaris said, playfully socking Hunter in the arm.

"Everyone has," Kanyn said to Hunter, the same playfulness completely absent from his face.

"I would have killed to see everyone's faces," Amaris chuckled. "I'm sure the pipsqueak won't be stepping out of line again any time soon."

Kanyn flashed Amaris a look, then looked back at the younger Order. "Hunter, you were too rash."

"Yes," he said with a nod. For the entire conversation he'd been staring at the ground, not making eye contact with either of them.

"Who was in that class?" Kanyn asked.

"Kids," Amaris replied dryly. "Why do you want to know?"

"I think it would only be wise to assess each one about what they witnessed and how they're feeling regarding."

Amaris took a challenging step toward Kanyn. "You care about them?"

"I care about them not going into mass hysteria because one of us held a knife to a student's throat without touching it."

Amaris looked like he had something else to say, but decided against it. "Fine. If you feel like that, you can handle it. Let's go Hunter." Without waiting for a response, he took off on a stride down the hallway.

Hunter looked at Kanyn before following Amaris.

I tiptoed back over to the bench. Obviously Kanyn wasn't fond of what Hunter had done. Amaris, the sadistic bastard he was, loved every minute of it. And Hunter, well, he seemed both remiss and regretful of the situation. But none of that gave me any peace of mind. Not one of them talked about how they shouldn't be threatening us with knives. And no one gave an explanation as to Hunter levitating a knife in the air.

I became so engulfed in my thoughts, staring at my feet, that I didn't notice the Order walking up to me until he stood right in front of me. At the sight of another pair of shoes in my vision, I quickly looked up.

Kanyn stood in front of me. "Could I speak to you in my office?" he asked.

I nodded. Apparently I was to be his first subject. I wouldn't have minded making a scene of mass hysteria. It would certainly feel better than acting like everything was fine.

6

I followed Kanyn down the hall to his office. Most of the other rooms we passed looked to be offices too, but all their doors were closed. Apparently, no one opted to work as late as him.

We arrived at his office—what I assumed to be his since he opened the door, but there was no nametag or other indication of the room belonging to him.

It was a small space, no bigger than a master bedroom closet. A wood desk stood in the middle, his chair on one side and a chair for guests on the other. Unlike any office I'd seen in the last ten years, there was no trace of technology on his desk, only a pale brown leather notebook. The only other items of furniture in the room were two bookshelves, a tall one opposite the door and a shorter one behind his desk. He kept it neat, not a book or paper out of place.

He sat down first, then motioned for me to do the same. Without even waiting to make sure I did, he opened the notebook and began writing on one of the pages.

Waiting for him to speak, anger bubbled up inside me. His face was expressionless, and he just scribbled in his stupid notebook. Why wasn't he asking me questions immediately, trying to calm my nerves, anything? I saw one of them holding a knife to a girl's throat with two feet of space between his hand and the handle. And Kanyn had the nerve to bring me in here and make me wait to release all my panic.

Finally, he looked up at me, and when he did, my frustration brimmed just below my ears. I could feel the strain in my eyes as I looked at him, the tautness around my lips.

"What did you see in your philosophy class today?" he asked.

"I saw Hunter almost kill someone." My answer was curt, but I could think of it no other way.

"How did you feel in that moment?"

"Like I was about to see someone die."

"And how do you feel now?"

My frustration had risen over my ears, and I felt like I was looking at him sideways. How did I feel now? A hundred words came to mind to describe my current mental state, but none of them could break past the wall of stupidity building up by my makeshift therapist. "Like I almost saw someone die and that this is stupid."

Kanyn looked up at me, seemingly a little surprised by my sardonic tone.

"I'm sorry, would you like me to use descriptives?" I asked. "Scared. Bored. Appalled. Exhausted. Untrusting."

A few seconds ticked before Kanyn found his next words. "Are you scared of Hunter now?" he asked.

"I was scared of him before. He isn't exactly approachable," I replied. I was scared of this whole place I wanted to add, but I remembered Kaisa's words about letting them into my thoughts. "Clearly he's dangerous. Why isn't someone as unpredictably violent as him kept on a leash or something?" To my surprise, I thought I saw a hint of a smile at the edges of his lips.

He closed his notebook and stood up from his desk, motioning toward the door. "That's enough for today."

"That's it?" I asked as I stood up. My frustration knocked against the underside of my skull. "Are you going to do anything? He's a psychopath."

"I don't think that's for you to judge," Kanyn said.

I had every right to judge. I'd seen the man throw—or hover or whatever—a knife at a classmate. "What about the way he did it? He wasn't holding onto that knife, it was just floating."

"Maybe you thought you saw that," he said.

My hands went to my hips. "I didn't think I saw anything. I saw it clearly. He wasn't holding that knife."

"It's best you return to your room, Number Five Hundred and Seven."

I wanted to challenge him on it but truthfully, laying my head down on a pillow sounded better than standing there arguing. I didn't turn my back on him until I was out the door of his office.

As I started down the halls, I realized I should have curbed my attitude just enough to ask for directions back to my room. Surely, I'd find it eventually, if not wander into some occult ritual beforehand.

I was just about to turn a corner when I caught sight of three people in the next hallway. Immediately I pulled back, flattening myself against the wall and praying none of them had seen me. When I didn't hear footsteps coming my way, I peeked around the corner.

As I'd suspected, they were members of the Order, one of them Hunter. The other two with him were taller than him by at least a head. One had dark brown hair and a pointed nose, with a metal bar industrial piercing at the top of his ear. The other had blond hair so light and void of yellow tints, it was the color of wax. The most prominent thing about him were the bags under his eyes.

"Come on Hunter, tell us," the one with the piercing said. "What caused you to snap like that?"

Hunter didn't respond, keeping his eyes directed to the side of his opposer.

The same one used a single hand to shove Hunter. "Why didn't you kill her?"

Hunter didn't even move back to the spot he'd been in before. He continued to look past him.

"Damn it, answer me, Hunter!"

Finally, Hunter spoke, but even then, he didn't look at the Order. "I just wanted to remind her of her place, Jutas."

Jutas scoffed, but that answer seemed to appease him. "You know Incencio is seething over what you did." He grabbed the end of Hunter's ponytail and ran his thumb across the ends. "Wouldn't be surprised if he made you chop off this beautiful hair for it."

Hunter glared at him but didn't pull away.

Jutas held his gaze, then dropped the hair. He crossed his arms. "If you ask nicely, I'll do it for you."

Hunter still didn't say anything, side stepping him, beginning to walk away.

"Walk away Hunter!" Jutas called after him. "Just keep walking, right on out of this place, you coward!"

My heart was trying to leap out of my chest. Hunter was one thing, but this other Order, Jutas, he seemed well near malicious.

I didn't exhale until I couldn't hear Jutas and the other in the hallway anymore. Compared to everyone else here, Hunter seemed to be the youngest. Whatever they were, clearly they weren't immune to simple behaviors like bullying.

Eventually, I found my way back to my room. Meg was already asleep, and I was too exhausted to do anything that might wake her. Any thoughts about Hunter's browbeating were quickly forgotten as I drifted off to sleep.

✶ ✶

I woke up in cold sweats. The first thing I remembered was the interaction between Hunter and Jutas. The second thing was being in Kanyn's office. The third was the girl and the knife.

Sleep hung under Meg's eyes as she got ready that morning. If she had heard about the knife incident, she didn't say anything. I was bursting to tell her what I'd gone through the evening before, but I held it in. She wouldn't hear me with fatigue clogging her ears, and her general anxiety strumming in her brain. As far as I knew, she hadn't found Ben yet, and that was the only thing that mattered.

When we arrived at breakfast, the same nervous energy as every morning filled the air. We took a seat across from Chance, Shauna, and Airi. We were becoming our own little group.

"Damn, you look exhausted," Chance commented as Meg drooped into her seat.

She glared at him, but barely, the skin around her eyes quivering to move. "That's not how you greet someone."

"I'm just saying," he said. "Did you sleep at all?"

"No," she snapped. Her irritation made me wonder if she'd been waiting for me to come back to talk to me. "It's been six days and I still haven't seen Ben. This place isn't that big."

"Maybe he's in another facility," Shauna said.

"You think there's another one of these?" Airi asked.

Shauna shrugged. "I mean Hitler had how many camps."

I didn't want to compare our situation with the Holocaust, but she did have a point. For all we knew, there could be other facilities housing more like us. But the thought sent a shiver down my spine.

"How do you know he was even brought here?" Chance asked.

Meg glanced at me. "Well, we were all together when they kidnapped us ..."

Chance shrugged. "I don't know. Maybe he's keeping a very low profile. Or maybe he's not even here. And if he's not, you don't need to keep worrying."

Meg stuck a spoonful of cereal into her mouth, but I knew her well enough to know nothing but Ben's face would keep her from worrying about him.

Out the corner of my eye I spotted Kaisa standing at the front of the cafeteria, holding a tray of food and looking around for a place to sit. I waved her over.

"Hey, new person," Chance said. He introduced himself and the rest of them followed suit.

"I'm Kaisa," she said. One of her fair eyebrows poked upwards. "One guy and all these girls? What kind of group did I walk into?"

Meg rolled her eyes and I wanted to as well. Just what we needed, someone to feed his ego.

"Did you guys hear what happened yesterday?" Shauna asked before Chance could let his ego shine.

"Was it real?" Meg asked. "It sounds kind of ridiculous. Holding a knife without holding it?"

"That's what I heard!" Shauna exclaimed. "That's why it's so crazy."

"Maybe she just thought he wasn't holding it because it was so close," Meg said. "You know your vision gets weird when objects are close."

"I was in the class," I said, barely loud enough for them to hear, but everyone's attention immediately turned to me.

"What did you see?" Airi asked.

" I ... It happened like you heard. Hunter jumped across the room. Well, I guess he jumped. One minute he was leaning against the wall and the next he was in front of her." I exhaled through my nose because I still didn't know what to make of the next part. "He held a knife at her, but he wasn't holding it. There were at least five inches or so between the knife and his hand."

I noticed Meg's mouth gaping beside me. She aired more on the skeptical side, so I knew hearing her best friend talk about such fantastical elements didn't sit right.

"How could he do that?" Airi asked, her voice a whisper.

"Strings?" Chance asked. "Maybe he's some kind of magician?"

Kaisa chuckled. "I see why you're able to have so many girls surrounding you. Do you really think that's it? That he's a magician?"

He shrugged. "There are kids running around here thinking this is Hogwarts."

"And they're pathetic," Kaisa said, bringing everyone's attention to her. "This is not a magical school, and on the one percent chance that it is, it's not the friendly version from the movies." She looked around, then lowered her voice. "None of you should underestimate them. They're smart. And there's nothing normal about this place or anything they do."

Icy chills pricked my arms and back. I wasn't underestimating them. But I also didn't understand, and that dulled my other senses, those instincts

I'd normally have. I'd seen someone have a knife at their throat and I hadn't run out of the room.

Kaisa was right to warn us, and she was right to think smarter than them. The problem was how many others could do the same?

✳ ✳

At least one person whispered about the incident from yesterday in each of my classes. I stuck my ears out to see if I'd hear anything different, but it was all the same. Gossip more than facts, speculations and rumors. Some people truly believed they had some sort of magical ability to levitate objects, while others refused to budge past the notion of a trick of the eyes.

But one thing was clear. Hunter threatened that girl—one of us—with a knife. And if he did it, the others were just as likely to.

By the time free period rolled around, the buzz had pretty much died down. But I still remembered it, and I remembered my meeting with Kanyn, in addition to what I'd witnessed between Jutas and Hunter. It prickled inside me, but it didn't seem like there was a single right person to talk to.

For a brief moment during the day, I considered approaching Kanyn, asking for a more composed discussion where maybe he could answer my questions. But if he'd wanted to actually give me answers, he would have last night. Instead he just probed, like he was studying me.

I met Meg at the doors of the room and we walked in together. Seeing an open table, we took that, setting our books down on top.

"I swear, people here are nuts," she said, following her sentiment with a long breath.

"Who are you referring to?"

"Our peers," she replied. "I've only talked to a few but dang, it's like they're living in la-la land."

"What do you want from them?"

"Answers. Intel." She shook her head. "I mean, we've been here almost a week and I feel like I'm getting dumber by the moment, even with these stupid high school classes. Have you noticed these classes don't even make sense? We're learning a random variety of different topics. It's not even like school. What's the point?"

That's what I wanted to know, among other things. Glancing around the room, I could see her point. Our peers were too comfortable, spending their free period just mingling or doodling. There was no homework to be done, no tests to cram for.

Meg's voice brought my focus back to her. "Do you see that?"

I tried to follow her eyes. "What?"

"That boy over there. He's wearing Ben's hat."

"Ben's hat?" Before I could explain to her that other people probably owned the same hat as her boyfriend, she was already marching in the boy's direction.

"Hey!" she snapped at him, louder than needed.

Glancing over my shoulder, I saw her shout had gotten Kanyn's attention. There was no clear expression on his face, but he was watching. His words floated back to me. You don't want something to happen.

I jumped up from my seat, quickly making my way over to Meg and the boy.

"Where did you get that hat?" she was asking him.

"What? I don't know," he replied. "They gave it to me."

"That's my boyfriend's hat."

"Meg," I hissed, trying to get her to lower her voice.

"What are you talking about?" the boy asked.

"That's my boyfriend's hat," Meg snarled, but at least she'd dropped her voice a few decibels.

I glanced over my shoulder again, and Kanyn was still watching us. I put my hand on Meg's shoulder. "Meg, people have the same hat."

"No." She ripped the hat off the boy's head, turning it around in her hands so that the brim faced her. Then she pointed at a pronounced pink lipstick mark right above the brim. "That's where I kissed his hat the day he first got it, so that no harm would come his way." She looked at me, and I saw the conviction in her face. "This is Ben's hat."

The boy put up his hands. "Look, I'm sorry, I didn't know. Like I said, I wanted a hat, they gave it to me. You can have it if it belongs to your boyfriend." The boy shoved his hands in his pocket and walked away.

Meg squeezed the hat in her hands. "Where is he, Cori? It's been six days and I haven't seen him. Or Mark."

"I don't know. I … Maybe they sent them home. Some of the kids who have been here longer have said people go home—"

"Why would he leave his hat?" She squeezed the hat even harder. "Even if they let him go, he wouldn't leave his hat."

I bit my lip, harder than I should have as I felt the blood pooling at the sides. I didn't have an answer for her. I couldn't think of even the slightest sentiment to comfort her. But I wanted her to shut up, she couldn't draw so much attention to herself. Not after yesterday. "Maybe they took it from him. They took things from all of us. Maybe they got confused when they gave certain items back."

Her knuckles were white against the navy hat, and I worried she might give herself a strain holding it so tightly. "Maybe."

I put a hand on her shoulder again. "Don't worry. Don't let yourself worry. I'm sure he's fine." I could see her start to steady, which meant I too started to steady. My heart had been racing, images of Hunter flying up with a knife swirling through my brain. He wasn't even in the room, but nothing seemed predictable around here.

We walked back to our table, plopping down in the chairs.

Meg stared down at the hat in her lap. It didn't even look like the wheels in her brain were turning. She was just staring.

I probably should have been more concerned about Mark too. But truthfully, without him present, it was hard to worry about anything outside what was right in front of me.

Like Meg looking like a lost puppy just brooding over a hat she'd stolen.

I stood up, sighing. One of us had to get answers, and I seemed to be the only one with something of an advantage. I made my way through the crowd over to Kanyn, keeping my gaze off him until I was right in front of him.

He looked down at me, his expression as unchanging as ever, but I thought I caught a glimmer of surprise in his eyes. "Can I help you?"

"Maybe," I replied, hearing my tone sour. Him leading with a question reminded me of how our conversation went last night.

"Your friend seemed very upset."

The question about the hat came just short of my lips. Then I remembered what Kaisa had said about not letting them into your own introspection. "Just a little homesick," I said.

"That's understandable," Kanyn said. "Maybe next time she doesn't have to be so loud about it? And so confrontational?"

I nodded once, refusing to look him in the eyes. The question came back. Maybe he'd actually give me an answer if I asked. Instead, I pivoted my thoughts, now looking directly at him. "Do you think she could call her family? Or send a text? An email, anything."

His eyes slid away from me. "That's not possible."

I raised my eyebrow. "Why not?"

"There is no cell or wireless service available in this location," he replied.

My eyebrow didn't drop. His answer sounded rehearsed. Repeated. Like he'd answered the same question a hundred times.

"There's nothing?" I asked. "Are we in a third world country?"

He didn't reply.

That was either as much as he felt like sharing or as far as his rehearsed answers went. I scoffed. "Then I can't promise she won't be loud again," I muttered. I felt his eyes return to me, his gaze burned the top of my ear.

After a few seconds, he said quietly, "That's understandable."

I refused to look back up at him, but my fingers curled into fists at my side. That's all he could say? That the situation was understandable? There was nothing understandable about a bunch of young adults being kidnapped and kept in a prison. "You can't keep us here with nothing," I muttered.

He didn't say anything, I didn't even feel his gaze anymore. Tears burned my eyes and I turned away from him, quickly making my way back to Meg.

She didn't even look up when I sat down. It was just as well, I didn't want to explain why there were fresh tears in my eyes. Explain how I wanted more than Kanyn was clearly willing to give. Explain that I thought one of them could help us.

✳ ✳

I didn't want to spend another afternoon sitting in the library. If I was going to be stuck here, I could at least try and learn my way around.

The halls for the dormitory weren't that exciting. They all looked the same, lined with doors and every so often a bathroom. They were on the east and south side—the only reason I had any directional sense due to the sunrise. All the classrooms and offices seemed to fall in the middle, but directly next to the dormitories. Which left the north and part of the west side.

Their quarters had to be on that side. Their bedrooms—if they slept—and bathrooms and whatever wicked possessions they kept.

We hadn't strictly been told we couldn't go to that part of the building, but it didn't seem wise either. They clearly wanted to keep their lives separate from us. We were their prisoners.

I found myself walking down the hall of offices, where I'd come just the evening before. And there was his office, steps away, with the door cracked open. I was coming from the left, so he couldn't see me approaching. I tiptoed to the outside doorframe and strained my neck to just barely get a look inside.

Kanyn sat at his desk, scribbling away in his notebook. In a way, he almost looked approachable.

"Did you need something, Number Five Hundred and Seven?"

I squeezed my eyes closed before walking through the doorframe, fully into the office. "No, I don't."

He delivered me that same confusing half tender, half rigid gaze. "How is your friend?"

"Meg?" I squeaked, surprised he'd even ask about her. "She's fine."

He nodded, turning his attention back to the notebook on his desk.

"She'd still like to hear from her family," I added.

"That's still not a possibility right now."

I stepped further into his office.

His full attention was on me. "Yes?"

"You're not human, are you?" I asked, narrowing my eyes.

"What makes you say that?"

"You just don't ... Seem it."

"Because?"

"I've never seen someone your height."

"Never? That seems unrealistic, there are plenty of people my height."

"I've never seen so many people your height in one place."

"Birds of a feather."

"That still doesn't prove you're human,"

"I believe Merriam-Webster defines a human as a bipedal primate mammal," Kanyn said. He motioned to the entirety of his body. "Which as you can see, I am."

"I'm not going to decide that just based off your looks," I said. "I'm sure you've heard of aliens. You know, Invasion of the Body Snatchers."

"Last I checked, there was no proof extraterrestrial life existed."

"Are you a vampire then?"

"No," he replied. "That should be obvious by my lack of fangs."

"A werewolf?"

Kanyn's lips parted into a smile, and I dare say a faint laugh escaped. "I didn't realize I looked that hairy."

I couldn't help the smile that came to my lips as well. "Sorry, just covering all the mythical creatures I know."

"Is that the extent of your knowledge?"

"For now," I replied.

"It's silly for you to waste your time thinking so much about what I am."

"Trust me, I'm thinking about other things," I mumbled.

"Good. Focus on yourself," Kanyn said. "It's for the best."

7

It started at breakfast.

I sat alone for the first time, since Meg decided to skip and I couldn't find any of the others. Although I sat alone, energized whispers surrounded me. At first, I thought it was me. But no one was even looking in my direction, just whispering among themselves. When the bell rang, the whispering didn't stop, but the energy increased.

My eyes rocked back and forth as I walked down the hall toward my math class. Everyone was buzzing, and I was the only one outside the loop.

I only made it through two classes before I felt like I was going to explode. I wanted to be in on it, whatever it was.

Physical training was the class I'd bonded with the least amount of people. It did still feel weird, after all, trying to take a P.E. class against our will. Still, I had to get answers from somebody.

I picked out a boy with freckled arms, tapping him on the back of his arm. "Do you know why everyone is so antsy?"

"You haven't heard?" he asked.

I shook my head.

"There's a guy who's escaping."

"Escaping? As in right now?"

The boy nodded. "He's been hiding since this morning, none of the Orders can find him."

I immediately thought back to my first night of laundry duty. "Is it Ermis?"

"I don't have a name." The boy's attention redirected as another boy entered the courtyard, high-fiving him.

I wanted to ask him more, but being that I didn't know him, it was probably better I didn't. As Trainus started his lesson, my mind stayed on the escapee, as I assumed many others did too.

It couldn't be Ermis, not with the way he'd completely folded that night. But he was the only person I'd met who even talked about escaping. Still, there were plenty of other kids here, it could be any one of them.

The escapee must have been weighing heavily on Trainus too because halfway through class he cut us loose, giving us the rest of the time to mill around in the courtyard. Though he didn't leave us, he stood in the walkway, his eyes searching.

When the bell finally rang, I jogged to the cafeteria. Spotting Chance, Airi, and Shauna at a table, I practically ran to them. "Have you guys heard?" I asked as I dropped down next to Chance.

Shauna raised her eyebrow with a smile. "You were one of those in high school who was always the last to know something, weren't you?"

"We've heard," Chance replied. "Frankly, I don't believe it."

"You don't believe that someone is trying to escape?" I asked.

Shauna shook her head. "With this many people talking? No. Probably someone said he was thinking about it and now everyone's talking like it's real."

I frowned. I'd waited half the day to be included in the gossip, now they didn't even want to talk about it. I glanced at Airi. "What do you think?"

She looked at Chance and Shauna before quietly answering. "I think it's possible. I've heard things too. It sounds to me like it's real."

"People are saying he's hiding, and waiting for the perfect moment to escape," Shauna said. "Waiting? Why would you wait? Go now. You've been in this hell long enough."

"Maybe it's not that easy," Airi said.

"I give him props for hiding, if he really is," I said. I still didn't know anything about these Order members, but it seemed like a game of hide and seek would be quite easy for them.

"If he makes it ..." Chance trailed off, his grilled cheese halfway to his mouth.

"You think it's real now?" Shauna asked.

"I'm just saying," Chance continued. "If he escapes, well, it would change your view of this place. Wouldn't it?"

Shauna rolled her eyes. "We'll see."

The rumors inside me were still buzzing, and they weren't going to be quelled with this group. A thought popped into my head, someone who might just have the information to assuage me. I would just have to find him again.

Although I could still feel the excited energy around us, our group didn't discuss the escapee for the rest of lunch. As soon as the bell rang, I was up and out of my seat.

There was no reason or rhyme to how I could find him, I could only pray that some power would bring us into each other's sights, and before everything was over.

As I was about to walk by where one hallway intersected with another, I just barely missed getting knocked over by two members of the Order. I recognized them as the ones who'd bullied Hunter, Jutas and the one with wax-colored hair.

"Watch your step," Jutas barked at me without stopping. "If you need help, I'll teach you how to walk straight."

I glared at them as they kept going, but neither of them bothered to look back. They must have been searching for the escaping kid too. I continued walking, and finally I saw the person I was looking for.

"Yannis," I called to him.

He looked up from his spot by an open window, holding a burning cigarette out the window. "Hm?"

I couldn't push down my own excitement anymore. "Is it Ermis?"

"Is what Ermis?"

"The guy hiding out, waiting to escape."

Yannis shook his head, a laugh on his lips. "He's not that smart."

He may not have been smart, but he'd tried escaping before. I felt the experience like an ice block against my back. "Do you have any idea who it is?" I asked.

Yannis shrugged. "I've heard a few names thrown around. But no one who for sure knows who it is. At least no one who I've talked to." He puffed twice on his cigarette then hung it back out the window. "Better that way probably."

The one person I thought could give me information hadn't given me anything. I wanted to be part of the hype, and not because I felt like I was missing out. Whoever this person was was really going against the grain, defying the odds. For that alone, whether he made it or not, I was interested in who he was. "Do you think he'll do it?" I asked.

"Escape?" Yannis asked. He shook his head then took a long drag from his cigarette. "Maybe if nobody knew. But everyone is talking about it. They know about it. They'll find him."

I deflated. Not that Yannis determined this boy's fate, but he had been here longer. If he didn't believe this boy had a chance, what would it take for someone to? A sense of dread creeped in just by my shoulders as another question came to mind. I didn't want the answer, but I had to ask it. "So, you don't believe anyone could escape here?"

He took another long pull. "I'm not going to say that. The idea that escape is possible certainly isn't on my mind though." He paused, staring out the window for a moment. "It's probably possible. Less than ten percent chance or something, if you're a numbers person. But I can't say I see it happening. Either they'll stop you or your own doubts will."

I pressed my feet into the floor to keep steady. I'd asked the question and expected as much for the answer. But it still stung to hear it. Yannis exhaled another puff and I asked, "They don't mind you smoking during the day?"

"They do," he replied. "But they're also a little busy today."

"I better get to class. I'll see you around."

Yannis offered a small wave before turning his attention back out the window. As I started away from him, I noticed he didn't move to leave his spot. I guess he thought they were too busy to notice his absence also.

The class they called expressive learning was still the most laid-back class we had to attend. This particular one felt even more so since Kat barely gave us any attention at all. As the class chattered, she stayed by the open door, watching the hallway.

I wondered if she was patrolling, or if it was something deeper that made her watch motionless. Like the others, she didn't wear a definable expression. But her eyes looked duller than usual.

Expressive learning passed by in what felt like only fifteen minutes, and I flowed with the ever-whispering crowd toward the room for free period.

I found Meg in the center of the room, standing and holding onto her books like she'd been waiting for me to arrive to get comfortable.

"You've heard?" I asked as I approached her.

She nodded. "I don't even have words."

I felt myself deflating. The lunch group had been a bust, Yannis didn't have anything to add, but I definitely thought Meg would want to blather wild scenarios. If we were anywhere else, that would have been the first thing out of her mouth. "You think he'll make it?"

"That's not really my concern," she replied. "I want to know what made him think he could do this. Is he that scared being here?" She shook her head. "But I also don't want to have the answer to that. I would hate to hear that being here is so ... Awful."

I'd been so caught up in the excitement of someone escaping, defying the system, I hadn't put any thought into what Meg was talking about. They'd told us not to try to escape and succeeded in terrifying more than half the kids here. So, then what could drive this kid to take such a big risk?

"It's probably just a dare," Meg said. "Some frat boy kind of thing. Saw it all the time in college."

I bit my lip, watching a calm Meg but her eyes moved around the room like there was a fire. She could talk herself into a rational explanation for anything—or at least try to.

"Anyway," she said, "I'm going to go to the library. I'd rather try and get something done than think about this craziness."

"Go ahead. I wouldn't be much help if you're trying to take your mind off things," I said. Too many thoughts and questions still swirled in my head, and in the silence of the library, I'd have to let them out. As Meg walked away, I looked around the room.

My gaze settled on Kanyn, standing and watching from a corner. For as much excitement that buzzed around the room, he didn't seem bothered by any of it. He probably knew more than anybody else, at least a name, or in their case, a number.

I took a step toward him and my muscles locked up. He may have been a bit nicer than the others, but he was still an Order, and apparently it was all Orders' duty to keep us here. Me asking about the situation could make it seem like I knew something, or maybe even like I was planning something myself.

He looked in my direction and I quickly turned away.

Either way, I couldn't let myself think even for a moment that I could trust Kanyn. He was an Order first, his job was to study me, or whatever they wanted us to believe.

I spent free period, much like I had expressive learning, against the wall doodling in my notebook and analyzing with myself the explanations I thought I would have talked out with Meg.

It was almost the end of the day, and no new information seemed to be feeding through the tubes. I took that to mean either the boy hadn't escaped yet and was still hiding, or he had escaped and no one knew yet. Something had to give. As much as I wanted to stay on the bandwagon of escape being possible, if he didn't make it by nightfall when the halls would be completely empty, I didn't give him much chance.

When the bell rang, I was one of the first people out of free period, making a beeline for my last class. I needed to be in a class where at least someone was trying to keep my mind on other things.

I managed to stride past two classrooms just before the crowd filed out, feeling their energy unfold behind me. I looked up for just a moment and saw him.

The escape artist. He ran like a skinnier version of Tom Cruise, but blood ridden terror gripped his face. I just managed to step out of his way as he sprinted by. Out of the corner of my eye, I spotted Amaris come from around the corner, chasing after him.

The kid ran into the large herd of people changing classes, assuming he planned to lose Amaris in the crowd. Unfortunately, seeing Amaris storming after him caused the sea of people to part, making a clear path for the kid.

Amaris passed me at a speed that made my hair fly up on the sides of my face, loudly muttering, "Enough of this shit." Without stopping, he raised his hand and pinwheeled it in the kid's direction. At the same time, following his movements, one of the crossed spears on the wall flew off, directly aimed at the kid, impaling him mid-run.

The boy teetered, dropped to his knees, then crumpled face forward to the floor.

Silence fell on the hall, all eyes either on the boy or Amaris as he strode over to the body.

The muscles in my right hand hurt, and I realized how tightly I'd been clutching my pen.

The mood in the hall was surprisingly empty. Assumingly, for the majority of us, myself included, our brains were still trying to process what had just happened. This kid was dead. Amaris killed him, he impaled him with a spear off the wall. The rules had been clear, a severe punishment for trying to escape. I don't think any of us expected an outright murder.

Amaris stood over the body, a satisfied expression across his face. Finally noticing the silence around him, he glared at the group. "Let this be a lesson to all of you."

Two other Order members ran up. One of them was Traygus, I recognized from the long scar down the left side of his face. Amaris stepped back as Traygus bent down to examine the boy.

I needed to get to my next class, but my feet were frozen to that spot. I wasn't the only one. Not a single person in the hall moved.

The other Order member, whose graying hair was in a thick braid, finally addressed the crowd. "Clear out. Now. And don't forget what you saw here."

No one moved a muscle.

"I said now!" This time he made his voice even louder and the crowd didn't hesitate to disperse.

My feet took me in the direction toward my philosophy class, but a part of me stayed planted at the scene. That part of me wanted to understand, try to process, what she'd just witnessed.

A boy was dead. A boy no older than myself, dead.

And how Amaris had done it. He'd just moved his hand, swung it around in a circle, and he'd controlled an object hanging on the wall. No strings, no trick of the light. The spear came off the wall and flew at its target, controlled by one of them.

That part of me didn't leave the scene until my backside hit the chair in my next class. It came reeling back, smacking me in the forehead. Keeping my head low, I glanced around the room.

For the amount of kids in my class, only two others had witnessed the same incident, and they were easy to spot. One stared straight ahead, like he didn't see anything, and the other had glued her forehead to the desk.

Word would get around soon, it was only a matter of time. And what would happen then?

If he knew, if somehow he'd been telepathically informed, Viscount didn't act like it. He went about his class like normal, and I did my best to keep my attention on him and his notes.

To keep in the screaming.

When the final bell rang, I made a beeline for the library. I didn't have the energy to be around a lot of people, to once again be surrounded by an agitating buzz. My path to the library took me past the spot of the spectacle, and my knuckles tightened on my books as I hurried by. It was clean now, like nothing had ever happened. The memory remained. I left a slowly gathering crowd in my wake.

✳ ✳

I returned to our room only about an hour after my last class. The library had been too quiet, to the point where I could hear the spear cutting through flesh and bone as the scene replayed over and over in my head. When I opened the door, Meg jumped up from her bed and threw her arms around me.

"Oh Cori, I'm so glad you're okay!" she exclaimed.

"Why wouldn't I be?" I asked, shrugging out of her hug. Even that was still too much interaction.

She blinked at me. "You've heard, haven't you? Everyone's talking about it. Well, whispering."

More whispering. For most of the day it had been all excitement, but now it was quiet, uncomfortable whispering. I closed my eyes for a moment and sat down on my bed. "Yes, I've heard about it," I replied softly. For a second, I considered telling her I was there, that I'd seen it with my own two eyes, but I didn't want to relive it any more than I already was.

"They killed him," Meg said breathlessly. She was short of having a panic attack, or she'd spent the last hour in here having one. Tears dribbled down her cheeks. "God, where are we? What do they want from us?"

I couldn't look at her, and my eyes dropped to the ground. I didn't have answers for her, and apparently no one here had answers for us. But one thing was clear. We were prisoners and they were the jailers who would do whatever they pleased.

Meg wiped away some of the tears from her eyes and sat down next to me. "I just wish Ben was here."

Ben. Mark. My parents. Law enforcement. Hell, I would have taken my sixth-grade math teacher at this point. Just anyone who didn't seem like they were trying to keep us under lock and key.

8

The next morning, to our surprise, there were two new schedules posted outside our door. Looking down the hall we could see everyone else also had new schedules taped to their doors, and kids stood in their doorways looking just as confused.

We had no one to ask, not that I think anyone wanted to approach an Order at this point, so we just went with it. Physical training was my new first period class, and since everyone's schedules had been shifted around, I had a whole new group of people in class with me.

I'd barely slept the night before, and from Meg's whimpering I knew she hadn't either. But Meg could be a beauty queen when she wanted to, so she hid the bags under her eyes well. I on the other hand did not, and one boy with a buzz cut was kind enough to point it out.

"You look like you haven't slept a wink," he said as he and another boy with floppy brownish-blond hair and glasses walked up to me.

"I didn't," I muttered, annoyed he'd thought I wanted him to point that out. He reminded me of Chance.

"He's really good at introductions," the boy with glasses said. "I'm Sherman, and the one who points out flaws is Theo."

Theo did something of a bow. "I couldn't think of any other opener."

"How about hello, how are you?" I asked. Despite my irritation, I figured it would be nice to get to know some new people. "I'm Cori."

"Man, I can't believe they changed our schedules around," Sherman said. "Not that I was used to the other one."

"You're not excited about PT being the first class of the day?" Theo asked us.

"Not really," Sherman replied.

"I don't like it in any part of my day," I added.

"Yeah, this is like freshman year of high school all over again," Sherman said, and he put his hand to the side of his head. "God, I don't want to relive that."

"None of us do," Theo said, his voice quieting as Trainus walked out into the courtyard.

Surprisingly, Trainus gave us a relatively easy day. We all ran five laps and then after we were free to mill around until the end of the period.

As much as I dreaded having Physical Training as my first period, I quickly realized I would learn to like it. My next three periods—free period, philosophy, and lunch—were just me. Not a single person I'd created a relationship with shared those classes with me.

My spirits immediately jumped when Theo walked into math class.

"Well, hey stranger," he greeted, taking the empty desk next to me.

"Are you good at math?" I asked.

"Pretty good."

"Great, we're best friends now."

"Does that make up for me pointing out your tiredness earlier?"

"No," I replied, but I laughed. My only laugh in what felt like weeks.

Although the mix-up of schedules was refreshing, my exhaustion weighed heavily on me. I heard Meg's whimpers from last night. I saw the spear pierce that boy's chest. I felt empty and rigid, like a cocoon. My spine was stiff. I was blind through our shift in the laundry, operating solely on muscle memory to load and unload clothes.

In my fog however, a new prospect was building. I was no escape artist, but maybe I could be. I needed facts, I needed answers, and yesterday's events made it clear where dependability laid. If I wanted answers, I couldn't wait for someone to tell me. I'd have to get them myself.

As Meg and I trudged out of the laundry room, I took the lead, starting down the hallway toward the library.

"Where are you going?" Meg asked, increasing her trudging just enough to be beside me. "Our room is this way."

"I'm going to the library," I said. "You're welcome to come with me."

"I thought you were tired."

"I'm exhausted," I replied. My muscles felt like they were dragging against the ground. "But I want to do some research."

"On?"

"Them."

I heard the air leave Meg's lips in a huff. "Do you really think they're going to have books on themselves?"

"I'm not sure," I said. "But it's a library, so they have books. Maybe some kind of history book or Greek myths will have something about them."

Meg rolled her eyes, but she didn't stop walking beside me.

She should've, and I should have turned and followed her to our room. We spent our hour before curfew roaming around the shelves of their library, looking for some sliver of paper that might give some information about them. But all we found were regular books, most similar to the ones we had back in college, and others older pieces.

By the time we returned to our bedroom, I was drained. To help ourselves, we needed to know about them. But the only way I knew to find information without Internet was through books.

They had us in a cage, one big cage with room to move about. They had us, and we had nothing.

Those thoughts lulled me to sleep, but when my eyes opened again the next morning, I felt like I'd been awake all those hours. Although my eyes were closed, my thoughts were running like a factory.

I dragged myself to breakfast, barely seeing anyone until I sat down across from Chance.

"Whoa," he said as he paused with his fork halfway to his lips. "Are you getting more tired?"

I shot him a glare.

"Sorry," he said. "You looked tired yesterday, but today it's like you've never even heard of a pillow."

"Sorry I haven't been sleeping well," I said. I added, "I spent an hour looking at books I thought could have some information about them, but nothing."

"You're looking for stuff in the library? Talk to Zahir."

"Who's that?"

"He works in the library," he replied. "He can probably show you some books you didn't think to look in."

I wanted to tell him I'd looked at every book in that room, but my eyelids could barely open wide enough to look at him directly. "Thanks," I mumbled.

He smirked, and I knew another undesirable comment was about to leave his mouth. "Maybe you should ask him for some books on getting some shut eye too."

I dragged through my classes, my eyes open without seeing, my brain too rundown to retain anything from the day. But when the final bell rang, I still walked to the doors of the library to meet Meg. Once she arrived, we entered, walking straight up to the counter where a taller boy stood sorting through some books. He had caramel colored skin and tar colored hair that slightly curled at the ends. Tar peppered his squared jaw.

"Can I help you?" he asked without looking up.

"We're looking for a guy named Zahir," I said.

The boy looked up with a raised eyebrow. "Why? Did he do something?"

"No, my friend Chance told me if I needed help finding something here, he was the person to ask," I replied.

"That sounds about right," the boy said as he walked out from behind the counter. "Well, you found me. Whatcha looking for, kid?"

Before I could respond, Meg asked, "Where are you from?"

The question caught him off guard for only a second. "Mohandiseen. It's a neighborhood in Cairo, Egypt."

Meg nodded, and I couldn't discern from the expression on her face why she'd asked.

Zahir's eyes danced on Meg before returning to me. "You're looking for?"

I glanced around the library. The only Order in sight was Truli, and she was standing in front of one of the stacks putting books away. Lowering my voice, I asked, "Do you have any books on them?"

"Them?" Zahir's eyes shifted over to Truli for a moment before he answered. "Honestly I don't think so. I've perused these stacks several times and, not that I even know where to start, I haven't seen anything that could be about them."

I wanted to slam my fist into the counter but didn't have the strength to pick up my arm. "Well, are there any books you notice them reading a lot?"

"They don't really check out books. I'm inclined to actually say they never do," he said. "Well, except for Kat and Hunter. They're always getting books, and they used to get stacks at a time."

I leaned against the counter, rolling over the shelves and shelves of books. A whole library here, practically a scholar's dream with some of the works I'd come across, but nothing that interested them to read. My brain was slowly coming back to life, the cogs starting to click against each other. "So," I said, "whatever it is they are reading, whatever information they do have, they're keeping it to themselves."

Meg looked at me, then put both her hands in my face. Only she could look at me and see the path my brain was leading me toward before I even spoke it. "No, Cori. You are not thinking about raiding their personal quarters to find stuff."

The gears were already back up to full capacity and turning inside my head. "That's where the answers are," I said, straightening up. "It would be simple."

She crossed her arms. "How is it so simple?"

"We know the ones that teach subjects will almost never be in their rooms during the day."

"Yeah, but we will be in class," she said.

"Not during free period."

Meg and I looked at Zahir, surprised he was still listening to our conversation.

"Sorry," he apologized. "I can't say I'm not interested in what they spend their time doing. Or why we're here in the first place."

I nodded. "Would you help us to find out?"

"I'd love to," Zahir replied. "But I don't get a free period, that's when I work in the library. I couldn't be the one to sneak around for you."

"No one can sneak around for you," Meg said to me. "In case you've forgotten, those guys watch us like hawks during free period. They'd notice if one of us sneaked out."

"Then we don't go in the first place," I said. "Just never show up to free period. If anyone asks, we were in the library." I looked at Zahir. "You can verify that, can't you?"

He nodded with a smile.

"Then it's a plan," I said. "We can trust you right?"

"Of course, you have my word." To drive home his promise, he put his hand across his heart.

"Thank you. My name is Cori, by the way, and this is Meg."

"Cori. Meg." He moved his eyes respectively. "And you're both friends with Chance. Got it. If I hear any questions about your whereabouts, you were here in the library."

I motioned to Meg and we exited the library. When we were just past the door, I said to Meg, "I think he was checking you out."

She scoffed, tossing her curls. "He was checking you out too. Trust me, he's not someone either of us should ever entertain."

I wasn't entertaining any thoughts besides finding out more about the Orders, but I didn't need to start in with her. For the moment, my fatigue had been lifted, the fog cleared, and I wanted to utilize every precious moment of this temporary clarity. "I'm going to do it tomorrow," I said.

Meg halted in her steps, grabbing my arm. "You're really going to do this, Cori?" she hissed. "Did you not hear what happened to that boy who tried to escape? And now you're going to try a stunt like this?"

She still didn't know that I'd done more than heard, I'd seen it happen. And that memory itself was more than enough motivation for me to go through with a stunt, as she called it. "Why are you so surprised? You did stuff like this all the time in college, in high school. Ever since I've known you, Meg."

"I've never risked my life. And I've never asked you to either. I just wanted you to live a little."

"Well now I am," I snapped.

She let go of my arm. "What a great time," she huffed, but I knew there was more concern than frustration behind her words. She stalked away, and I let out a sigh. She would fume over it, but she would still help me. That's what best friends did.

✳ ✳

Holding onto my courage became more difficult as the hours passed and the time for action drew closer. At breakfast the nerves started to nip, and I tried to focus on every flake in my cereal and every crunch of my toast.

Before Meg and I separated for class, I asked if I would meet her at the library. She only nodded, then walked away. Still fuming, but still loyal.

If physical training wasn't outside, I would have spent it watching the clock. If I knew how to read the sun, I would have done that for the whole fifty minutes. The movement eased my nerves, as did listening to Sherman and Theo complain about every exercise we did.

The bell rang, and a calm current of confidence washed over me. I wasn't thinking about what could happen, what would happen, or even about what I might find. I was focusing on putting one foot in front of the other.

I paused in the hall to let a group of kids pass by, and at the tail end went Kanyn. Headed toward free period, and any other day, I would be too.

He didn't notice me, thankfully, because had he looked at me with those brown eyes I didn't think I'd be able to hold on to my resolve. Turning in the opposite direction, I headed toward his office. I had to retrace my exact steps from the bench I'd been sitting on that night to get to the office, but I made it without anyone noticing. To my dismay, the door was closed and as I neared my heart sped up from the anxiety of my entire plan falling through due to it being locked. I sighed as the doorknob turned, pushing the door open and quickly stepping inside, closing the door behind me.

I had an hour, but I didn't want to spend the entire hour in here in case someone did go looking for me. Looking around the room, I decided to start with the bookshelf first. Scanning the shelves, it only looked to hold old works of literature—Aristotle, Homer, the Oresteia. I pulled a few out in a feeble attempt of finding a secret passageway or something of the like. As far as I could tell, there were no books on them, no untitled or unbounded loose-leaf that might hold such secret information.

I crossed the room over to the other smaller bookshelf behind his desk. This one was lined with leather notebooks I'd seen him write in before, all the exact same shade of brown.

I removed the very first one.

The first page had only two inscriptions, a number and a name. Flipping through the pages, my lips formed a hard frown. There only seemed to be miscellaneous notes, and they stopped not even a third of the way through. I took out the next one, but only found the same results.

They were collecting information about us, this was proof, but I already knew that. Kanyn never stopped writing it seemed, except for when he was in free period or walking.

Disturbing as it was, I still wanted information on them. I turned in a circle, looking for the next spot I'd search. My eyes fell on Kanyn's desk behind me.

As I'd noticed before, he kept his desk well organized, clear except for one leather bound journal. Glancing back at the shelf with the rest of them, there wasn't an empty spot for the rogue notebook.

My hand hovered above it. If this was any other situation, I would never look through someone else's private thoughts. But this wasn't a normal situation. My best friend and I had been kidnapped, as well as everyone else here. I had to do it for them.

I opened the cover of the journal. A sigh of relief escaped my lips. There was nothing written on the first page and although that didn't give me any information, it eased my discomfort of snooping. I flipped to the second page, again finding it empty. I flipped to the third page and my stomach did a flip flop as my gaze landed on the first entry.

#19
#7   #408
#28 #396
#35
#22 #451
#13
#14 #500

I turned the page but only found more blank lines. This was the only entry in the whole journal.

"Nineteen, seven, twenty-eight ..." I read them aloud, like they would spark meaning if I did. Nothing, and I glanced at the clock. I hadn't been gone that long, only ten minutes, but it felt long enough. I didn't want to risk being there any longer. Silently, I repeated the numbers to myself, straining myself to memorize them in seconds. This would have been the best time to have my phone. Closing the journal, my eyes jumped around to make sure I hadn't left anything out of place.

Scampering to the door, I cracked it open, checking to make sure there was no one to witness me coming from one of their offices. With the hall clear, I jumped out into it, barely closing the door behind me before scurrying down the hall toward the library.

When I strolled through the doorway for the library, a wave of relief washed over my sweating back. On the second shelf I passed, I grabbed a random book. Zahir and I met eyes before I slunk into a chair and pretended to bury myself in reading.

✳ ✳

My trip to Kanyn's office didn't leave me as shaken up as I'd expected. I spent the better half of my time in the library staring at the pages in my book while wracking my brain to figure out the numbers. I wrote them down on a scrap sheet of paper, but even having them physically in front of me again didn't help. Maybe I should have spent more time reading his text in the other journals, but he was so verbose, it would have taken forever just to find something useful.

The numbers had to be important, I just had to figure out why. And why didn't every number have a counterpart?

The rest of my classes I split my time between taking careless notes and trying to crack the code between the numbers. They weren't all evens or odds, they weren't prime numbers, and they didn't correlate to letters in the alphabet.

By the time I got to expressive learning, now my last class of the day, my patience waned. I'd risked my neck for a puzzle I had no idea how to solve. I needed another pair of eyes to look at it.

I looked up from my desk, my gaze immediately landing on the only person standing up. He stood by himself in the back corner, hovering over his wood creation with a hammer and nail.

I'd noticed him working diligently from the day before, and he'd made great progress since then. Someone who was smart enough to put that together might be able to put numbers together just as well.

I crossed the room over to the space he was working at. "How do you know how to build that?" I asked.

"To be honest, I don't really know," he replied with a small shrug. He stood back, admiring his work. "It's kinda weird, but certain pieces just feel like they go together you know? Like I can feel how it's supposed to work."

My eyebrows rose. "You're saying you think you have some sort of sixth sense for building?"

"Sixth sense or …" The boy didn't finish his sentence but shrugged again.

Sixth sense, magical ability, or whatever he was alluding to, any other day it would have sounded like a quack joke. But after recent events, nothing was too farfetched. "Okay, explain to me how you think you have a special ability to …" I stopped as he flashed a grin at me. "You're joking."

"Yeah," he said, chuckling. "It's a bird respite. I've built one before. That was on a much smaller scale, so I thought I'd try my hand at a better one. After all, it seems I've got nothing but time." Grinning, he added, "Sorry about my little joke. I have a weird sense of humor. And this isn't really the place for it."

"No, it's okay," I said. "Honestly, some humor would be good around here. So what are you, a genius or something?"

"Maybe in another life," the boy replied. "I'm Nicolas by the way. You?"

"Cori."

"Let me ask you something," he said, and I noticed he was moving the materials in front of him around without any real rhyme or reason, only appearing to be doing something. "This whole situation is weird, right?"

"Yeah."

Nicolas's eyes darted around the room for a moment before settling back onto the table. "Well, when I first got here, I thought this might be some kind of experiment. But things feel wrong here. Like, really wrong. I can't be the only person who thinks that, right?"

"I guarantee you're not," I said.

He sighed. "Good, I thought I was crazy. People just carry on here like it's normal."

I suddenly had every desire to tell him about what I'd discovered in Kanyn's office. But I pressed the feeling back down, I didn't know this boy well enough yet. I was still figuring out who I could and couldn't trust. "Where are you from?"

"Gothenburg. You?"

"Atlanta."

"Not familiar with that," Nicolas said. "America?"

I nodded.

"Ah," he said. "I've heard many things about there. Still not as bad as here. I heard ... Never mind. I'm sure you've heard by now."

"The boy who was trying to escape?"

He nodded. "There's something really wrong here. We need to wake up."

The feeling didn't go away, in fact it felt like it dug its claws into the back of the bottom of my throat. I took the crumpled piece of paper out of my pocket and set it on the table for him to see. "Do these numbers mean anything to you?" I asked.

Nicolas slid the paper in front of him. His brow crinkled and he rested his chin on his pointer finger. Finally, he shook his head. "No, sorry. What are they supposed to mean?"

"I don't know," I replied, taking the paper back. "That's why I was asking."

"Maybe if the numbers on the right weren't missing, it'd make more sense."

"That's how I found it," I said. If the numbers on the right weren't missing, I could probably figure it out. "Thanks for looking at it. I better get back over to my spot and work on my project."

He waved me away as I walked back over to my spot.

As it stood, so much for learning about them. Even after taking the risk to find something, we still had nothing.

✸✸

I had to tense every muscle to keep from running to the dining hall. When I arrived, Chance, Airi, Kaisa, and Shauna were already sitting at a table closer to the back wall. I picked up a tray of food and headed over, Meg meeting me as I walked over to the table.

"You're not getting dinner?" I asked her, noticing her lack of a tray.

She shook her head. "I overheard some kids today saying the dinner tonight had rat poison in it."

"There's the girl," Chance said to me as we sat down next to Shauna.

"The girl?" I asked.

"Yeah, we all know about your little plan to break into Kanyn's office," Chance replied.

I glanced at Meg, who had been the only person I'd told about my stunt. She only shrugged.

Chance elbowed Kaisa, who had only looked up from the book she was reading when I first sat down. "Alright, you can take your nose out of that book now. She's going to tell us what she found."

"Aren't we waiting for Zahir?" she muttered to him.

"Zahir?" Meg repeated, just a few seconds before the tan skinned boy saddled up to the table. He took a seat on the same side as us, on the other side of Shauna.

"Sorry I'm late," he said. "Did I miss anything?"

"No, she hasn't started yet," Chance replied, and Kaisa closed her book.

"Uh, question," Meg spoke up. "Why is he allowed to hear?"

"Oh, come on, I figured he ought to," Chance said. "He did cover for Cori."

"He didn't cover for her, no one caught her," Meg said.

"Can hear both of you," Zahir said. "And as much as I love people talking about me, I'd rather hear about the interesting things Cori dug up."

A scowl found its way onto Meg's face, but she didn't say anything else.

I explained to the group everything I'd seen in Kanyn's office, making sure to be as detailed as possible about the journal. No one said anything immediately when I finished, in fact from most everyone's faces it seemed that they were all trying to digest what I'd told them.

"A journal with only one entry," Kaisa murmured, tapping her finger to her chin. "And it's just numbers."

"That's what stands out to you?" Shauna asked. "How about the fact that they've got pages of notes about each of us. Why in the world would that be?"

I looked at Meg. "In a creepy way, it gives validity to your idea that this is all just one big psychological experiment."

She scoffed. "I think we all know that idea went out the window when ..." She didn't even have to say it, we all knew what she was referring to.

I noticed Zahir pressing his hand against his forehead. "Is something wrong, Zahir?"

"Huh?" He opened his eyes, removing his hand from his forehead. "Oh, it's nothing."

"Are you sure?" Airi asked. "If you need some aspirin, I have some in my room."

"No, no, it's not a headache."

Airi and I exchanged glances. He couldn't just leave it at that. "Then what is it?" I asked.

"Yeah, are you sick man?" Chance asked.

"No, it's not anything health wise ..." Zahir blinked a few times before attempting to explain himself. "It's weird, but I just keep hearing this voice in my head."

Meg tossed me an incredulous glance and I tried not to smile.

"Voices?" Chance asked, arching an eyebrow.

Zahir shook his head. "Not voices, just one voice. It just started today, like this morning. And the weirdest part is it's a friend of mine's voice."

"What's he saying?" Meg asked, resting her head in her hands and leaning forward like she was truly interested.

"He just says my name, and occasionally he says help me." Zahir shook his head again, dragging his hands up his face. "I know it sounds crazy, I'm just telling you what it is."

"Well, you're right," Meg said, "it sounds crazy."

"As does everything lately," I muttered.

"Forget it," Zahir said.

"You're probably just not getting enough sleep," Shauna said. She turned her attention to me. "As I won't be now that I know they're writing novels about us."

My eyes dropped down to my tray. I'd wanted to provide some kind of answers, but even I felt like I'd dug up more questions.

9

I hadn't stopped thinking about what I'd found in Kanyn's office, but I also hadn't been able to come up with any explanations either. We'd thrown a few around at dinner but none with any weight. My forehead throbbed as I lay in bed, only dulling when I lay face up with my eyes closed. There had been so much stimuli in the past few days and my brain couldn't work fast enough to process it all, at least not without a large degree of suppression.

The throbbing suddenly intensified to three loud knocks, and I clenched my eyelids. As I felt them again, I realized it wasn't my head, but someone at the door. I glanced over at Meg, but her focus stayed on her book, so with a grunt I rolled myself out of bed and answered the door.

"Chance, Zahir, is something wrong?" I asked the two boys I found waiting outside.

"Is Meg there?" Zahir asked, and I couldn't read the expression on his face.

I nodded.

Zahir flashed a look at Chance.

"Can you close the door?" Chance asked me.

Quietly, I pulled the door shut behind me. "What's going on?"

"Zahir says the voices—"

"Voice," Zahir corrected before wincing.

"Right, the voice, has intensified. It's louder and more frequent."

"So ... Are you going to the infirmary?"

"Are you crazy? I don't want anyone to know about this, especially them," Zahir replied. He winced again.

"I suggested for once Zahir just let this voice talk," Chance said. "If it's calling to him, maybe he should answer, you know? Or at least figure out where it's coming from."

"You're going to follow this voice inside your head?"

Zahir nodded. When I didn't reply within a few seconds, he scoffed. "I knew she wouldn't come with us. Forget it, I'll go by myself."

"No, I'll come," I said quickly. "Are we going now?"

Zahir and Chance nodded.

I sighed. "Let's go then."

Chance looked at Zahir. "Alright man. Whatever direction the voice gets louder in, that's where we go."

Zahir nodded and started walking down the hallway. Chance and I followed, but stayed a few steps behind so he could lead the way.

"What exactly do you think we'll find?" I whispered to Chance.

He shrugged. "I don't know, but I understand him not wanting to consult them about this ... Problem. Ignoring it obviously isn't working, so he might as well meet it head on."

We wandered through the halls, surprisingly void of any Orders, and I could tell as we kept going, we were getting further and further away from any frequented area. The hallways became darker and somehow, quieter. Finally, Zahir stopped in front of a doorway. He opened it, and I expected us to find a boy shivering in some sort of a supply closet, but instead we were met with descending stairs.

Zahir stepped back, clearly apprehensive to the idea of heading down into the darkness. He looked at Chance and me. "What do we do now?"

"This is your friend's voice, correct?" I asked.

Zahir nodded. "We came here together. They let him go maybe a week ago."

I took a deep breath, then took one step down. "Let's go then."

Zahir put his hand on my shoulder, stepping around me to take the lead.

Chance closed the door behind us and we descended. My eyes adjusted to the darkness, and it turned out to be the way into a basement.

I scrunched my nose at a foul odor wafting our way, like spoiled meat or bad eggs.

As we came to the bottom of the stairs, our eyes landed on the scene before us simultaneously.

On the right side of the room, paling bodies were stacked on top of each other, appendages twisted and sprawled out around them. On the left side of the room, long black garbage bags lay in stacks. It wasn't hard to put the pieces together of what was inside those bags.

Bile rose in my throat and I swallowed hard to push it back down.

"What is this?" Chance hissed.

The only response I could give was to shake my head, I had no words. I'd never seen a dead body, let alone so many. I had gone from a nightmare to a horror movie.

A guttural yelp escaped Zahir's lips and he dashed over to the pile of bodies.

Chance and I followed him, despite my repulsion of the corpses. Some of their eyes had even been left open.

The way they were stacked, not every full body was visible. Heads or arms stuck out while the rest of the body melded in with the pile.

Zahir cradled one of the protruding heads against his chest. A boy the same complexion as him with dark brown hair and bleached tips. His putrid lips were closed, but his eyes were wide open.

"Is that ...?" But the way he stopped, Chance knew the answer already.

Zahir barely bobbed his head up and down to nod, tears brimming in his eyes. He bent over the head and gently closed the eyelids. "I thought he'd gone home," he said hoarsely.

Averting my eyes, I covered my mouth with my hand to keep the smell off my tastebuds. I wanted to run, scream, anything but be in that rotting room.

As I shifted around the room, trying not to really look at anything, I stopped on a pile with a fresh body resting on top. The boy who tried to escape. His eyes were closed and his hands had been placed over the hole in his abdomen.

One arm poking out from the midsection of the same pile caught my attention. Slid all the way down to the wrist, only in tack by the width of the hand, a gold chain bracelet with one thin section, with an embedded diamond stone. The piece of jewelry seemed so familiar. Its origin was on the tip of my tongue, but I couldn't remember.

"We should go," Chance said. He put his hand on Zahir's shoulder. "I'm real sorry about your friend."

"Me too." More should have been said, but the question was what. As if we weren't already in the worst situation we could ever find ourselves in. And then people were dying, decomposing right under our feet.

✻ ✻

Meg asked me where I'd gone when I came back to the room, but I couldn't answer her. I crawled straight into bed and let images of the room play over and over like an old school stereoscope until I fell asleep.

When I woke up the next morning, again Meg tried to get an answer from me, but I ignored her, and honestly barely heard her. Every dream I'd had that night was me walking down some hall in this godforsaken building, always to end up at the same set of stairs, always to discover the same gruesome sight.

Meg trailed behind me as I got ready in the bathroom, then back to our room, then down to the dining hall. I didn't have any connection with my senses until I put a spoonful of warm oatmeal into my mouth.

It wasn't just me moping. Purple circles framed Zahir's eyes and he stared down at his bowl of oatmeal, stirring the oats around but never actually taking the spoon out. Chance's usually somewhat kempt hair looked like he'd raked his hands through it several times this morning and never bothered to fix it after. He too stared at the fruit and cereal on his tray, every so often taking a bite.

Kaisa sensed our melancholy. "Is something wrong?" she asked, her eyes bouncing between Chance, Zahir, and I.

Zahir let out a shaky breath that sounded like he'd been holding it since he woke up this morning.

"Last night we found something very disturbing," Chance said. His gaze shifted around the room before continuing. "Yesterday, the voice Zahir was hearing started affecting him more."

I noticed the 'oh great' eye roll from Meg.

"I suggested he try to follow the voice, since he didn't want to get help," Chance explained. "Cori and I went with him. And it led us to this basement."

"What was in there?" Shauna asked.

Chance closed his eyes and swallowed. "Bodies. Dead bodies. Zahir's friend and the boy who tried to escape were down there."

Our section of the table fell quiet, all eyes on Chance.

"E-Explain," Kaisa said after a minute.

"They were all people who we thought got sent home," Zahir said, balling his fists on either side of his tray. He was struggling to hold himself together. If he started crying it would surely draw attention from an Order. "They didn't send anyone home. They killed them."

"They're killing people?" Airi gasped.

"Why are you so shocked?" Shauna asked. "Amaris killed that boy and Hunter threatened to kill that girl."

"I know but ... I guess I wanted to believe that was just, you know, an incident," Airi replied quietly.

Chance shook his head. "And that's our problem. That's the problem. They hid these murders and just told us people were going home. Everything bad that happens here just seems like an incident. But they're not, these people are murderers and they're waiting to do the same to all of us."

"All of us?" Kaisa asked, and our attention shifted to her.

"You don't think it's all of us?" Zahir asked, his eyes red now.

"If it was all of us, there wouldn't be any of us left," Kaisa said. With all eyes on her, her voice quieted. "Chance is making it sound like we're all here like pigs waiting to be slaughtered."

"That's what it feels like now," Shauna said.

"If that were the case there should be more people ... Gone." Kaisa shook her head. "I just don't think we should jump to conclusions."

"We shouldn't jump to conclusions?" Chance hissed. If he didn't have to worry about being heard he would be shouting. "Are you crazy? People are dead."

"I understand that," Kaisa said, articulating each of her words. "I'm just saying that instead of panicking and ending up like them, we should try to be logical about this. We should find out about these people and their true intentions."

Chance crossed his arms and averted his eyes, his lips set in a frustrated line.

Kaisa turned her attention to me. "Cori, when you went into Kanyn's office, all you could find were notes about us, right?"

I nodded. "It really wasn't much."

"Depending on how you look at it," she said. "We know they're studying us. And in depth. Maybe they're looking for someone? Or something? A behavior of some sort?"

"And how does that help us?" Chance asked, but he didn't meet her eyes.

Kaisa glared at him. "I'm not sure yet. But it could be that if they are looking for something like a behavior, they're dismissing those who don't fit the bill. Or the ones who do."

Chance didn't respond.

"Not dismissing," Zahir spoke up. "Killing. Call it what it is."

Kaisa nodded. "Yes, I'm sorry."

Silence lingered over us for a few minutes.

"And this voice led you to that room?" Shauna spoke up. "Just so I'm clear."

Zahir nodded. "I can't explain it. I just heard him. How about we give the subject a break."

Another silence fell on us, and it wasn't until Chance stood up to put away his tray did the moment feel like it had been broken.

The day absolutely dragged on. Sherman and Theo sensed 'tension' around me, so they kept their complaints at least a foot away from me. Nicolas dared to ask if something was bothering me, but I simply shook my head without looking at him. I didn't want to sit in any of my classes, all taught by blatant murderers. And what disturbed me more was that no one else in my classes knew.

When I came across Kaisa and Chance at the end of the day, it seemed they had had similar days. The three of us sat together at the edge of the patio, not speaking, just staring.

"Do we tell someone?" Chance asked after a few minutes.

"Who would we tell?" Kaisa replied softly. She was right. They, the people who were holding us hostage, were the killers. And they were the only authority.

Chance shook his head. "I can't get that image out of my head."

"Same," I murmured. I'd seen it last night, but it played across my mind like I was back in that basement.

Another lapse of silence fell over us. I wanted to break it, and I'm sure they did too, but there was really nothing to say.

I turned when I noticed out of the corner of my eye a figure coming toward us.

"There you are!" Airi exclaimed as she sped-walked toward us. Her cheeks were blush against her pale face.

"What's up?" Chance asked, scooting over so she could sit between me and him. His expression visibly shifted a few notches upward, closer to smiling.

"I've been looking for you guys," she said. "I think I found something that could help us understand them."

"Really? What?" I asked.

"I went to Kat's office to talk to her about something, and I noticed on her bookshelf was this book called The Order. That's what they call themselves."

"Perfect," Kaisa said, any trace of weariness leaving her too. "Airi, we need that book."

"I figured, but I couldn't take it then," Airi said. "Kat was right there. And even though she's pretty nice, she's still one of them. I doubt I could just ask her for it."

"Sounds like we're going to have to steal it," Chance said.

"Steal?" Airi asked. "From them?"

"It's the only way," Kaisa said. "We need to see if there's anything about them inside that book."

Airi's already pale face had turned even whiter, I expected to be able to see her veins any moment. "But to steal from them?" she asked in almost a whisper.

Chance put his arm around Airi's shoulder and gently pulled her closer to him. "Hey, I know it seems scary," he said in a soft voice. "We can completely leave you out of it if you want."

"No," she said, but the way she rubbed her eyes, she looked like she wanted to cry. "I want to help."

He nodded, removing his arm but keeping his attention on her for a moment. He looked at Kaisa and I. "Should we steal it tonight?" he asked.

Kaisa shook her head, her eyes darting back and forth as she thought. "We don't know what this book is. What if it's a ritual of some sort? What if she reads it every night? She'll see that it's missing and then they'll just search our rooms or something."

"Well with that kind of thinking it seems like there's never a good time to steal it," Chance said.

"Of course there is," Kaisa said, standing up. From our seated position, we watched her walk around a few steps, checking to make sure no one was listening. When she was done, she sat down in front of the three of us. "From nine to four we know that Kat is busy teaching. Every fifty-minute period slot is a class. That's the perfect time for us to be reading the book."

"Except that we're also in class," I pointed out. "Those guys are like hawks. I don't think I could ever get away with reading under my desk."

"Lunch time," Chance said. "Or free period. We could read it in the library."

Kaisa nodded. "Here's how I see it. We get someone to meet with Kat before her first class, somewhere outside of her office. One of us slips in, gets the book, and we can read a bit in the library during breakfast. They won't be too suspicious if we're not there or show up late, a lot of people skip breakfast. Then we can hand off the book during the day so we can read it during our lunch times or free period."

"And putting it back?" Airi asked.

"We put it back after our last class, during the bustle of everyone getting out," Chance said.

"I'm in her last class of the day," I said. "I'll do it."

"You sure, Cori?" Chance asked. "You already broke into Kanyn's office. You don't have to do everything." He grinned. "Unless you've got a past as a criminal you're trying to restart."

I finally felt a hint of a smile trying to creep into my lips. I didn't, but I wasn't putting it past myself now. Although terrifying, sneaking into Kanyn's office had given me a rush better than any last minute studying or a well deserved A on a test. "I'll do it, it makes the most sense."

"If Cori is going to return it," Airi said, "then I'll distract Kat in the morning."

"You're okay with that?" Chance asked. "You really don't have to."

Airi nodded. "Yeah, I'm sure it'll be fine."

"And I'll get the book in the morning," Kaisa said. She looked at each of us, nodding. "It's a good plan, right?"

The three of us nodded back. But even I could see the slightest of nerves behind her eyes.

✳ ✳

My foot tapped an indentation into the carpet of the library. I sat across from Chance, trying to keep my attention on my math notes, but every two seconds my attention jumped back to the doors of the library, hoping to see Kaisa walking through.

If Chance was anxious, he hid it well. He sat still with his notebook open, resting his chin in his hand. I hadn't noticed him look even once towards the door.

"So Chance, where are you from?" I blurted out.

He glanced at me, giving me a sheepish grin. "Does it matter?"

"Just trying to make conversation," I said. A movement at the doors of the library made me look past him.

Kaisa strolled in, holding her books to her chest. From the table, I couldn't see if she'd succeeded or not. She pulled a chair over to the head of the table between Chance and I.

"Did you find it? You weren't there very long," Chance said.

"I didn't have to be," she said, finally separating her books from her chest. She looked around, then set her books onto the table in a stack. The topmost and smallest book was a moss green leather-bound book with the title Ordinem was spelled out in beautiful cursive on the front cover, no author.

"Ordinem," Kaisa said, "it means 'the order' in Latin. Sounded perfect."

I could have smacked myself for being so stupid. Of course Ordinem meant order in Latin, and I'd seen the same book among Kanyn's collection on the first bookshelf, but I'd overlooked it as more old literature.

"Well crack it open, we don't have that much time," Chance said.

He and I leaned in close as she opened the book to the first page. It was blank, and she flipped to the next one. From my angle, I couldn't really make out the text. My foot started to tap again as I waited for Kaisa to point out something. She flipped the page again.

"Are you going to stay in the beginning?" Chance asked. "Nothing happens in the beginning."

Kaisa rolled her eyes and flipped to the middle of the book. She skimmed the page once, then again. Then she read it aloud. "The Orders will begin the process of entering their Orderly state by experiencing various changes. They may become very weak, sick, or confused. In addition, as they begin to awaken, they will become hyper focused on their identifying attribute, or a single number. This is the number within the Order that they will assume once fully awoken."

"This sounds like some book I would have read in middle school," Chance said, and Kaisa nudged his shoulder.

"That's what it says," she said.

"Well, it sounds ridiculous," he said. "I barely even understand what it's saying. And hyper focusing on a number? A number?"

"Maybe if someone didn't skip to the middle of the book, he'd understand what it means," Kaisa said. She looked at me. "Cori, what do you think?"

"I ..." I didn't know what to think, in fact I actually agreed with Chance's evaluation. I simply shrugged. "I'd have to read more, probably in order too."

Kaisa looked at her watch. "We'll have to finish it later. We've got six minutes before first period."

"Can I have it first? I'd like to read it during my free period at ten," I said as I stood up. "I can give it back to you at your lunch time."

"Sure, just be careful," Kaisa said as she passed it to me. "Who knows what kind of punishment we'd get for being discovered with it."

If I thought about what kind of punishment we'd get into, I'd throw the book in the trash. We already risked it all by taking it, there was no point worrying now.

For the first time since I'd been there, I put my all into physical training. I didn't hear a single word from Sherman or Theo, I put every ounce of thought into the exercises. First period went by quicker than usual, and although Theo and Sherman were right at my heels as the bell rang, trying to figure out if I was ignoring them, I darted down the hall for the library.

Finding a secluded corner, I settled into the chair, positioning the green book inside a larger one I'd grabbed off the shelf.

I only had fifty minutes, so I needed to be strategic with how and what I read. Kaisa read through at least the first three pages and hadn't shared anything, so there was probably nothing there. However, it was confusing when she skipped straight to the middle.

Opening the book to just outside the ten-page mark, I began reading.

... creating the Orders. Thirty-six fragments of his soul broke off and attached to thirty-six different human beings. The attachment would have been undetectable, nothing more than a particle of light penetrating the body. It is unclear as to when these particles of Dorroroch will awaken in the host, but when they do, the host will experience special abilities akin to your own. Among those, it is expected to see telepathy, telekinesis, teleportation, and other variations of these abilities. Other signs might include an increased level of intelligence, extreme feats of strength, prolonged sickness, seizures, and even premature death.

I closed one eye as I tried to count all the Orders I'd come across. At least fifteen.

But Kaisa had been right in her theory that they had some kind of special powers. And telekinesis explained Hunter holding that knife in midair.

It is unclear if the Orders will awaken at the time of birth, but it is more probable any abilities will manifest past puberty when the body can properly handle them. It is crucial all thirty-six Orders be contained before they are able to fully use their abilities. Without the proper regulation, the Orders could grow to become a threat to the human race.

I paused, setting the book down. The Orders were supposed to be contained. Sure, they were all in one building in the middle of who-knows-where, that seemed pretty contained. But if that were the case, who was containing them? Who put them all here? And who was letting them go out and round up all these young adults—

The realization hit me so suddenly, I said it aloud. "They're not The Order. We are."

10

That section of the book went on to explain how and why it was their sworn duty to eliminate all thirty-six Orders at any cost. I read it too slowly and too carefully, and the time quickly ticked away. When I looked up at the clock, I only had five minutes left. Five minutes for me to incessantly flip through pages, trying to skim all the parts I hadn't gotten to. There were theories on how the awakening would happen, potential qualifying attributes for Orders, as well as individual sections about each of the abilities possible to manifest.

I could only hope Chance or Kaisa were faster readers and could acquire more information than me.

When the bell rang, I jumped up, holding my notebook as close as possible to my chest to conceal the green book. I darted through the hall, taking extra caution not to even slightly rub up against another person, fearing the smallest bump would send my books onto the floor, exposing them.

I found Chance standing off to the side pretending to look through his own notebook. "Hey," I said, my tone jumping even in the one syllable word.

"Hey," he greeted, looking first around us, then at me.

I slid him the book, Chance using the same method to hide it. "There are some parts I didn't get to—"

"Got it," he interrupted. "Let's keep moving. See you later."

I nodded, though I wanted to explain everything I'd already learned. He'd read it himself, hopefully. Walking away from him, my lungs were on fire.

Calling themselves the Order, they'd so blatantly lied to all our faces. We were the Order, or at least thirty-six of us were. They were looking for the Orders.

"Dang it," I muttered aloud. Had I spent less time reading about their duty, I could have spent more time reading about who 'they' even were. And I'd have to wait all day just to talk about the book.

When the bell rang, ending sixth period, I was one of the first out the door. In the time between bells I'd have to locate Chance and this time I didn't have any idea what direction he'd be coming from.

I didn't have it in me to stand by myself in the hall like he had, but I would look odd walking up and down the hall. I tried to walk slow, like I was lost in thought. Finally, I spotted him coming down the hall.

"I was beginning to think you'd forgotten," I said, but my words tapered off as I noticed his face. His eyes stayed down as he reached in between his notebooks and slid the book from between them. He didn't look at me as he handed it off to me.

"Are you okay?" I asked, putting the book between my chest and my notebook.

"Yeah," he mumbled. "Kaisa said when you walk into Kat's office, there's a bookshelf to your immediate left. It was on the third shelf, exactly at the end on the right side."

"Got it," I said. "You sure something isn't wrong?"

"I got to get to class." Before I could say another word, he turned and started walking away.

I stood there for a moment longer, hoping for some reason he'd come back to tell me something. Then I turned to head to my own class. Taking short breaths, I tried to recall every exact word I'd read in the book. I didn't know what Chance had read, whether it was more or less than me. Was there something deeper into the book that had unsettled him? Maybe just the realization that they weren't the Order and that some kids here were was bothering him, if he'd figured that out.

As I walked into class I pushed my questions to the back of my brain. Just one more class, then we could finally talk about it.

It had been easier to focus on my classes earlier in the day, when I knew I had hours before I was free. My leg bounced under my table as I tried to make it seem like I was working on something. And I was, I'd started a poem the day before. But I couldn't keep my attention on the poem and off the clock.

I looked up and the clock finally read three-forty. Ten minutes and the bell would ring. Ten minutes and it would be a mad dash to Kat's office. My foot tapped harder. I should have asked Airi exactly where her office was. It only seemed obvious that it would be in the same hallway as Kanyn's, but there were multiple offices, and no name markers.

I glanced back at the clock. Three-forty one. My gaze dropped down to Kat, writing in her journal.

What if she was planning to head straight for her office? What if she had something to do or something to grab in there? I needed time, to get to the hallway, to find which office was hers, and then to put the book back.

As if on cue, Nicolas plopped down in front of me, birdhouse and all. "Hey, what do you think?" he asked, rotating it on the table for me to see all angles. "Flat roof or slanted roof? Or multiple roofs?"

"Uh, slanted," I replied. "Think it looks better that way."

"I see," he mumbled, eying his piece.

"Could you do me a huge favor?"

He looked up at me. "Sure, what is it?"

"When class ends today, could you talk to Kat for a few minutes?"

He furrowed his brow. "Talk to her?"

"Yeah, you know, ask some questions," I replied. "I'm not super sure what this class is all about or what we're supposed to achieve so maybe some questions like that or just anything—"

"Anything to distract her."

"Yeah," I said, surprised he'd predicted it, but relieved he'd said it. "I know it sounds fishy, but I'd really appreciate it. I would tell you why if I could—"

"You don't have to tell me what for," Nicolas said. "I got it. How long do you need?"

"Ten minutes tops," I replied. "And I just need her to stay in this room."

"You can count on me."

I glanced at the clock. Six minutes left. Glancing back at Nicolas, I asked, "Why are you so willing to help without any information?"

He shrugged as he fiddled with his birdhouse. "Seems like you might know something or at least are trying to know something. And it's not like being here is so exciting."

"I ..." I paused, making sure I was sure about sharing this information with him. "I might know something. Maybe."

"Cool."

"There's a group of us," I continued, still unsure if I was blabbering because I wanted him included or I just wanted to talk to someone. "I think you should meet them. We've been discussing some things."

"Just tell me when."

The bell rang.

Nicolas got up first, taking a few seconds longer to collect his things, then walked over to where Kat was standing in the doorway.

I didn't wait to hear what conversation he struck up with her, scooting past them with the other kids exiting. Although, I knew exactly which hallway to go, but I'd never been to any other office except Kanyn's.

I breathed the heaviest sigh of relief when my eyes came across something I hadn't noticed in the few times I'd been down the hallway. On one of the doors, three down and on the opposite side of Kanyn's, was a small, green chalk sign hanging off the doorknob. Written in fancy cursive was the name Kat.

As I had with Kanyn's, I checked to make sure no one was even turning down the hallway, before darting into her office.

Bookshelf on the immediate left, third shelf, right at the end on the right.

As I slid the book in place, I let out another quiet sigh of relief. I paused for just a moment in her office, looking around. Her space was the complete opposite to Kanyn's prim and proper. There were bright colors everywhere, stacks of books and papers, even statuettes. Either she too was something of an anomaly, or they had more character than I was giving them credit for.

As much as I wanted to look around, to note every difference between what Kat kept in her office versus Kanyn, I swept out of there, and out of the hallway altogether. I didn't need to have any ties with that area for the day, just in case.

Making it back into the classroom hallways, I spotted Kaisa, and jogged up to her. "Hey! So tonight then—"

"Let's not do tonight," she said. "Just in case we have piqued anyone's suspicions."

"Okay," I said, immediately disheartened.

"I'll see you at breakfast tomorrow." She didn't wait for me to respond before walking past me.

I figured I'd check back at Kat's classroom, just to see how far she'd gotten. I spotted Nicolas and Kat still standing right inside the door. Kat twirled the ends of her hair between her fingers, looking fascinated in whatever they were discussing.

In the briefest of moments, Nicolas noticed me. He said something, what looked to be a thank you, and walked out of the classroom. "Everything work out?" he asked as he walked up to me.

I nodded. "Again, thank you." I promised him the next time we all sat together in the cafeteria I'd call him over, then we parted ways.

Given that we weren't going to meet, I skipped dinner altogether, spending the majority of the night in the library and then going to my room.

I sighed something heavy when I made it back to my room. Meg wasn't even there, and she was the only person left I thought I'd be able to share all my theories with. It seemed the only thing to do was to go to bed early, if anything to put a pause on creating more theories.

Meg came just before I closed my eyes, speaking to me as if I wasn't halfway buried under the covers. Something about Airi feeling sick and her and Chance helping her. The constant prattle rocked me to sleep faster than the silence had.

But when my eyes opened, they stayed open. Squinting at the clock on the wall, it was a little after six in the morning. I considered going to the library, but after reading the book, I didn't want to be anywhere where there weren't a crowd of other humans around.

Closing my eyes, I tried to will myself back to sleep. When that failed, I fell back on counting backwards from one hundred. Over and over again, until the clock read seven twenty, what I felt was an acceptable time for me to head to the bathroom to get ready.

By eight-ten I was walking into the dining hall. Meg refused to get out of bed, so I'd left her. Chance and Kaisa had pushed off this conversation, but I wasn't going to let them do it again. I found Zahir in line to get food, and the two of us sat at a table already occupied by Kaisa and Chance.

"I've got to say, it still feels a little unfair that I helped with this whole research thing and I didn't get to read any of this book," Zahir said to no one in particular.

I expected Chance to respond, but he kept quiet. "There wasn't time unfortunately," I replied to Zahir. "Maybe we can get it again."

He waved his hand, dismissing me. "Kaisa already told me a little about it yesterday. Sounds like a boring read anyway."

I looked over at Kaisa and Chance. I was bursting to talk and they were sitting like stones. "You guys have been pretty quiet," I commented, trying to prod them.

Kaisa looked over at Chance, but he didn't look up from his plate. Then she turned to me. "Cori, I don't quite know how to say this. Chance and I were talking. Remember that small part I read in the library about the Orders and their awakening?"

I nodded, although that part was a little fuzzy in my mind. "The numbers thing and being confused?"

She nodded once. "We read more into that, the section with examples on how the awakenings would happen. Did you read that?"

I shook my head.

"Well, Chance and I agreed that … We've both had those experiences."

I blinked, trying to comprehend. "What do you mean?"

Kaisa took a deep breath before continuing. "We both have had experiences similar to those described in the book. About a year ago I got really sick. It lasted for almost a month. The doctors never found out what it was, so they chalked it up to some random bug." She chuckled to herself. "Just a bug. I felt like I was dying, I couldn't even turn on the light in my room. But I remember I kept having these … Hallucinations? I don't know. Sometimes they were dreams but sometimes I'm sure I was awake. I would see this number at the edge of my vision. Twenty-five. Like it was singed onto my eye, I would see it everywhere. And Chance—"

"Mine wasn't like that," he cut in, finally looking at the rest of us. "It was a weekend when my mom wasn't home, so I was the only one there. It started Friday night, I kept hearing the number twenty-six. Sometimes it was a whisper, like a ghost. And sometimes it was like someone was standing right next to me shouting it. It lasted all weekend, I thought I was going crazy. Then it just got better. I didn't know what it was, but I've never forgotten. This kind of explains it."

I stared at them, a steady stream of air making it through the slight crack in my lips as I continued to suck in air until I couldn't hold it anymore, and let it out. "Are you sure?" I asked, finally.

"We're sure those events happened to us," Kaisa replied. "And we're here, aren't we? Is that a coincidence?"

"Sure doesn't seem like it," Chance muttered, turning his attention back down to his plate.

Kaisa sighed, moving some of her food around her plate with her fork. "So, if this book isn't just a cruel joke, that would mean that we're two of the people they're looking for," she said.

Chance looked at Zahir. "You too."

Zahir leaned back in surprise. "Me? Why me? I've never seen any weird numbers."

"Never? None?" Chance asked.

"Or you've never gotten sick or something for no reason at all?" Kaisa added.

"People get sick in Mohandiseen all the time," Zahir said. "That doesn't mean anything."

"Why do you think Zahir is one?" I asked Chance.

"When he heard his friend," Chance replied. "The book said Orders have special abilities. I bet that's why Zahir could hear him."

"So shouldn't my friend be in the Order, not me?" Zahir asked.

"He might be too," Chance said. "We can't ask him, now can we?"

"He probably wasn't," Kaisa said. "They're looking for Orders—us—so they wouldn't have killed him if he was."

"Well, I don't think I'm an Order," Zahir said, crossing his arms. "What number would I even be?"

"I don't know, you've got about thirty-four possibilities," Chance snapped at him.

I looked at Kaisa. "Who else?"

"What?"

"Who else do you think is an Order?" I asked. "Did you read why they want to find the Orders?"

She shook her head.

"Then all we know is that they want to find them. Whoever 'they' are. They're killing people who aren't Orders, so I can only imagine what torture they have for Orders. I don't want anything to happen to them—to anyone. I think we should find as many as we can."

"We?" Zahir asked, his eyes darting between Kaisa and I. "Why us? And if they're Orders, maybe they should just tell them."

"There's no way you believe that," Chance said. "I don't know what your time here has been like, but mine has been less than pleasant. We were kidnapped. Why would we trust our captors?"

I nodded. "I agree. I think it's best to keep this here for now."

Kaisa bit her lip and nodded. "Maybe ... Airi?"

Chance looked at her.

"She's pretty sickly. The book mentioned sickness being a sign of an Order." Kaisa shrugged. "I also get this weird vibe when I'm around her. Not bad, just weird."

"Anyone else?" I asked.

"What about your friends Sherman and Theo?" she asked. When I gave her a look she quickly added, "We're in philosophy together. Got to talking and they mentioned you."

"You get a vibe from them?" I asked.

She nodded. "It's weaker, but a vibe all the same."

"How many is that so far?" I asked, opening my notebook and turning to the very last page to write down the names.

"Six."

Zahir looked over my shoulder. "Does my name have to be on the list?"

"Yes," Kaisa said.

"Well what about Cori?" Zahir asked.

Hearing my name felt like lightning striking the tops of my ears. I shook my head. "I've never even mildly experienced anything like that."

Chance looked at Kaisa. "Do you get any kind of vibe from Cori?"

Kaisa looked at me and slowly shook her head. "I'm sorry, I don't. But I wouldn't rule you out just yet."

Still, I refrained from writing my name on the list.

"That's thirty-one Orders left," Chance said. "So, it's decided, we find the others."

Zahir's eyebrows jumped into his hairline. "Like seek them out? What for?"

"They're looking for them," Chance said. He glanced at Kaisa and added, "For us. I think whoever these other Orders are should know about this too."

"So how do we find these Orders?" Zahir asked. "Just ask around if anyone's seen any random numbers lately or felt deathly sick?"

"Yeah," Kaisa replied. "But remember, they don't have to feel 'deathly sick.' It could be really minor, like a random ache."

"I'll make sure I specify," Zahir said, rolling his eyes.

Kaisa glanced at me. "You don't remember seeing anything that could help us find them?"

I shook my head, severely wishing I had used my time more effectively with the book. Was it worth stealing again?

"Don't worry about it," Chance said. "That thing was like a history book. Way too much information, not enough focus on the stuff that matters."

"I'm sure it all matters," I mumbled. At least for us it did. We needed to know who we were dealing with and what exactly they were looking for. And Kaisa and Chance deserved to know more about these "Orders" that they were.

"I wonder what our order is," Kaisa said.

We all looked at her.

"Remember?" she asked, glancing at Chance. "It said the Orders also fall in a certain order. It determines the level of their ability or something."

"I'm only in the Order if I'm more powerful than this guy," Zahir said, nodding toward Chance. "So, number thirty-six."

"I'm sure it's the number you guys saw," I said.

"Oh yeah, that makes more sense," Kaisa said, her cheeks reddening.

"That makes you twenty-five, Kaisa. And me twenty-six." Chance grinned at Zahir. "You have to beat twenty-six."

11

Not much happened between breakfast and the end of the day. I tried to see if I could 'feel' things like Kaisa claimed, but the only thing I felt was dwindling adrenaline.

I found Kaisa after my last class, and she invited me up to her room so we could talk more. Given all the information we'd recently dug up, it felt safer to hang out in small groups in our dorms instead of public spaces. Her space was perfect since she was lucky enough to have a room to herself, at least for now. Her roommate had been 'sent home' a few days ago. Chance was waiting for us outside the door.

Once inside, Chance reclined on the spare bed, Kaisa sat on her bed, and I sat on the floor next to her bed.

"Well," I said. "Did you find any more people?"

"I didn't," Chance said, raking his hand through his hair like he was searching for lice. "I still don't really know what I'm looking for."

"It's a feeling, remember," Kaisa said. "At least, it is for me."

"Well, I didn't feel anything except indigestion," he said. "I think it was the waffles this morning."

"It could be anyone," she said, tapping her chin. "It could literally be anyone here."

"Can't believe it was us," he muttered.

"That's why we got picked up in the first place," Kaisa reminded. "I wonder if that was in their book. Like, how they decided who to bring here."

"You guys got to a lot more in the book than I did," I said.

"That's only thanks to Kaisa," Chance said. "If it were up to me, I probably wouldn't have gotten anything. But she's Speedy Gonzales here, flipping through pages and skimming the text."

"Do you think we should try stealing it again?" I asked.

Kaisa shook her head. "Normally I would say so. But considering we've established they're looking for us, it might backfire. What if they catch us this time?"

Who knew what their punishment would be for that? They had no problem killing the ones who didn't even know why they were here.

"We'll have to work with the little that we have," she said.

"Which really isn't much," Chance said.

Our attention turned to the door at the sound of four short knocks. Our signal.

Kaisa answered, but before she could open the door all the way, Zahir scooted inside, closing it after him.

"Alright freaks," he said. "I brought you some presents."

"What are you talking about?" Chance asked.

Zahir motioned to the door. "I'm not saying I believe in all this crap," he said, "but I may have found some people who fit the bill."

"Let's see them then," Kaisa said. She opened the door and Zahir stepped back out, talking to someone just outside.

One girl with tight, coily, red hair stepped into the doorway.

Kaisa, still standing right by the door, looked back at Chance, but he shook his head.

The second person, another girl, stepped into the doorway. She had platinum blond hair with dark roots and a puggish face. Kaisa shook her head this time.

The third person, a girl with curly black hair and doe shaped hazel eyes, walked into the room. At the same time, in perfect unison, Kaisa and Chance mumbled under their breath, "Her." They shared a surprised look with each other.

"You … Felt that too?" Kaisa asked.

Chance nodded. "Yeah, I don't know how to describe it. I just … Felt it was her."

Kaisa nodded, then looked back at me. "She's one of us."

The girl crossed her arms and raised one of eyebrows. "What do you mean? He didn't explain anything to me."

"Nothing?" Kaisa asked Zahir.

He shrugged and shook his head. "Didn't really know how to."

Kaisa crossed the room over to her bed and motioned for the girl to join her. "This is going to take a few minutes. Zahir, do you mind dismissing your other friends?"

"I don't even know them," he said as he left the room, closing the door behind him.

I abandoned my spot on the floor to sit next to Chance.

"What's your name?" Kaisa asked the girl.

"You don't want my number?" she asked, her eyebrows lifted.

Kaisa shook her head. "It's all names around here. I'm Kaisa, that's Cori, and that's Chance."

"Azita Silvers," she gave. "What is all this?"

"This is going to sound ridiculous," Kaisa began. "In fact, it's still kind of crazy to us. But we think we know why we're all here, and it has to do with you."

"Me?" Azita asked. "I'm just a girl from Herat. This is something much bigger than me."

I could feel Chance roll his eyes beside me.

"Yes, you're right," Kaisa said. "These people that are holding us here, they're looking for other people. Some of us are special to them."

"Special how?"

"Well," Kaisa paused and looked at Chance and I, but neither of us had anything to offer. "We stole a book from them, and it informed us about this group of individuals that they are looking for."

"What, and you think I'm one of them?" Azita asked. "Based on what? And who are they looking for? For what reason?"

"We don't know why," Kaisa replied. "We only had so much time with the book before we had to put it back. Trying not to get caught. But there's these people and they're apparently called the Order. And these Orders apparently have some sort of magical powers. I know how this sounds, but we read it."

"I don't have any magical powers," Azita said.

"We don't either," Chance said with a scoff.

"In the book it explains how these Orders awaken. Chance and I both had experiences like what's described. And I know it sounds ridiculous, but we can sense others. Maybe that's our power. But we both sense something in you. You must be like us."

Azita stared at Kaisa for a few seconds, then glanced over at me. "What about her?"

"Undetermined," Kaisa replied. "But regardless, she's our friend and she's read the stuff too."

I squirmed under Azita's eyes, happy when she finally directed her attention to her own lap. I understood, the whole thing sounded ridiculous, like something out of a movie. People didn't have 'magical powers' and usually didn't find out by reading it in a book. But it wasn't like anything else around here was exactly normal, she had to give us that.

"Again, I know this sounds like the wildest tale," Kaisa said. "And you don't have to believe us. We just thought we should tell you because you could be in danger. These guys are … I don't know what they are. But they have killed people before and I don't know if that's what's in store for all of us."

Azita, still staring at her lap, nodded but she didn't offer a response.

Kaisa moved away from her on the bed. "We're not trying to keep you here either. You can walk out at any time. We just wanted to let you know."

The last word left Kaisa's lips and Azita stood up, crossing the room before any of us could say anything else. She stopped with her hand on the doorknob. "How many people have you told?" she asked over her shoulder.

"You're the first," Chance replied. He grinned sheepishly. "So, feedback is appreciated."

To my surprise, Azita turned back around to face us. "I wouldn't randomly bring people to your door and then judge them like models. This is something I assume you want to keep pretty private. You don't know that I or anybody else you tell isn't going to snitch. So, I would just be a little more selective."

"Appreciated," Kaisa said. "Does that mean you won't tell?"

Azita nodded.

"And that means, you believe us?"

She almost smiled. "I'm willing to believe I've got some magical powers, at least for now." She left the room, closing the door with the softest of thuds.

I looked at Chance and Kaisa. "That went pretty well, I think."

"You think it's a good idea telling people we're who they're looking for?" Chance asked. "What if we're wrong? Or what if they turn us in."

"I know, it just came out," Kaisa said. "I've never had to explain something like this."

"I wouldn't care as much if we had some of those magical abilities we're supposed to have," Chance said. "But so far, I got nothing. Except the ability to 'feel' others. And I'm not even sure that's something."

"Are you doubting that you're an Order?" I asked.

"I mean, we're only like fifty percent sure, right?" Chance said. "No one has confirmed. And like I said, no magic."

"But the awakening," Kaisa insisted.

"Could just be a fluke," he said standing up. "I already thought it was for four years."

Kaisa looked at me. "What do you think?"

I hugged myself, thinking. "I really don't know what to believe anymore. It all seems pretty real. I agree, I can't confirm you two are Orders.

But we do know that whoever they are, they might be in danger. I'm willing to find them and warn them."

Kaisa nodded.

✳ ✳

We informed Shauna, Meg, and Airi of all our conclusions the next morning at breakfast. It went about as well as I suspected. Shauna was in disbelief, Airi was quiet, and Meg was somewhere in between full doubt and crying.

"This is crazy," was the first thing out of Shauna's mouth.

"We know," Kaisa said. "But we think it's real."

"Where is this crazy book now?" Shauna asked.

"We had to put it back," Kaisa replied.

Shauna made direct eye contact with each of us. "Guys, we're not in a movie."

"We might as well be," Chance said. He stabbed his fork into a raspberry and popped it in his mouth. "Look, you don't have to believe us, Shauna. But Kaisa and I both had these ... Experiences."

"These 'experiences,'" Shauna said. She looked at Airi, Meg and I. "What about you three? Any 'experiences?'"

"I've never had anything like that," Meg said.

"Same," I replied.

Our eyes fell on Airi.

"Airi?" Shauna prodded.

She tugged at the ends of her hair, biting her lip. "I don't ... It's just that ... Well, I've been sick a lot. Different things, some unexplainable by doctors. It just seems that maybe ..."

"Maybe you could be an Order too," Kaisa finished for her. "I don't think everyone goes through the exact same thing. But being constantly sick and doctors don't know what's wrong, I think that could be something."

"She could just be sick," Shauna said.

Kaisa shook her head. "I don't think so. I have this little ... Feeling. This pulling sensation."

Shauna sat back in her chair and crossed her arms.

"This whole thing is weird, is it not?" Chance asked. "But this is kind of the best explanation we've gotten so far. As farfetched as it is."

I looked at Meg, who still wore the same mixed expression on her face. "You haven't said anything."

Meg ran the edge of her spoon across her bottom lip. "It seems to me that regardless of Kaisa or Chance's or Airi's status, there are a group of people here who could be in danger. And we need to find them, if not to at least warn them."

Kaisa, Chance, and I nodded.

"Then that's all there is really to it," Meg said. "We find these Orders. And Kaisa, if you have 'feelings,' I guess you'll use that to help."

"Of course," Kaisa said.

Meg shrugged and the bell rang. "Then that seems all there is to it." She had more to say, I knew her too well.

Despite my new objective, I went through my day normally. Although I had an eye out for anything obvious, I didn't really try to identify people who could be Orders. This sensation Kaisa and Chance were experiencing, they couldn't explain it and I had yet to feel anything like it around anyone. It seemed better to leave it up to them. They could walk past every kid here and identify the Orders. I could just support.

Meg and I said nothing that evening as we hung out in our room. Meg sprawled out on her bed, looking like someone who'd just collapsed after running a marathon.

I almost let her drift off into a late nap, then thought otherwise. "We haven't gotten a chance to talk about breakfast."

"What about it?" Meg said, raising her voice for me to hear her through her pillow.

"How you're feeling about it."

She flipped onto her side so she was leaning on her elbow, facing me. "I don't really have any feelings about it."

"Really?" I asked. "You?"

"I have thoughts," she replied. "But not feelings."

I stared at her, waiting for her to continue.

"Are we in a movie?" she asked. "Because that's what it seems like. Things that just don't happen in real life have been happening. We must be in a movie."

I laughed, dryly. "We're not in a movie. No matter how much you've always wanted to star in one."

She didn't smile. "I've lost all perception of what's real and what's fake here. A book about people with special abilities? And a prison to find them? It's crazy. And somehow we're in the middle of it." She sat up and crossed her arms. "This isn't how I planned my freshman year to go."

"Me either," I said. "And yeah, this feels absurd. But it's happening, at least I'm pretty sure. Unless we're in the Matrix and we're waiting for someone to wake us up."

The door opened, and Kaisa plowed into the room. "Hey, I have someone for you guys to meet." Before she could tell us more, a boy at least six feet tall walked into our room.

He looked at the two of us, then looked at Kaisa with a broad smile. "Oh, a four-way? That's pretty impressive, I didn't think that about you when I first saw you." A thick Australian accent cupped each of his words.

Kaisa rolled her eyes. "This is Hudson," she said to Meg and I.

"If you want our opinion on if Hudson is a pig, the answer is yes," Meg said with a smug frown in his direction.

"I think he's one we're looking for."

Meg looked him over once. "Him?" she asked. "Why?"

Kaisa twisted Hudson's right arm so we could see his wrist. The number six in barbed wire. "This tattoo." She looked at him. "Tell them why you got it."

Hudson twisted out of her grip. "I don't know. For like a month I kept thinking about this number, so I figured I'd get it tattooed. Not much of a story." He lifted up the corner of his shirt to reveal a shark tattoo that took up the greater part of his left side. "Now if you want to hear about this tattoo, that's a good story."

Meg gave Kaisa a look as if to ask if we really had to accept him, but I knew if Kaisa had a feeling about him, she was probably right.

Kaisa closed the door then directed Hudson over to sit on Meg's bed. "Listen, we have something really important to tell you and we're not sure how you're going to take it."

His eyes jumped around to each of us. "Are y'all into freaky stuff? I'll admit right now, I've never done anything, but I'm up for it."

Meg looked at Kaisa. "Do we have to?"

Kaisa ignored Meg, her focus on the boy. "I'm sure you've noticed some of the weirdness around here."

He snorted. "Some? This whole place is a looney bin. I feel like I'm trapped in an insane asylum."

"Yeah, okay, it's weird here," Kaisa said, and I could tell even she was beginning to lose patience with his demeanor. "But this is even weirder. These people, or whatever they are, that's keeping us here, they're looking for something. They're looking for us." Hudson's eyes again bounced between each of us. Before he could remark, Kaisa added, "And you." She gave him another moment before continuing. "We're different. How we're different is still a little unclear, but we are. You, me, them, and thirty-two others. And they are looking for us. That's why all of us are here in the first place. They're trying to sort through us to find the ones they want."

A shiver traveled down my spine. The Orders were the ones they wanted, Kaisa and Chance. That still hadn't settled in my head. They were hunting them, and we still didn't know for what. Yes, the book said 'to contain' them. But judging by their character, containing didn't seem like it would just be locked in a room.

"I'm different," Hudson said slowly, sounding every word out. "And I'm different like the three of you are different. How exactly am I—you—different?"

"Well, uh …" Kaisa glanced at us before answering. "Magical powers. Hypothetically."

He raised his eyebrows. "Magical powers? Like witches and all that?"

"More like X-men," Kaisa said. "Telepathy, telekinesis, stuff like that."

His gaze moved slowly between each of us before returning to her. "Did you find a way to get drugs in here?"

Meg rolled her eyes, throwing up her hands. "I think you're wrong on this one, Kaisa."

"I'm not wrong," Kaisa said. "There's no drugs here. Just concern. Can you at least agree to check in with us over the next few days? If this is all a hoax, then fine. But until there's proof of that."

"Fine. I've got nothing to lose, you're all attractive."

"And don't tell anyone," Kaisa said as he stood up.

"I'm not telling anyone you're all on some hard stuff," Hudson said. He winked. "I just might need some and the less people to share with, the better."

Kaisa motioned for him to leave.

"Him?" Meg asked when he was gone.

"You heard the story about the tattoo."

"It wasn't much of a story," Meg said. "There are plenty of people who think of an idea for a tattoo and then get it within a few days."

"But I feel it," Kaisa stressed.

Meg sighed. "Is he really worth saving then?" As if to answer, her stomach growled loudly. She stood up, stretching. "Whatever, let's just get some food."

"Sounds good," I said.

Meg proudly led the way, not paying attention to the two of us behind her.

I paused in the doorway, turning to Kaisa. "Why do you keep saying us?"

"What do you mean?"

"When you were explaining to Hudson. You included Meg and I, like we're Orders."

Her eyebrows knitted together. "Well, you might be. And Airi and Shauna too."

"You said you didn't feel anything from me," I said. "You also didn't say anything to Shauna, nor were you positive about Airi."

"I have a strong feeling about Airi," she said. "I didn't want to say anything this morning, didn't want to scare her. And I'm starting to think we could all be Orders."

"We can't all be," I said. "The book said there's only thirty-six."

"No, I mean in our little group. Me, you, Chance, Shauna, Zahir, Airi, Meg." Kaisa shrugged. "It's just a thought I had. You know, why we've all been kind of drawn to each other. The book said the awakenings probably started after puberty. Who's to say they don't happen later? Maybe some of you haven't gone through it yet, and that's why I don't sense anything."

"Maybe."

"Would you want to be an Order, Cori?" she asked.

I opened my mouth to answer but the answer died in the back of my throat, if I'd even had one at all.

Meg's head suddenly popped back into the room. "Wow, way to let me just walk by myself. I thought we were going to dinner."

"Sorry," Kaisa said, exiting the room.

I followed, but my mind stayed in the room, in that moment. Would I want to be an Order? Would I want to be one of their sought-after objects? Kaisa and Chance were playing their parts well, they didn't show a speck of apprehension being Orders. But could I do that like them? Would I even want to? It was nerve-wracking enough just being here as a normal person.

As we neared the cafeteria, the smells of dinner pushed my thoughts just far enough away. At the same time, we arrived at the doors of the cafeteria, Nicolas was walking in too.

"Hey stranger," he greeted.

"Hey," I said. "Care to sit with us tonight?"

"Sounds good."

We got our food and found Zahir and Shauna at a table.

"This is Nicolas," I introduced to the group. "He's in EL with me." I felt her staring at me, and I looked over at Kaisa. She motioned to Nicolas with her eyes, then nodded.

12

Kaisa continued to find people right and left. At this rate we'd have all thirty-six in maybe three days. But then what? Once we identified all the Orders, how would that change anything? Of the ones we assumed we found, none of them knew anything about any magical powers. Busting out of here like a prisonbreak was certainly off the table.

It was just Kaisa, Airi, and I at breakfast this morning, and the three of us mostly kept to ourselves. From the way Kaisa's eyes kept bouncing around, I assumed she was scoping out new Orders. Airi doodled in her notebook, working on shading in a giant tree. And I was focusing on my pancakes like they were the last ones I'd ever eat.

"Oh!" Airi suddenly exclaimed, looking up from her notebook. "I just thought of someone who might be an Order. Her name is Dara. I remember when she got really sick, that was maybe a week after she first got here. She's a tiny thing, so I thought maybe she just had a really weak immune system."

"Sounds worth checking out," Kaisa said. "It fits the bill."

"After classes then?" Airi asked.

Kaisa and I nodded.

"Let's meet at the library."

I spent another day keeping one eye open for obvious Orders, but ultimately having no luck. The more time that passed from reading the book, the more it felt like a young adult novel.

Maybe this still was some psychological experiment, and that book had been planted. Maybe they were all wearing stilts to be that tall. And maybe those bodies ...

The bodies were the toughest part. Of course, fake bodies were created all the time for movies. But they had looked, even smelled, so real. And the boy who tried to escape. Some people could possibly cross that off as some kind of special effect, but I had witnessed it. There was no special effect that could mimic that spear flying off the wall and penetrating that boy's back.

I went to the library early that evening to review some of the concepts we'd gone over in math. Although we never had any homework, and there didn't seem to be any tests scheduled, I still tried to review and understand, at least to pass the time.

A flurry of blond made me look toward the doors. Instead of Kaisa, it was Amaris who'd walked in. He walked like an asshole. Being so different than a human, he carried himself just like the pretentious frat boys and jocks I saw in college.

As his gaze swept over to me, I lowered my eyes. Him seeing me staring would have only heightened his pretentiousness, that's how it always worked. And by god I was not going to give him any fuel for his low burning fire—

"You looking at something?"

I looked up to see him standing a few inches closer to my table, his beady eyes holding all of me in his gaze. "No," I replied dismissively, lowering my gaze back to my notebook.

I didn't have to look up again, I felt him step closer. His voice raised as he asked, "Is there a problem?"

I looked up again, but I wasn't seeing him in the same threatening way I usually saw him or any of the others as they strode through the halls. I only saw him as one of those old school bullies. Intimidating, but weak if addressed directly. "Do you have a problem?" I fired back at him.

He was at my table now, the ends of his hair brushing against the top of it. "You better watch yourself."

"It seems like you're the only one watching me, that's why you're over here," I said.

Amaris snorted, though only one side of his mouth moved. "We're all watching you. Don't think for a second we're not."

I couldn't help but roll my eyes. "I don't think anyone thinks that. Every corner, one of you is there. But thanks for reminding me I'm trapped in a concentration camp."

He snorted again. "Worse."

My next comment came out without a thought toward danger or repercussions of any kind. Just a good old clapback. "Can't be worse than this conversation, asshole."

I heard it the same time he heard it, and he immediately reverted back to my captor.

"That's a shot," he growled.

My mouth was working overtime, faster than my good sense. "That's not a shot."

The expression on his face flashed from utter surprise I'd spoken back to him, to outright anger. "Oh, it isn't?"

Before I could respond back to him, out of the corner of my eye I saw Truli coming over. She directed her attention at Amaris. "Amaris, you're causing a disturbance."

"I'm causing a disturbance? This little—"

"This is a library," she interrupted him.

His chest puffed out so much he looked like he wanted to choke her. He shot a hot glare at me, then without another word, strolled out of the library.

Truli glanced at me before returning to her position at the front table.

The moment Truli sat back down, a haughty smile rested on my face. Talking back to Amaris felt too good. The anger across his face had been downright delicious. These bullies didn't scare me. They were all talk, all about intimidation. Without that, they had no power. A shot? To hell with his shot.

To my dismay, it turned out that was a shot because within twenty minutes of Amaris leaving, another one of them came to me telling me to report to see Kanyn. I grumbled under my breath as I packed up my books and the entire walk to Kanyn's office. The door was slightly ajar when I arrived, open enough for me to see him sitting at his desk. I knocked as gently as I could, still trying to keep my frustration at bay.

"Come in," he said.

I walked in, trying not to stomp, and closed the door behind me.

"You may be seated," he said without looking up from his notes, but my butt was already halfway to the seat. He continued writing for a few minutes longer, then finally looked up.

A chunk of my frustration melted away as his attention rested on me. I forced myself to keep a calm disposition. "You asked to see me?"

"Yes," he said. "It seems you got into an altercation with Amaris in the library?"

My frustration multiplied. "I would hardly call it an altercation."

"What would you call it?"

"Amaris coming in and yelling at me for no reason."

Kanyn wrote that down, hopefully word for word. "That's your second shot," he said.

I blinked, obviously not hearing him correctly. "Second?"

"The first one was for leaving your post during laundry duty."

"When did I ..." My words trailed off as I put together what he was saying. "You knew."

He didn't satisfy me with an answer, but his lack of one was answer enough.

"Why didn't you say something then?"

"I wanted to see what you would do if you thought you'd gotten off."

I folded my arms and sat back in the chair, a scowl crawling across my face. "Guess I failed. I got another shot."

"It wasn't a pass or fail, just to see what you did."

Restlessly, I sat up straight in the chair again. "Where's Amaris's shot?"

"We don't get shots."

"Well, you should," I said. "Some of you are real assholes."

"If we did get shots," he said, "how many shots would Amaris have?"

It was a ridiculous question, like he was talking to a toddler. But I answered anyway. "Sixty-five," I said.

Kanyn raised his eyebrow.

"Just throwing out a number. He's a jerk so I figure by now he'd have a lot." Without thinking, I added, "Hunter probably would have some too."

"Because you think he's impulsive?"

I nodded. "Jutas and his blond friend would have a couple too," I added.

"His blond ... Do you mean Astaroth?"

I shrugged. "I guess. He's always with Jutas."

"That's him," Kanyn said. "You don't like them either?"

I shook my head. "They're both jerks as well."

"Why?"

I opened my mouth to reply, then stopped myself. The only reason I thought those two were jerks was because I'd seen them bullying Hunter. Which meant I was bothered that one of them was being bullied. I should have felt no pity for any of them. "They're just malicious," I replied.

"They're young," Kanyn said. "Those three are the youngest here. As I understand it, Jutas has something against Hunter. Astaroth is just an instigator."

"What's young?" I asked. "How old are they? They look like they're in their twenties."

I noticed the pause before he answered me. "Hunter is twenty four. Jutas and Astaroth are both twenty-five, though Astaroth is older."

"How old are you?"

Another pause. "Twenty-seven."

Young murderers. Maybe this was a cult.

"Anybody else deserving of a shot?" Kanyn asked.

I shook my head, beginning to feel uncomfortable with the conversation. He seemed to be joking with me, and although comforting, all things considered, it felt inappropriate.

He sighed. "Well, you have two shots, versus zero for everyone else on your list. And I don't see them getting any soon, not that there's any competition. Try not to get any more. You don't want that kind of attention."

I hadn't wanted Amaris's attention in the library, but he gave it to me free of charge, with a complementary shot. But I was done talking, at least for tonight.

I stood up to leave, and with my new height I could see better over Kanyn's desk.

He was writing in one journal, but another one was open at the edge of his desk. It looked to be the same one I'd opened myself, but now there were two new numbers.

#3   #470

I glanced at Kanyn to see if he'd noticed me looking, but his attention was on his own writing. I didn't wait to be dismissed to leave.

Reluctantly, I headed back toward the library. Hopefully I hadn't missed our meeting. Turning the corner, I stopped short of running smack dab into Kaisa.

"There you are," she said, grabbing my arm and pulling me off to the side of the hallway. "I've been looking all over for you."

"Sorry, I was in Kanyn's office. I got a shot."

She shook her head like my mother. "Smart, Cori."

"It wasn't on purpose," I protested, but there was nothing I could say to make it go away. "Have you been waiting on me to go meet Dara?"

Kaisa paused, and her grip on my arm stiffened. She cleared her throat before whispering, "We're too late. She's dead."

It was like she'd hit me with a bag of bricks. "She's dead? What do you mean she's dead? Airi just told us about her today—"

She shushed me. Not here.

We didn't speak again until we made it to the dormitory hallway, huddling against the wall.

"She left class early I was told, she didn't feel well," Kaisa explained in a strained whisper. "I went to see her right after my last class. I was the first one back in these halls." She shook her head. "I saw them taking her from the room. Her neck, it was … Purple. Like she'd been strangled. I hid so they wouldn't see me, but I think they did it to her. I don't know what they did, but I'm sure they did it."

I leaned my head back against the wall, digesting what she was saying. Strangled. They went to her room and strangled her. Had she screamed? There would have been no one around to even hear her.

"But why?" I mumbled.

"It's not their first time," Kaisa said.

"No, but why pick her? Because she was sick? Did she know something? I mean what about her would make them—" The answer hit me so hard my legs almost collapsed from underneath me. "The numbers."

"What?"

"I told you I saw seven numbers in that journal in Kanyn's office." She nodded, and I continued. "When I was there today, he had it open on his desk. Just before I left, I looked at it, there was another number added, number three. And it had a correlating number, I can't remember what it was." The answer was growing more apparent to me the more I spoke. I took a shaky breath. "I think … I think the entries are the members of the Orders that they've killed. Dara was killed today, a new entry."

Kaisa stared at me for a moment, either stunned or trying to form her next words. "What about the other number?" she asked finally. "You said some had it and some didn't,"

"I know, I know," I said. "I don't know, they could be …" A light switch turned on. "They're assigned numbers." I looked right into Kaisa's eyes. "The numbers we're assigned when we get here. That's what they are. They were killed here. Number three was Dara, she was killed here."

"What about the ones without assigned numbers?"

"I don't know. Maybe they were never assigned numbers? Maybe they weren't even brought here, that's why they don't have numbers." My palms were sweaty from how fast my brain was processing information. "Yeah, that makes sense. They're bringing us here looking for members of The Order. It's easier to just find us if we're all locked up here. But the ones without assigned numbers, maybe they were too obvious, maybe they slipped up. I don't know, but they were never brought here."

Kaisa turned away from me but pressed her weight into the wall. "So, they're killing the Orders. They're killing us."

I hesitated before nodding slowly. "Maybe not," I then added. "I mean … I can't imagine everyone we saw in the basement were Orders. I only saw seven, now eight, entries in that journal. There were more than eight bodies."

She ran her thumb across her chin. "So what, you're saying they made a mistake?"

"Maybe," I replied. "The book made it seem like the Order is kind of important. So maybe they've found eight members of the Order already. And maybe I'm wrong, and Dara isn't even one of them, it's just a coincidence she was killed the same day."

"Or she was, and it was a mistake to kill her," she said.

"Maybe they didn't kill her," I said, but I was just spouting off words now. "You said you didn't see anything. I mean she could have … Killed herself."

Kaisa pressed her thumb into the middle of her chin. "That's a lot of possibilities."

"It is," I replied. And I'd talked myself into not knowing which one was the most probable.

"We keep this between us until we know for sure," she said. "About the possibilities."

I nodded.

She offered the palest of smiles. "Guess you're glad you're not one of us."

"Kaisa—"

She put her hand up. "Just a joke." She turned and headed down the hall toward her room.

✳ ✳

It took me two hours to fall asleep. No matter what thoughts I tried to have, my mind kept returning to Dara. I'd failed her. If I had just kept my mouth shut, I could have been there for her. I might have even stopped her death.

I finally did lose myself in my guilt and drift off to sleep. At six twenty in the morning, my stomach clenched so hard it woke me up, sending me tumbling out of bed. Meg didn't even stir, but I couldn't attend to that. My stomach unclenched, and a rush of liquids surged through my body.

Stumbling, I ran out the room, leaving the door wide open, and rushed down the hall to the bathroom. As soon as the door closed behind me, the liquid feeling ceased, and my stomach clenched again. Tight pain shot from my heel up my legs, causing me to drop to my knees and curl up in a ball on the tile floor.

I laid there in my fetus position for a full minute. By then my breathing was returning to normal, and I figured in a few more seconds, I could uncurl myself. At that moment, all my muscles seemed to unclench at once, and a wave of nausea hit me face first. I scrambled to crawl into the nearest stall, just barely making it to the toilet before the bile juice waterfalled out my mouth. I threw up until I was sure I was starting to see bits of yesterday's lunch.

A reprieve, finally, and I used the last bit of strength I had in the moment to flush the toilet. I looked up at the space of wall directly above the toilet. Though my eyes were half closed, I could very clearly make out what I was seeing.

The number 15.

13

By the time I'd finished emptying my stomach and the sudden aches subsided long enough for me to crawl back to my room, it was almost seven. I laid face brown in my bed, agonizing over the fact that I felt like crap but would still have to get up in a few too-short minutes. I considered using a sick pass, but now that I knew for sure I was part of the Order, I didn't want to draw any suspicions my way.

Our way. I was part of the team now. I couldn't do anything that risked the safety of the others. I would have to just pull it together and make it through the day.

Meg woke up at her usual time, at seven ten. Usually by the time she came back from the bathroom around seven twenty, I would be out of bed, if not already dressed. This morning however, when she came back to the room, she was greeted by the sight of my half out-of-the-covers body still in bed.

"Cori, it's almost seven thirty. You're not up?" she asked, switching on the light.

I groaned in response to her, an action that hurt my vocal cords.

"Alright sleepy head. Don't blame me when they run out of French toast."

I heard her open the door, but not shut it. After a few seconds, she spoke, which meant she was still standing there.

"Huh, they gave us new schedules again."

I looked up, which hurt my neck muscles, all the way down my spine. "Again?"

She nodded, and I saw she was holding a printed schedule in her hand. The other, mine, was still taped to the door.

"Do we have anything together?" I asked.

"Um, no."

"What's my first class?"

"Science."

"How wonderful," I muttered as I laid my head back on my pillow.

"There's also a note at the bottom," Meg added. "No more extra duties. So no more laundry duty."

I thought I said 'great,' but I didn't hear it past the intensely firing synapses in my brain.

"Get up soon," she called to me before closing the door behind her. She didn't even bother to turn the lights off.

I ended up staying in bed past eight, not venturing out of the room until eight forty-five. I stopped by the dining hall just to see if there was any food left and managed to snag the last apple in the basket to eat on my way to class.

Thank God my first class wasn't physical training anymore. The effects of becoming an Order hadn't worn off enough for me to run even one lap around the field.

I threw the apple core away as I entered the class and claimed a seat in the middle. My other classmates filed in, taking their seats. I eyed them, enviously curious. Did any of them feel like their limbs were going to separate from their torso at any moment? Like their skulls had become a drum in a seventies rock band? And were they struggling to hide their symptoms like I was?

A drum solo began, and I bowed my head until it was over, clenching my jaw. After thirty seconds it ended, silent until the next song started.

I looked up at the same time a boy with brown hair that gleamed red at the end with the light entered the room. The second my eyes landed on him, every single hair on my body stood at the alert. Cold shivers vibrated through my body, and a humming started in my ears.

The closer he got, the louder the humming became, and the more the shivers reverberated. He sat two desks in front of me, and I felt like I was pulsating.

He had to be a member of the Order, I was undoubtedly sure that's what was causing those sensations. But what number? His radiance was so strong.

Throughout class I focused on steadying myself so I could talk to him, but when the changing bell rang, my stomach did somersaults, and the only question I could get out was for his name.

Killian.

My stomach continued its gymnastics routine as I tried to get to my next class, and my legs felt like jello the more I walked. Finally, I couldn't take it anymore and sat down on one of the cushioned benches in the hallway. I squeezed my eyelids shut to keep the world from spinning and clenched my teeth to keep my breath steady. A slow crest of calm finally came through, and I opened my eyes.

Then I blinked, disturbed by what I had first seen. But clear as day, on the ground was the number fifteen. Or, it was for me. I moved my eyes back and forth across the floor, and the number moved with them, like it was burned into my pupils.

I closed my eyes again. There was no point in trying to will it away. I knew what this was, I knew why it was happening.

"Are you sick?"

Weakly, I tilted my head up, expecting to see Chance. Instead, Kanyn looked down at me.

"So what if I am? It's not like another shot is going to make me feel better." I forced myself to a standing position and tried to confidently stride away from him, though it probably looked just as sick as I felt.

By the end of the day, I was actually deciding between continuing on as a walking corpse or just letting them know I was sick to get some kind of medication.

Limping into my last class, now philosophy, I was happy to see Kaisa already there. I took the empty desk to her left as she conversed with a boy I didn't recognize on her right.

She turned to me with a wide smile. "Hey, glad you're in this class," she said.

"I'm glad you're in this class," I said. "At least you came in with a friend."

"Yeah, this is Jheremy," Kaisa introduced the Spanish boy sitting beside him. He offered a small wave. "We had free period together in our last schedules."

"Can't believe they switched them again," Jheremy said. "It's a little frustrating."

"And convenient," I said, locking eyes with Kaisa.

She chewed on her lip, and her eyes looked me up and down. "Are you sick?"

"You could say that," I replied. I'd answered her honestly, but her eyes didn't leave me. "What, do I look that bad?"

"No." She didn't stop staring, inspecting.

I sighed. Clearly, I would have to pull it out of her. "What is it then?"

Kaisa glanced at Jheremy, who wasn't paying attention to us, then looked back at me, dropping her voice to a whisper. "I'm getting the vibe from you now."

"Great timing," I said. "Yeah, I'm pretty sure I'm an Order too, based on this morning. Number fifteen to be exact."

"What happened?"

"It was awful, I don't even know how to describe it," I replied. "And I still feel crappy."

"I'm happy you're one of us," she said, giving a small smile.

I mirrored her smile as best as I could with the muscles in my face twitching. "Yeah, me too."

✳ ✳

The aches and tremors settled enough for me to not wish I was dead. After class I tried scouting out the boy from my first class, Killian. If now I could experience the same sensations as Kaisa and Chance, then he wasn't just an Order. He was a strong one. Which meant he needed to know what we did.

Even through doing a loop twice around the classroom hallways and the dormitory hallways, I didn't even catch a glimpse of him. I figured I'd wait in the library in the hope he'd pass through. Studying to pass the time, I became so engrossed in my notes, I didn't notice the two people walk up to the table until they were pulling chairs out to sit across from me.

Airi and another girl with perfectly caramel skin, brown almond shaped eyes, and straight black hair swept into a bun sat down. The girl's eyes were red like she'd recently been crying. Airi looked like she'd shed a few tears as well.

"Hey," I said, pushing my notebook to the side, "is something the matter?"

"This is Srey," Airi replied. She paused before adding, "Dara was her best friend."

"I'm so sorry."

With her chin high, Srey said, "Airi explained everything to me. It's not fair what they did to her. I want to help you. Us."

I blinked, processing what she was saying. "Are you ...?"

"A few months ago, before coming here, I got really sick. I was bedridden for a week. While I was sick, I kept catching glimpses of the number ten. I didn't know what it meant then, I thought I was hallucinating," Srey explained. She glanced at Airi before continuing. "Then I came here. They kidnapped Dara and I together, we were out at a club in Vietnam. Dara got sick here, she went through the same thing I did. She told me she kept seeing the number three. We didn't think much of it, just a weird bug we'd both caught, probably stress. But it all makes sense now."

I nodded, because truthfully that was all I could do. I didn't have the right words for this situation. We needed to find other Orders, but why had Airi brought her to me? Kaisa was better at this stuff. "We are so sorry we couldn't save Dara."

"It's alright," Srey said softly. "She is watching over us. What matters is that we find the others and get everyone out of here, right?"

"Yes, of course," Airi replied. Her eyes glossed over the open books in front of me, then stood up from the table. "You look like you're busy, Cori."

Srey stood up, flashing me a weak smile. "Thank you. Good to meet you."

Before I could say anything, the two were walking out the library. For the best. The more we found, the less we needed to be around each other in groups.

I looked over a few more pages of notes with no sight of the redhead coming through the door. By that time another headache was chipping away at my stamina. I gathered my things and headed out the library, running smack dab into Chance headed toward the dining hall.

"Hey, I haven't seen you all day," he said cheerfully. "You headed to dinner?"

I shook my head. "Honestly I just want to go to bed."

"Need someone to walk you back to your room?"

"Yeah, it's such a dangerous neighborhood." The words came out sarcastic, but I realized their weight seconds after they were out. I looked at him. "I'm sorry. I didn't mean it like that."

"It's okay," he said. "How was your day?"

"Awful," I replied. "I got sick this morning and I've been sick all day. But in other news, Airi found someone else."

"She did?" he asked excitedly. "Number?"

"Ten."

"Hm." Chance began counting on his fingers. "So, we have ten, twenty-six, twenty-five, six ..."

"Twelve out of thirty-six."

"Out of thirty-five."

I raised an eyebrow at him.

"Dara, she was an Order, wasn't she?"

"I ..." I thought back to my conversation with Kaisa. "I never met her."

"I didn't either, but I trust Airi's judgement. She seemed certain."

As did Srey. I considered sharing with Chance the same possibilities I had with Kaisa. But we'd agreed to keep them just between us, until we had more evidence either way. And on top of that, if I shared the possibilities with Chance, I was pretty certain which he'd claim to be most likely. I knew too which was most likely. I just wasn't ready to admit it.

A door to one of the dorms opened in front of us and Kaisa walked out. "Oh, hey," she greeted us, pushing some loose strands of hair into place.

"Where'd you just come from?" Chance asked.

"Just visiting a friend." She motioned for us to keep walking, not that she knew where we were even headed. "You guys?"

"The library," I replied. "Chance is so kind to walk me back to my room. I'm skipping dinner tonight."

Kaisa's eyes narrowed. "You should eat."

"Really, I can't."

"Okay," she said. "Anyway, I think I found someone else."

"How do you keep finding people?" Chance scowled.

"I don't know. I pay attention to what people are saying, what happened in their lives," Kaisa replied. "That and these weird feelings I keep getting. Anyway, it's Jheremy."

My eyebrows raised. "Jheremy? In our philosophy class?"

She nodded. "We had free period together in our previous schedules. I don't know, I've always got an interesting vibe from him. But today we were talking, and he told me this story where in high school he was playing soccer and at the end of the game, he missed a goal because his vision became all cloudy and he kept seeing the number thirty-one."

"Sounds like a winner," Chance said.

"How many people is that now?"

"Thirteen."

"Maybe fourteen," I said.

"Who?"

"There's this boy in my first period. I didn't get a chance to really talk to him since I feel like death, but his name is Killian."

"What's he look like?" Kaisa asked.

"Red hair, paler features. He looks young, maybe fifteen or sixteen."

"We'll keep an eye out for him at dinner," she said.

"So, this friend you were visiting," Chance said. "Any chance it was this Jheremy fellow?"

Kaisa noticeably hesitated before answering. "Yes."

Chance grinned at her. "Do you and Jheremy ..."

"What about it?" she snapped.

He held up his arms. "Nothing. Just seems like you spend a lot of time together. I imagine a girl can get kind of lonely being locked up in a concentration camp."

"You're immature."

I laughed under my breath, and that small action made my ribs hurt, reminding me of how I really felt. But it was nice to be in a moment that felt normal.

Meg wasn't in the room when I arrived, and I made quick work slipping into my sleeping clothes and sliding under the covers.

The clock read five after nine when Meg returned. She realized her mistake as soon as she turned the light on. "Are you still sleeping?"

I shook my head sluggishly. Had she not returned at just that moment I probably would have slipped into a deep slumber, but I hadn't seen her all day. Pushing myself into a sitting position, I wiped my eyes.

She sat at the edge of her bed, playing with a strand of hair. "Are you feeling better? If I'm being honest, you only look slightly better than this morning."

"Thanks," I mumbled, chuckling. "I'm okay. This nap helped. What about you? You okay?"

"I think the definition of okay has changed in this place," she replied, starting to braid that strand of hair. "I was just thinking about Kaisa and Chance and all of them." She shook her head, her eyes pointed toward the floor. "I can't imagine how they feel knowing ... Everything. I just wish there was something we could do. This is so unfair, nobody deserves this."

My body hummed as I nodded weakly. "Yeah, I agree."

"What do they want them for? I mean these people are kidnapping people, combing through to find them," she continued. She finished her braid, then immediately started unbraiding it. "How long until they find all of them?"

"All of us," I said.

Meg's gaze jumped up to me.

I let out a short breath. This was as good a time as any to tell her. "I'm one of them. I'm an Order."

"What are you talking about?"

"This morning. Whatever awakening they have with the sickness and the number, I experienced that this morning. I still feel sick."

"Tell me you're joking."

"I wish I could," I replied. "But my tongue has tasted like fuzzy acid all day. And my head is pounding and my joints feel like they're splitting apart."

"Aren't you supposed to have a number?"

"Pretty sure it's fifteen. I've seen that a few times. So ..." There didn't seem like there was anything else to say. The danger she'd just mentioned, I was a part of it. They were after me too.

Meg crossed the space between our beds and knelt at my feet, taking my hand in hers. "I'm not letting anything happen to you."

"Thanks," I said, but there was no comfort in either of our words.

✳ ✳

Waking the next morning, I finally felt better. My body cramped at random times, but I could definitely get up and go to breakfast. I sat at a table with Shauna, Airi, Srey, and Nicolas. Across the hall, Meg, Kaisa, and Azita were sitting together.

"Man, I can't get used to these schedule changes," Shauna said. "I went to philosophy last period yesterday instead of math."

Airi nodded. "Yeah, they're pretty annoying."

"Switching up our schedules probably helps when people disappear," Srey muttered.

I noticed Nicolas rub his jaw quizzically. "What is it?" I asked him.

He looked surprised that I'd picked up on his perplexity. "It's nothing. I mean, I just think the mixing up the schedules might be more than just trying to cover up disappearances."

"Then what is it?" Shauna asked.

"I think ... I think it might be a sorting technique."

"Keep going," Srey said.

"Okay, look at it like this," he explained, moving his fingers along the table as he talked. "If you have a bunch of data, and you're trying to figure out how to connect it, what do you look for? Patterns, some similarities. Well, when you have a lot of data, the patterns or similarities might not be so obvious, so you try different sorting techniques to find that pattern. I think the constant mixing us up are various sorting techniques, and they're trying to find some way to find Orders. I assume they haven't found the right one yet, which is why they keep trying new ones."

Shauna rolled her eyes. "Great, they actually have a strategy to find us. We're doomed."

"Don't say that," Airi scolded.

I looked over at Nicolas. He looked like he wanted to say more, like there was one more piece he was mulling over.

"So, what do we do with that information, genius?" Shauna asked.

He shrugged. "Nothing really. I don't know that there is a pattern that identifies Orders. But if they're looking for outliers, then it would be best to just act like everyone else. Be as normal as possible."

"Normal, right," Shauna muttered. "I thought I was normal."

I had too. It was still crazy how quickly I'd gone from 'normal' to not. I hadn't even fully accepted it yet.

It wasn't until my fourth period that I started thinking about what Nicolas had said. The patterns in each class. As Brunhild droned on about something—geometry things I think—my eyes wandered around the room.

What could be the pattern here? It wasn't anything glaringly obvious, like gender, race, or even hair color. Maybe our eye color? I strained my vision to see the color eyes of the boy next to me. When he finally looked up, they were green. Mine were brown.

It could have been age, but I spotted a girl in the back who looked no older than a freshman or sophomore in high school.

Maybe we were from the same region. Or maybe our parents had the same job. I scribbled down the possibilities on the side of my notebook. I would need to talk to people to find out, and that wasn't a possibility with

Brunhild lecturing. A class like EL or even physical training would be better, where there was more room to talk.

I was happy when the bell rang, so I could stop creating new pattern possibilities. I quickly found Nicolas in the hall, heading to free period. "Did you find anything?" I asked. "I couldn't get a lot because no talking in class. But from what I did get, I don't see any similarities at all. It seems as random as where lightning strikes. I wrote down all my possibilities, but all I got was—"

"It was our numbers," he interrupted. "Everyone in my class had a middle number of two."

I could have slapped myself. I hadn't even thought about our assigned numbers.

"In my third period class, it was a bunch of people who had lighter features. Paler skin, lighter eyes, et cetera," Nicolas continued. "And in my second period, it was all left-handed individuals."

"So, what does all that mean?"

"I think that each class at each time is a different sorting," he replied. "So, if last period was our numbers, everyone in lunch with me had a number where the middle digit was two. Simultaneously, everyone in math with you had assigned numbers middling with the same digit." He tapped his chin with the tip of his pen. "It's a random sorting. Not one that would really help them find similarities between the Orders considering they assigned us the numbers solely based on our time of arrival. And I don't think its perfect either because technically Meg should have been in class with you. You two arrived at the same time and would have the same middle number. But it's a sorting all the same."

My lips turned upward into a grin. This kid was too smart for his own good, maybe he was a genius. "Since you're so smart," I asked, "what's the sorting for this period?"

Nicolas shrugged with a grin. "It could be something as simple as the first letter of your last name. The best way to find out is by talking to people, asking them questions."

"Hey, was there something you didn't get to say this morning?" I asked. "You looked like you wanted to say more."

"Oh ... No," he replied, but his tone didn't match his words.

Before I could say more to him, a girl moving past me caught my attention. She glided through the incoming crowd and out the doors. My feet were after her before I had time to process. In our previous schedules, she'd been in the same free period as well, although I only noticed her a few days before the switch. As she was doing now, she would leave at the beginning of the period, covering herself with the wave of kids entering.

She didn't go very far, taking a direct path to the bathroom. I stepped through the door, easing it back into place so it wouldn't slam behind me. There was a short L-shaped hall before the bathroom opened to the sinks and stalls, and I stood just at the crook, peeking at her.

My jaw dropped.

She stood in front of the second sink, her hand stretched out in front of her. Three pieces of silverware, obviously stolen from the dining hall, floated inches off the counter around her hand. To both my shock and awe, she slowly took two steps back from the counter, and the silverware moved with her, fully hovering above the floor.

"What are you doing?" I blurted out, stepping into the light.

My voice broke the girl's concentration and the three pieces of silverware clattered to the floor. Panic flashed across her face, but a scowl quickly replaced it. "Don't you knock?"

"For a public bathroom?" I had to ignore her crude tone. "Seriously, what were you doing?"

"None of your business," the girl replied as she bent to pick up the silverware.

"You were levitating it."

"That's ridiculous."

"I saw you," I said, plainly. "Is that why you're always coming to the bathroom during free period? To practice?"

"Look, could you just drop it?" The girl tried to march past me, but I defiantly stepped in front of her.

"You need to listen to me. I know what you were doing, and I know why you can do that. I also know that you sneaking in here to practice is not safe for you. They're looking for people like you." I stepped back from her. "People like us."

"Who is 'they?'"

"Them. The ones running the show here. The ones who call themselves the Order," I replied. "They're not the Order, we are. But they're looking for people like us. That's why all of us are here. They're sorting through everyone until they find all thirty-six of us."

The girl crossed her arms. "You're telling me there's thirty-five other people here who can levitate things?"

"I'm not sure all of them are here, but there's definitely thirteen."

She continued to stare at me, her arms and her mind refusing to open to what I was saying.

"I can tell you more tonight if you need more convincing," I continued. "We can all be there."

The girl delivered an even harder stare before exhaling and uncrossing her arms. "Alright. Where do I need to go?"

"I guess we can meet in our room. We try not to be all together too often," I replied. "We're the room that's for five hundred and three, and five hundred and seven. Come around seven thirty."

The girl nodded then headed toward the door. Before leaving she turned back to me and said, "My name is Jacqueline."

"Cori," I said back, but the door was already closing after her. Sighing, I leaned backwards into the wall and stared at the spot on the floor where the silverware had fallen. She'd actually been levitating them, just like Hunter had done with that knife. It was one thing to have read about it, but to see it in action. Questions streamed in and out of my head. How had she even discovered she could do that? How could she do that?

I didn't want to spend too much time away from free period. Out of habit of being in a public restroom, I washed my hands before leaving. As I walked back through the entryway, I glanced around the room. My heart skipped a beat when my eyes moved over Kanyn.

He was watching me, standing perfectly still as he always did.

14

My back stiffened as I forced myself to stare straight at the table I was heading to where I'd left Nicolas. My heart thumped as I slowly dropped down into the seat. I could feel Kanyn's stare on my back. Closing my eyes, I exhaled. It wasn't weird for me to be walking in, I'd simply gone to the bathroom. I went to the bathroom.

I didn't look in his direction again until the bell rang. He wasn't looking at me as I left the room, and at that point I didn't know for how long his attention had been off me.

I spent the first part of physical training replaying myself walking out of and into free period. Had I walked in a weird manner, something that piqued his attention? Had Jacqueline said something when she came back? Maybe she complained that I'd cornered her in the bathroom.

Kanyn wasn't there. For all he knew, I'd just went to the bathroom. As humans do.

The unease didn't start to die down until I walked into philosophy, seeing Kaisa and Jheremy waiting for me. My mind jumped back into puzzle mode.

"Kaisa, what's the last digit of your number?" I asked.

"Seven."

I turned to Jheremy. "What's the last digit of your number?"

"Two."

I sighed. That wasn't the common factor this time.

"Who wants to know?" she asked.

"Oh, it's an idea Nicolas came up with this morning," I explained. "That each class is a type of sorting. They're looking for patterns to identify Orders."

Kaisa nodded. "That makes sense. Have you found any patterns?"

"I haven't, I was trying," I replied. "Nicolas did. He's really sharp, you know. He said it was our assigned numbers in fourth period, and the hand we write with in second."

"So, what's this period?" Jheremy asked.

"If he was here, he could probably already tell you," I said. Looking over at Jheremy, I noticed him writing in his notebook. He was right-handed. I looked over at Kaisa and rolled my eyes, seeing she was a lefty. Nicolas should have been here, I wasn't good at putting together random pieces of information. A random idea popped into my head. "Kaisa, what's your middle name?"

"Ansa."

I turned to Jheremy, who was already paying attention to me.

"Aron," he said.

"And mine is Andrea," I said. "We've been sorted in this class by the first letter of our middle name."

"Are you sure?" Kaisa asked.

Jheremy turned around in his seat to the guy sitting behind him. "Hey, man, what's your middle name start with?"

"A," the boy replied.

Jheremy looked back at Kaisa and I. "Seems like it."

"So, what can we do with that?" Kaisa asked me.

"Nothing," I replied. "Yet." I lowered my voice as Viscount walked into the classroom. "But we should keep our eyes out. I don't think our middle names are going to identify us, but you never know what could. We don't even know what the pattern is."

"If there's one," she said, straightening in her chair to focus on the coming lecture. "It could all just be completely random."

It sure felt random. Of the small selection we had, I couldn't think of one obvious similarity except for the fact we'd all been unfortunate enough to be brought here. So far, only four of us were even from the same country.

I spent most of class doodling on an almost blank page. Above my doodles I wrote down the patterns Nicolas identified as well as the one for this period. None of them seemed to be anything serious, nothing that would give us away any time soon. But how many other sorts had they tried already? What if the next one was the right one? I was pulled away from my thoughts by the girl directly in front of me asking a question.

"How do you say that name?" she asked.

Viscount glanced at the chalkboard behind him. "Parmenides," he replied, sounding each syllable.

"Oh," the girl said, "so you just ignore the two at the end?"

Viscount looked at the board again, then back at her. "A two?"

The girl nodded. "There's a two right after the 'S.'"

Viscount looked back at the board with an eyebrow raised, then looked back at the girl.

I glanced at Kaisa, but she didn't look back at me. Her attention focused on the girl, her muscles tense.

"A two?" Viscount asked slowly. "As in, the number?"

The girl looked around, pure confusion all over her face. "Am I the only one who sees it or something?"

I wanted to jump up and slap my hand across her mouth, but that would only serve to draw attention to both of us. She didn't know any better, but she was practically outing herself. And if Viscount read the book cover to cover, he'd know she was too.

By the grace of God, another kid, this one with a smug face, leaned back in his chair and said, "No man, I see it too."

Another boy in the back, who would have made a great partner in crime to the first, spoke up next. "Clear as day. You're not blind, are you, Viscount?"

Viscount actually gave his back to us so he could fully stare at the board.

"It's right there," the first boy said. "Like right there. I don't know how else to say it. Right there."

Viscount stared, and the strain swelled on his face.

One girl giggled, and that started a chain of laughter throughout the classroom.

Glancing at Kaisa again, she was looking at me now. She gave me a small nod, and I returned it. But why hadn't Kaisa sensed the girl before? She was sitting right in front of us.

Viscount gave the class a sizzling glare and the laughter halted instantly. "Very funny," he growled.

The bell rang, saving us from his wrath.

I stood up, but moved my things around on my desk as I waited for the girl in front of me to get her things together.

When she walked, we walked, Kaisa and I practically tailing her out of the room. Viscount didn't watch us leave, sitting at his desk writing in a notebook similar to the ones in Kanyn's office.

Once out in the hallway, Kaisa and I managed to step in front of the girl, blocking her from getting lost in the sea of changing students.

"Quick question," I blurted out. "What's your middle name?"

"Uh, Adelmo," the girl replied. "It's my father's name."

I tried to keep the smile off my face, proud that I was figuring out their little sorting game. The smile drooped as I noticed Kaisa's humorless face.

"What was your name?" she asked. "Your real name, not your number."

"Yelena," the girl replied.

"Right." I noticed Kaisa's eyes slip toward the classroom door, then back to Yelena. "That was weird, right? What you were seeing in class today, the number."

Yelena nodded once. "I'm not sure why those two boys made it into a joke. I really—"

"Don't talk to anyone about it," Kaisa said firmly. "No one. But look for us in the dorm hallways this evening. It's important." Before Yelena could ask any questions, Kaisa walked away.

Yelena looked toward me and immediately I knew why Kaisa had looked back toward the classroom. Yelena had made her episode public, in front of one of them. She might become a target, as would anyone associated with her. But I didn't have the balls to look back to see if Viscount had stopped writing to come watch.

I only gave her a small nod, then walked away. If she was smart, I'd see her tonight.

✳ ✳

Kaisa and I went to dinner together early that evening. As we were leaving, I spotted Jacqueline about to walk out, and I invited her to walk with us as we looked for the girl from philosophy.

We came across her walking up and down the dormitory halls, trying not to look out of place. She didn't, she looked like a ghost was after her, but I wasn't going to tell her that. Not when we had so much else to explain.

We brought the two to Kaisa's room, spreading out to start our summary.

"I guess we should start by introducing ourselves officially," Kaisa started. "I'm Kaisa." She pointed to me. "That's Cori." I offered a small wave.

"Yelena," the girl from philosophy introduced.

"Jacqueline. I thought you said there was thirteen."

"Well, we're not all here. We don't like to be together very often just in case." Kaisa looked at me before continuing. "Also, one is already dead."

"Maybe," I felt the need to throw in. But as soon as I said it, I knew the possibility was hardly possible.

"Maybe they're dead?" Jacqueline asked.

"Maybe she was an Order," Kaisa replied. "We can't really ask her now."

"Because she's dead?" Jacqueline pressed.

Kaisa hesitated before nodding. "They killed her. We don't know why. It could be because she was an Order or because she wasn't. Regardless, they're killing people."

Yelena gasped, an appropriate reaction. Jacqueline on the other hand didn't change her bored facial expression, stopping short of rolling her eyes.

"Was that not obvious?" she asked.

"You knew?" I asked.

"I speculated," Jacqueline replied. "People disappear and not one of them bats an eye. You have to ask, and their only response is that people 'went home.' I'm not stupid. People aren't usually kidnapped to just be sent home."

Yelena shakily raised her hand, and Kaisa motioned for her to speak. "Um," Yelena said quietly. "I think I missed something. What is an Order?"

"Right," Kaisa said. "Us. Me, Cori, you, and Jacqueline. And about nine or ten others here that we've found. We've done some snooping around and we found out that these people who are keeping us here, they're looking for these Orders. And an Order is, well, someone with special abilities, according to the book we read."

I nodded. "And I'll admit, it's all been a bit far-fetched, even with the weird predicament we're in. I mean magical powers or whatever, this isn't a movie, right? But then Jacqueline ..."

Jacqueline fully rolled her eyes now. "Right, the silverware."

"Silverware?" Yelena repeated.

Jacqueline motioned with her head to a pen lying on Kaisa's bed. Kaisa handed it to her, and she set the pen on the floor in front of her. She stretched out her hand, just like she had in the bathroom. Slowly, the pen rose off the floor until it met the palm of her hand, and she closed her fingers around it. She handed the pen to Yelena. "No strings," she said.

"Telekinesis," Kaisa said. "Exactly what the book said."

"But I can't do that," Yelena said.

"Neither can we," I said. "Like I said, Jacqueline has really been the first proof that all this is real and not one big joke."

"I mean, I never thought this wasn't real," Kaisa mumbled.

"So, I'm an Order," Jacqueline said. "So what? What does that mean?"

Kaisa and I exchanged glances. We really should have kept the book to show people.

"We don't know. We only had so long with the book before we had to put it back," I replied.

"But it means you're part of the reason for this whole setup. They're 'sorting' through kids to find Orders. We don't know for sure what they plan to do when they find you but ..." Kaisa paused. "I doubt its good."

Yelena raised her hand again and Kaisa gave her the floor.

"That sounds great and all. Well not great, pretty scary actually. But how do I fit into all of this?"

"Your incident in philosophy earlier," Kaisa explained. "We read about how Orders awaken. Each Order is tied to a number, and there's thirty-six total. Part of the awakening process is to start seeing or obsessing over the number you're associated with. You were seeing the number two on the board even though it wasn't there. Those boys playing along like it was a joke was a fluke, wasn't it? They were trying to pull a joke, but you actually saw the number."

Yelena nodded.

"You're awakening, you're finally seeing your number," Kaisa said. "That's what alerted Cori and I about you."

My attention returned to Jacqueline. I couldn't tell if she just looked perpetually bored or if she was still skeptical of the whole thing. "What do you think?"

"I hear you. I mean I guess I experienced something like that. Nothing that made me look like a maniac in front of people. There was a period where I was obsessed with the number twenty-seven," she said. "Decided that would be the age I'd get married, buy a house, and all that. I also requested a monthly allowance of twenty-seven thousand dollars." She shrugged. "Kind of my lucky number at the time. I figured it was just a phase."

"I would bet anything you're twenty-seven," Kaisa said. I glanced at her, surprised she could just gloss over the fact that this girl received an allowance of twenty-seven thousand dollars.

"Okay," Jacqueline said, her attention turned to levitating the pen. "What are we supposed to do with this information?"

"For one thing, not sneak off to the bathroom every day to levitate objects," I said.

Jacqueline rolled her eyes again, but Kaisa spoke up. "Cori is right. You don't have to do anything. We just wanted to inform you so that you don't draw any unnecessary attention to yourself. We don't have a plan. If you come up with anything, we're up for it."

Jacqueline and Yelena shook their heads.

"Well okay then," Kaisa said, standing up. "We'd love to introduce you to everyone else. Slowly of course. With our group getting larger, it's more important we spend more time apart."

As Jaqueline and Yelena stood up too, Kaisa gently took Yelena's wrist. "You especially be careful," Kaisa said. "You made your awakening public in front of Viscount. Hopefully he'll just think it's a coincidental prank, but I don't know."

Yelena visibly stiffened, but nodded.

"You had dinner?" Jacqueline asked Yelena.

Yelena shook her head. "I'm not particularly hungry."

"I'll walk you back to your room then." Jacqueline glanced at Kaisa and I. "For protection."

Kaisa closed the door behind them, sighing to herself as she did.

"I think that went well," I said.

Kaisa nodded. "Nice work finding Jacqueline. She should be more careful."

"She didn't know." I was honestly happier she took everything well. From her attitude in the bathroom, I really thought she was going to resist anything we had to say. "I wanted to ask you, do you know why you didn't sense Yelena? She sits right in front of us."

"I thought about it ..." she trailed off, hugging herself and tapping her index finger against her forearm. "I think that was Yelena's awakening. Literally in that moment. She didn't experience any pain or anything physical. Everyone else has already had their awakening a while ago. I think that's why I didn't sense her, because before today she hadn't awakened and today it was so new." Kaisa looked me in my eyes and shrugged. "It's just a theory."

"I feel like that's all we're working with lately," I said. "Theories."

"Should we take the book back?" she asked.

I bit my lip. I wanted to say yes. All of our answers could be right there in those pages, all we needed was time to read them. But I shook my head. "We should consider it luck our plan worked so well the first time. We don't know what they would do if they caught us, but we do know death is an option. I'm not willing to die over a book."

"Me either ..." Kaisa said, but she trailed off again, staring at the wall.

If there was anything I'd learned about her, she was a thinker. She could lose herself in her thoughts. At the moment, I preferred sleeping over thinking. Might as well get to the next day. The next obstacle.

"I'll see you at breakfast tomorrow," I said as I passed her out the room. The halls were empty as I headed to our room, giving my anxieties the stage they needed. I fought the entire way to keep them quiet.

Opening the door to our dorm, I found Meg curled up in a ball in the middle of her bed. "Hey, are you feeling okay?" But as I spoke, she lifted her head, and I could see her face was wet and blotchy. Fresh tears were still in her waterline. I flung myself down next to her. "What's wrong? What happened?"

"Nothing," she blubbered as she tried to wipe her eyes, but new tears kept taking the spot of the old ones. "Just feeling overwhelmed. Ha, that doesn't even describe how I'm feeling." She looked at me. They're killing people who aren't in the Order."

They're potentially killing people who are in the Order, I wanted to say, but that didn't seem very comforting either.

"There's only thirty-six Orders and maybe a hundred and fifty kids here. It's easier to find those who aren't in The Order. What if ..." Meg bit her lip. "What if they come for me?"

"Why would they come for you?" I asked.

"I'm not an Order, Cori. I'm sure it's obvious." she sniffled. "I've never been extraordinary or anything like that in my life. What if I'm next? What if I'm not cutting it, and they're about to come and here and kill me in my bed?" Her sniffling intensified until she sounded like she was choking.

"Meg," I said abruptly. As she tried to gain control over her sniffles, I softened my voice. "No one is on their way here to kill you, okay? So, get that out of your head."

Her sniffles quieted, but the tears returned. "If it's not now, it's later. It's coming."

"Then we don't let that happen."

She looked over at me. "How?"

I was the last person to come up with a plan. I said the first idea that sounded good. "They want the people in the Order. We're the focal point. So, we just have to make you a focal point too."

Meg used the collar of her shirt to try and dry her tears once again. She waited for me to elaborate.

"I think everyone in our group—besides Kaisa and Chance—assumes you're an Order, basically because no one has said differently," I said. "Let's keep it that way then. Just stay with the group."

My words were working. She wasn't sniffling anymore, and new tears weren't replacing the ones she wiped away.

I hugged her, something I should have done more often for my best friend. "I won't let anything happen to you," I said. "No matter what happens, I won't leave you."

15

I was jolted out of the euphoria of my dreams and back into the dark reality of my dorm room by knocking at the door.

"What time is it?" Meg mumbled, her voice changing volume with each word.

"It's like eleven thirty," I mumbled back to her as I stumbled to the door. I wiped my hand across my face before opening the door. The hall light blinded me for a second, but blinking through the pain, I could finally make out who was standing at the door. "Hunter?"

He didn't crack a smile. "Kanyn wants to see you in his office."

"Now?"

"Yes. Hurry up."

Meg yawned loudly behind me. "What is it? Who's at the door?"

"No one, go back to sleep," I said to her. To Hunter, I whispered, "Do I have time to change?"

"No."

"Can I at least put on my hoodie?"

"Fine."

My eyes, now adjusted to the light, made me blind in the dark room, and I groped around for the hoodie. Sliding it over my head, I went back to the door, and quietly closed it after me.

Hunter looked down at my feet. "Did you want shoes?"

"Do I have time for shoes?"

He paused, then replied, "No." He started down the hallway, confident I was trailing behind him.

I yawned to myself as we walked. It had to be way too late to be appropriate to visit with one of them. My fatigue kept my mind heavy and unable to conjure up any concern of why this meeting couldn't wait.

As we came to the end of one of the cut-throughs, Hunter suddenly put up his hand and I halted mid-step. "Wait."

I waited and after a second Hunter gingerly pushed me back into the shadow of the hall. He stepped forward into the main corridor. At the same time he stepped out, Jutas and Astaroth passed by.

I couldn't help but be a little thankful to him for hiding me from them, especially Jutas. At least they were only passing. Or so I thought.

My eyes barely caught his movements. In one fluid motion, Jutas whipped out a knife from his robe and pinned Hunter against the wall, the blade less than half an inch under his throat. A smile spread across Jutas's face.

"You flinched."

Hunter's only response was an unwavering stare.

Jutas scoffed, pushing himself back away from Hunter, the smile permanently etched on his face. "You're slipping, Hunter," he called as he and Astaroth walked away.

Hunter waited a few minutes, I assume until they were far down the hall, before motioning for me to enter the main hallway. Without a word to me, we continued toward Kanyn's office.

I however couldn't let that encounter go so easily. It was one thing for Jutas to push him around, but to actually hold a knife to his throat. I cleared my throat before softly asking, "Are Jutas and Astaroth always that way to you?"

"What way?" Hunter asked without turning around.

"Mean," I replied. "Complete jerks."

"I don't know what you're referring to."

"I overheard a conversation between the three of you. Jutas was grilling you about what you did in class that day," I said. "And what just happened. He blatantly threatened you—"

"Forget that happened," Hunter said shortly. "It's none of your business."

It was none of my business and I shouldn't have cared. But I did. From the short glimpses of him I got, Hunter was quiet and kept to himself. Jutas was vicious and domineering. He and Amaris must've gotten along great, though I had yet to see the two together.

Neither of us said another word.

As per usual, the door was slightly ajar when we arrived. Hunter waited a few steps outside the door for me to go into the office. And as usual, Kanyn sat at his desk writing God-knows what notes about any and everything. Even this late at night, he found stuff worthy of writing down.

I slumped down in the chair, struggling to keep my eyelids open. "It's kind of late."

"Good observation," he said.

I was too tired to appreciate his sarcasm. Yawning, I asked, "Why am I here? I haven't done anything."

"I just had a question."

"A question?" I asked. "As in singular? You couldn't have waited until tomorrow to ask me one question?"

"What were you talking to Number Four Hundred and Forty-Nine about?"

"Who?"

"Jacqueline," Kanyn replied. "You followed her into the bathroom during free period."

I kept my composure, which wasn't too hard with how tired I felt. "Not followed. How about I had to go to the bathroom?"

Kanyn looked at me briefly before continuing. "Alright. You went to the bathroom. Did you speak to her while you were in there?"

"I don't remember. I'm sure I did, it's a public space."

"What did you talk about?"

I shifted in my chair so that I was leaning on one arm atop the desk. "Interested in girls' bathroom talk are you? That's a new level of perverted."

He didn't break character for that one.

"Look, if I spoke to her, I don't remember what I said. Probably something short like hey."

"And you don't remember seeing anything odd about her while you were in there?"

I sat up straight. "Are you accusing me of peeping?"

"Cori, enough," he said tiredly. "I have a strong suspicion that you also noticed Jacqueline's strange behavior, going to the bathroom every free period."

I did my best not to squirm under his eyes. "How is that strange behavior? Free period is the best time to go to the bathroom."

Kanyn's only response was to maintain his eye contact with me, and I felt my muscles twitching to squirm.

"And why are you watching her like that? That's strange behavior. Which actually brings us back to perverted."

He sighed. "You are such a child."

"And it's past my bedtime," I said standing up. We could go in circles until the sun came up, one of us needed to end it.

As I reached the door, Kanyn spoke again. "You're eighteen years old, able-bodied and able-minded, one of your first acts here was to try and sneak out, but you can't remember whether a conversation occurred earlier today."

I should have just walked out and left the discussion at that. Obviously he was baiting me—and I fell for it. I turned back around and asked, "Are you asking me or telling me?"

"I don't believe that you don't remember," he said.

"Your opinion."

Kanyn's eyes narrowed just slightly. "You know, don't you?"

His gaze sent shivers through my bloodstream. "Know what?"

"That there's something off about her," he said. "And that there are others of which something is off."

I could feel my body starting to uncontrollably squirm, and I knew he could see. "I don't know what you're talking about."

"Cori," Kanyn said, and his gaze intensified on me. "I promise you it's much easier if you're just honest with me. I'm not looking to get you in trouble, or anyone you know. I just want to know what you know."

"Why?" The question came out hoarse from my dry mouth.

"It's easier to understand you if I know what's on your mind." He motioned to the open chair.

There was probably no consequence to me walking out the door, but still, I reseated myself across from him.

His gaze softened. "I can make this even easier for you. A trade. You tell me something, I'll tell you something."

My body was numb, I barely felt the chair underneath me. I didn't want to divulge a single word, risking outing myself or any Order. But knowledge was power around here. Especially for the Orders, we could use the upper hand.

I stared into his eyes, considering his offer. I should've looked somewhere else. His gaze was a sparkling galaxy I wanted to float in.

"I did speak to Jacqueline," I started slowly. "But it wasn't anything in depth. I just asked her about her ... Routine. As you said, it's noticeable that she disappears to the bathroom every free period." I let my eyes drift to the right of his, gazing at the wall behind him.

"What did she say?" he asked.

I shrugged, keeping my eyes away from his. "It's just for privacy. Or something."

"That's all?"

"She's not much of a talker," I replied. "Seems a little arrogant."

There was a pause between us, Kanyn not taking his eyes off of me. Then he said, "It's interesting that you picked up on her behavior. Clearly you're good at observing people as well."

"Maybe," I said. The more time I spent with him the more I'd say. Being here, he was a danger to me and I was a danger to the Orders. I swallowed, and pushed forward. "What are you going to tell me?"

Kanyn's eyes flickered to the door, then he exhaled through his nose. "You may not believe what I'm going to tell you, and that's completely up to you. But I promise you what I'm about to tell you is the truth."

My gaze returned to him. The numbness was subsiding, I could once again feel the weight of my body pressing into the chair.

"I'm sure you've wondered why you're here."

I nodded.

"It's because we're searching for something. Not something, someone. Thirty-six someones to be exact."

"Thirty-six someones," I repeated. Information I already knew.

"There are thirty-six individuals around your age who possess special powers."

"Special powers?"

Kanyn nodded. "Yes, like the ability to levitate objects in the air and teleport."

I had to act like this was the first time I was hearing about such magical powers. I forced my eyebrows to raise in surprise. "I'm supposed to believe this?"

"You don't have to," he replied. "But they do exist, and we're looking for them. I know Caecilius said that we were the Order. He misled you, and I apologize for that. These individuals are the Order. They're special beings, and it's important that we find all thirty-six of them."

"For what?"

The light in Kanyn's face seemed to fade as he answered my questions. "To protect them."

He was lying.

I shouldn't have been able to tell. I shouldn't have noticed something so subtle on him. But I did.

He continued. "You noticing little things like that about people made me think you already knew somehow who we were looking for. Clearly you didn't, you're just a keen observer."

"I guess."

I could tell he was forcing the smile, little as it was, on his face. The light hadn't come back to his eyes. "That's a good skill."

Shifting my legs, I realized how uncomfortable I was becoming. I was an Order, Kanyn didn't realize, he thought I was looking for Orders, and for some reason thought I was now trustworthy enough to tell me about them. Also, I hated watching him have to lie. As much as I wanted to ignore it, I couldn't unsee the dim lights in the pits of his eyes.

And that risked everything.

"Are we done?" I asked. "It's still late, and only getting later."

"Yes, you may go," he said, leaning back in his chair. He stared at the notes in front of him, but without focus.

Again, I stood up and headed for the door. Something inside screamed at me, tried to push me back to the chair. Compassion as some called it, and it wanted me to go back and console him, to coax him into confessing what he knew and what was wrong. But I couldn't let it win. I couldn't be the reason my friends got hurt. I closed the door behind me with a shaky sigh.

I tried not to think about the entire exchange until I returned to my room, simply to make sure I actually got back to my room and didn't absentmindedly wander into some other hallway—or into Amaris or Jutas. When I reached the room, Meg was fast asleep. I wondered if she'd even tried to stay up.

As I lay on my back in bed, I couldn't remove the image of Kanyn's face when I'd asked him what they wanted the Orders for. A lie, but a lie that disheartened him. What did they want the Order for? Did they want to make us into an army and use us against the world? That couldn't be it. Even thirty-six humans with special abilities couldn't take on an army of ten thousand with AKs and nukes. And they'd possibly killed some of us. I didn't know that for certain but the dread of that reality being true weighed more and more heavily.

Why hadn't Kanyn just told me the truth? Maybe I could wear him down with more office visits. Maybe if I just asked directly.

Hey Kanyn, what is it you want these Orders for? Could it have something to do with all these people who suddenly disappear? What about all those bodies down in the basement? Does that have anything to do with it—

A sudden realization struck me, so forcefully every muscle in my body locked. The gold bracelet I'd seen in the pile of dead bodies. At the time I couldn't remember where I'd seen it before, but now I did. It was the same bracelet Gianni had been wearing, the one he said his mother had given him.

I sat up, my mind racing to put all these pieces together. The basement full of dead bodies. The journal with Order entries. Gianni. Dara. This place.

Dara was an Order, there was no reason to doubt it. She was sick, and they took that as enough of a sign to come for her. Gianni was an Order, I was sure, and he had been killed a while ago. But how did they know about him? What had he done? I closed my eyes as I thought back to the few interactions I'd had with him, searching for any kind of clue he could have given.

He was exceptional in physical training. He could run miles without tiring, do push-ups in the hundreds. A gifted athlete, that's what I'd chalked it up to. I'd overlooked it, that was probably the first indication for them. But that alone couldn't have identified him.

Fourteen. He had said his favorite number was fourteen, that it was his number in sports. He had it fricking tattooed on his beefy arm. That had to be it, what confirmed their suspicion. I didn't know for sure, But I did know fourteen was another one of the numbers in the journal.

A stifled cry escaped my lips, and I looked over to see if I'd woken Meg.

I'd ran my mouth that night to Kaisa and convinced her they'd made a mistake with Dara. They were searching for us and killing others in the process. But the reality was clear.

They were killing people who weren't Orders to find us. And when they found us, they killed us too.

✳ ✳

I couldn't fall back asleep. I did out of sheer exhaustion, but it was like falling unconscious instead of drifting into a peaceful slumber.

The next morning, I rushed Meg to breakfast, but left her at the doors when I spotted Kaisa. I gave her a quick overview of what happened last night, pointed out a table for us to sit at, then left her to round up the others. Of the fifteen of us, only Chance, Zahir, Shauna, Jacqueline, Nicolas, Srey, and Sherman were in the dining hall already. I didn't have time to wait for the others.

"Cori, we shouldn't be in a big group like this," Kaisa whispered as I sat next to her.

"I know. But we need to talk, all of us," I said. I glanced around the room. There weren't any of them in the dining hall yet. "It'll be quick." I met each of their eyes before starting. "There's something we need to talk about." I swallowed hard. I'd had the thought for days, never speaking it aloud, not wanting it to be true. But it was—Kanyn lied, it was in his eyes. Gianni had been an Order and he was among the bodies killed. We all deserved to know the truth.

"They're killing everybody." I'd said it. Laid it out on the table for everyone to do what they would with it.

The questions fired.

"Excuse me?" Shauna asked.

"What are you talking about?" Meg.

"Wasn't that obvious?" Chance.

I glanced at Kaisa. In light of our private conversation, she would know how to help me explain.

She cleared her throat and began. "I think there's been some ambiguity on what they're looking for."

"Orders, I thought," Zahir said. "Isn't that the whole point?"

"Yes," Kaisa said. "And who here was under the impression that since they're looking for Orders, they are safe from ... Murder."

Meg, Zahir, Shauna, Sherman, and Srey all raised their hands.

Kaisa nodded at them. "And the rest of you?"

"Figured we were all dead at one point or another," Jacqueline replied.

"Not as morbid, but I assumed they were killing Orders," Chance said. "One extreme for another."

"How did you assume that?" Shauna asked. "We don't have any proof of that."

Srey looked around with a gaping mouth. "But Dara—"

"Getting there," Kaisa cut her off. "Dara was an Order, there's no denying."

"We don't know that," Zahir said.

"She absolutely was," Srey said.

"She more than likely was," Kaisa said. "And she is dead."

"There was another," I spoke up. "His name was Gianni, I don't know if anyone else here knew him." Jacqueline raised her hand in accordance. "I didn't know him very long, but I'm sure he was an Order too. At first, I just thought he was a conceited athlete or something like that, but that was my fault."

"You didn't know," Kaisa said.

I hesitated before continuing. "His favorite number was fourteen, he mentioned that. That could just be a coincidence, but I don't think so. And if he went through the same things the rest of us has, that would make him the fourteenth Order. I've been to Kanyn's office many times and he has this journal with numbers in it. I believe it's a list of found Orders. Number fourteen is listed. Gianni was among the bodies found in the basement. So, either they didn't think he was an Order ..."

"... Or they did know," Sherman finished. "And that's why they killed him."

"Dara too," Srey added.

"Right," I said. "They knew or they assumed and got lucky. Which brings me back to my opening statement, they're killing everybody."

"So, they're killing Orders." Zahir said. "They're searching for us, killing those who aren't us, and then killing us."

"This should count as genocide," Shauna muttered.

The table fell into silence, forks and spoons scraping the bottom of plates.

"It makes sense," Nicolas spoke up.

Everyone's attention turned to him.

"It makes sense?" Chance asked. "What the hell about any of this makes sense?"

"I mean, it makes sense with my sorting theory," Nicolas said. "They're searching for thirty-six or so of us here. And they're trying to find some kind of pattern between us to identify us from the rest. But why keep looking in a large crowd? Eliminate the ones that don't fit, make the sample smaller."

"You're sick, aren't you?" Zahir asked him with a sneer.

Nicolas shrugged. "Just telling you how they're probably thinking."

The table fell into another silence.

Kaisa suddenly stood up, her hands on either side of her tray. "We've been together too long," she said. Without waiting, she took her food and went to sit at another table.

Jacqueline stood up next with a wry expression on her face. "Guess the question is how long until they get to us." She was almost laughing as she too walked away for another table.

Zahir went next, muttering about not being hungry anymore.

I didn't feel the strength to get up, so I kept my position. But everything tasted like cotton as it hit my tongue, so I ended up getting up early anyway. As I made my way to the doors, I noticed Kaisa getting up from her new spot.

She met me outside the doors. "That was a good decision," she said. "To tell everybody. We all need to be on the same page."

"I didn't tell everybody."

"We'll share the message."

Jacqueline's words ran though my head. How long would it be? If Nicolas was right, and they were constantly whittling down the number of people here, it would only be a matter of time. The question was how much time.

Airi scurried up to us, the look on her face urgent. "There you are."

"What is it?" Kaisa asked.

"I heard two people were rushed to the infirmary yesterday."

"Okay, and?"

Airi looked around before answering in a low voice, "They're both having very specific symptoms. That's how one of them put it anyway."

I looked over at Kaisa the same time she looked at me.

"We should check them out," she said.

I nodded and looked at the clock on the wall. "We have some time now before classes start."

Airi took a step, but Kaisa grabbed her arm. "You should see the others in the dining hall," she said.

Airi looked at her, then me, but she didn't ask questions. She nodded and passed us into the dining hall.

Kaisa and I hurried as fast as we could without sprinting to the infirmary.

It was a room similar in size to the one for free period, with seven beds lining one wall. Three of them were occupied. One by itself at the very end, someone hidden deep under the thin covers. The other two were closer to the door, one bed between them.

The girl held a sun-kissed tan, with hair the color of the sandy beaches she probably laid out on, and matching thick eyebrows. She sat upright, stretching her lanky legs the length of the bed. She noticed us the minute we walked in, but pretended to be more interested in a string on her pants.

The boy reclined in bed, and I didn't get his features until we were right up on him. Pale skin, sharp lines in his forehead and jaw, a thick torso. And he carried one of those faces that looked perpetually distressed.

"I am not even sick," the boy was saying. "This is bullshit."

"Yeah, you're not sick, that's why you look like a piece of *mierda*." The girl's eyes moved to us. "If you're looking for Phaenna, she's not here."

"Did she say when she'll be back?" Kaisa asked.

The girl shook her head. "What do you need?"

"We actually want to talk to you," Kaisa said, stepping closer to their beds. "Maybe. Were you two just admitted?"

They nodded.

I glanced at the last bed. "What about him or her?"

"*No te preocupes*," the girl replied. "She just has a problem *con su cama.*"

"I'm sorry, my Spanish isn't very good," I said.

"How you say, a bed wetter," the girl said.

"What are your names?" Kaisa asked.

"Stepan," the boy replied.

"Valentina Ruiz de Neuquen, Argentina," the girl replied. "*Y tu?*"

"I'm Kaisa and this is Cori," Kaisa said. "You two are sick?"

"We're not here for fun," Stepan said.

"If you don't mind us asking, what kind of symptoms are you having?" Kaisa asked.

"None," Stepan replied curtly.

Valentina rolled her eyes. "Well unlike the Hulk here, everything hurts. I was getting really dizzy and vomiting."

"That's it?" Kaisa asked. "Nothing else? No ... Numbers?"

"Numbers?" Stepan asked. "What are you talking about?"

"Never mind," I spoke up, shooting Kaisa a look. Looking back at Valentina I asked, "Are those your only symptoms? Nothing weird?"

"Besides getting dizzy from sitting down?" Valentina scoffed. "Why are you here again? Are you a nurse?"

Phaenna walked in, going over to the desk on the opposite wall.

"We just wanted to see the infirmary," Kaisa said. "We've never been here." She motioned with her head for us to go.

"Hope you feel better," I said to them.

"I don't feel anything now," Stepan said, loudly for Phaenna.

I waited until we were steps away from the infirmary to speak again. "What do you think?"

The bell rang and kids poured into the halls.

"I feel something. Faintly," Kaisa replied. "They can't stay there."

"We'll have to go back after classes?"

She nodded. "We have to tell them as soon as possible."

16

As soon as possible unfortunately became the next day. Kaisa found me before I even made it to the infirmary, telling me Phaenna told her there couldn't be any visitors for the rest of the afternoon.

That night I prayed, under my covers with my eyes squeezed shut, that nothing happened to the two of them before tomorrow.

The next morning, we headed straight for the infirmary. Every footstep vibrated in my chest. All I wanted was to see the two of them still cooped up in their beds. Crossing through the threshold of the infirmary, I breathed a deep sigh of relief.

As soon as Valentina noticed us however, she rolled her eyes. "Oh, you two again."

"Yeah, we're back to check on you," I said.

"You did such a great job before," Valentina said. *"Un par de doctores de verdad."*

"We just want to know if there's anything odd about your sickness," Kaisa said. "Anything at all. Your life could be in danger."

Stepan shot up in his bed. "Our life? Phaenna told us it was probably just a virus."

"It could be," Kaisa said. "But it could be something else, and they won't tell you. That's why you have to tell us if you're experiencing anything out of the ordinary."

"I mean, this whole thing is out of the ordinary for me," Stepan said. "I rarely get sick, even living in Voronezh."

"Yesterday you said you weren't experiencing any symptoms," Kaisa said. "What are you sick with?"

Stepan crossed his arms and looked away.

"Oh, just tell them, strong man," Valentina snapped.

After another second, Stepan, reluctantly, said, "I just threw up."

"How many times?" Valentina pressed.

"Five."

"In *una dia*," Valentina said to Kaisa and I. "In one hour. He threw up five times in one hour! If that doesn't say something is wrong with you, I don't know what does. But no, he wants to complain that he shouldn't be here."

"I haven't thrown up since and I feel fine," Stepan said.

I glanced at Kaisa. Throwing up five times in one hour did sound relatively serious, but not like anything for an Order.

"And you, Valentina?" Kaisa asked.

"No sé," she said, twirling a strand of her hair. "Like I said, getting dizzy and vomiting the past few days. But something strange? I mean, one of my girls told me something. The last time I got dizzy, I fainted, and that's when they finally brought me to the infirmary. Anyway, this girl said that she could tell I was starting to get dizzy because my eyes weren't focusing, and my head started to rock. I don't really remember all that. She also said—and this is really hard for me to believe—that once I entered into this dizzy spell, weird things started to happen."

"Like what?"

"Apparently everything on my desk started to float. *Los lapiceros*, my notebook. And she said that after that, it started happening to the people right next to me. And just before I passed out, everything that was floating just went flying around the room. Then boom, I fainted." Valentina shrugged. "That's what Danielle came and told me. I didn't believe her, she's not really coping so well being here. Taking shots of *detergente* and all that."

Kaisa and I exchanged glances.

We then stood there for about thirty minutes explaining everything to the two of them. Stepan was easy to convince, in fact he seemed ready to jump out his bed. Valentina took a little more convincing, and we had to promise Jacqueline would stop by to give her proof about what we were saying.

"Now you guys understand that you're in danger," Kaisa said. "We all are. Valentina, you don't know if your friend told Phaenna about that episode, right?"

She shook her head. "But even if she didn't, Brunhild was teaching so he probably told the others."

"Just get better quickly," I said. "Even if you have to fake it just to get Phaenna to let you return to your rooms. If anything happens, scream for help."

✳ ✳

In a day's time, both Valentina and Stepan were released from the infirmary. Unfortunately, their release didn't free them from the eyes of our executioners. Us Orders were running out of time. The longer we stayed, the more we'd tell on ourselves, and then it would be too easy for them to pick us off one by one.

The weight of the situation hung over all of us, it was obvious by the silence and meaningless sliding of silverware at dinner.

Chance, Nicolas, Sherman, Hudson, and I sat together at one table. I'd noticed Kaisa, Shauna, and Airi sitting together, but other than that we were spread out, if even present in the cafeteria at all.

I set my fork down, finally tired of moving the strips of chicken from one side of the plate to the other. I opened my mouth to break the silence, but Nicolas beat me to it.

"They're going to find us soon," he said, his voice just loud enough for us to hear.

Everyone's eyes lifted to him. Chance was the first to break contact, lowering his eyes and continuing to pick at his food. "Well, that's positive," he muttered.

"We aren't doing anything," Nicolas continued. "And they're continuing to learn about us, to figure out the algorithm."

"An algorithm isn't going to help them find us," Chance said. "We're all different, as you can clearly see."

I glanced at him. The frustration haloed around him, and if it was one thing I learned about Chance, he became more defensive the more boxed in he felt. But surely, he could see past his frustration to what was inevitably coming our way.

"What are we supposed to do?" Sherman asked. "We're behind the walls of a concentration camp. There's no way out, at least not one I can see."

Hudson took a sip from his can of soda, his eyes still on Nicolas. "You got something, string bean?"

"I've just been thinking," Nicolas replied. "You're right, Sherman. Looking around there's no way out. We can't escape this place, they've made sure of that."

Sherman slouched in his seat. "That's what you've been thinking about," he muttered.

Nicolas ignored him and continued, "So maybe we need to spend less time focusing on how to escape ourselves, and more time focusing on how someone else can rescue us."

"Someone would have to know where we are to rescue us," Chance said.

"I know. We'd have to tell them," Nicolas said. "So, what if we built a radio."

"A radio," Hudson repeated.

Nicolas nodded. "I've built one or two back home. It's not too hard, we just need the right parts."

Our only response was silence for the first few seconds. It was like we needed those seconds to let our misery lift so we could fully take in Nicolas's words.

"Are you being serious, Nicolas?" Chance asked.

Nicolas nodded, running his pointer finger along the table. "I've really been thinking about it. It's not anything certain, but it's something, and more than we have. I think I'd only be able to build a one-way radio."

"Which means?"

"We could send messages out, but not receive any."

Hudson groaned. "Well what good would that do us?"

"A hell of a lot," Chance said to him. "If we can let someone know we're in trouble and where we are, they can send help."

A radio. It was so simple, but being used to our phones and the internet, any of other type of communication hadn't even crossed our minds.

"What would we need?" I asked.

"Something for voltage. Something to be the switch. Some wood and some nails, some wire, and a steel plate if we could find one ..." He trailed off as he opened his notebook and began making a list. "And some other things."

Hudson looked over Nicolas's shoulder. "I'm going to be honest with you man, I don't know where to find those."

"That's alright. The switch could be as easy as just two paper clips," Nicolas said. "And for the voltage, you could use a battery. But I am thinking something bigger."

"There isn't exactly a store here," Chance said.

"All these items we can take from other things around the building," Nicolas said. "But we'll have to be very careful. Nothing someone would notice."

Chance tapped his cheek as he looked over Nicolas's list. "Okay. Alright, I think we can make this happen. Just give us some direction."

I looked across the room and met eyes with Kaisa. I'd tell her later, in the safety of one of our rooms.

We had a new chance.

⁎⁎

Nicolas didn't need all of us sneaking around to get him the parts for the radio. Even still, I found myself requesting my own item to retrieve.

I'd done it twice now, going into Kanyn's office and then taking the book from Kat. It was invigorating, feeling like we held the upper hand. Like we were smarter. Like it was us who held them here.

Of course, that was just a feeling, but enough to excite me over retrieving something as simple as a knife.

I waited until the arms on the clock both pointed to the twelve. Slipping out from under the covers, I held my breath, and the soles of my feet touched the floor.

I glanced at Meg, not that anything this deep into her sleep could wake her.

I took a deep breath as I closed the door behind me, alone in the dimly dark hallway. It was as quiet as it had been that night with Hunter, but haunting without him. Tiptoeing through the halls toward the kitchen, my head stayed on a swivel, constantly checking over my shoulder for one of them to melt out of the shadows.

We really had no idea what they did at night. I'd never dared before to sculk around by myself after curfew. Obviously, they were awake, evident from seeing Jutas and his friend out and about. The night was probably their time to move about freely, to shed their captor role. Maybe they didn't even sleep at all.

Arriving at the dining hall, I peeked around the doorway into the room. It was eerie, such a large and empty room completely dark. For the smallest of seconds, I debated if one of them could be hiding on the floor among the tables.

I launched myself into the room before I could dawdle anymore, darting across the front and through the open space into the kitchen area. Dropping into a crouch behind the serving well, I closed my eyes to try and slow my almost aching heartbeat. Just one knife, that was all I needed.

Opening my eyes again, I spotted a knife block on the counter. I would have to stand, or at least squat, to reach one. From my position, I glanced toward the door. My heartbeat was the loudest sound, and I strained to hear any movement over it. It was now or never. I needed to scoot over, pop up, and grab a knife.

One breath, and I launched over to the knife block, pulling one out in the same motion. I crashed back into the spot I'd been in before, awkwardly cradling the paring knife against my chest.

In an almost whimpered prayer, I begged my heartbeat to quiet just enough for me to hear my surroundings. It was one thing to sneak to the kitchen. But sneaking back to my room put me in even more danger, because now I carried banned paraphernalia.

I tiptoed to the doors first, peeking into the hallway. A pin could drop and it would have been the loudest noise outside my chest. A part of me wanted to run, at least sprint, but if I did run into someone, that would make me all the more suspicious.

One foot into the hall, then the next. I crossed my arms, gingerly holding the knife between my arms and my chest.

Every time I came up to a cross-section, my breath caught to the point where I could pass out. Each time the adjoining hallway was empty, and I took a quiet deep breath.

Maybe they did sleep.

I finally made it back to my room, closing the door painfully quiet behind me. I hesitated, back against the door, waiting to see if one of them would knock on the door.

No one did, and finally I eased over to my bed, situating the knife between the mattress and the frame.

My heartbeat, fast but finally steady, lulled me to sleep.

✳ ✳

When my eyes opened, my first thought was the knife delicately pressed under my mattress. I rushed to get myself ready, not waiting for Meg. Carefully tucking the knife in between the pages of my notebook, I then hurried to the cafeteria.

Just the two people I wanted to see were already seated when I arrived. I sat down with them, a big smile pasted on my face.

"What are you so happy about?" Chance asked.

"I got your knife."

"Already?" Nicolas asked.

I nodded, unable to wipe the grin off my face. "Got anything else?"

"Slow your roll, sticky fingers," Chance said. "Give the rest of us a chance."

Barely paying attention to him, I set my notebook on the table and flashed them both the concealed weapon.

"You're good," Nicolas said.

"Yeah, too good," Chance said. "And too hasty. Now what are you going to do, Einstein? Carry that around with you all day?"

My smile faltered. I hadn't thought of that. I couldn't really hand it off to Nicolas here in the cafeteria. For one thing, they might see. And for another, even if they didn't, Nicolas would have the same problem of carrying it around all day.

Nicolas squinted to see the clock on the wall. "You have time to run it back to your room, depending on how fast you move."

Chance folded his arms, a haughty smile now on his face. "Let's see it, Cori. You've got the pickpocketing hands. Do you have the feet to match?"

I shot him a glare, but I was already on my feet. It would be a stretch due to me sleeping in a little later. But I had no choice. Unless I wanted to steal another knife—or worse, get in trouble for this one—I'd have to make it.

17

An icy needle had stuck itself into my spine from the moment I'd been summoned to Kanyn's office to the moment I stepped over the doorframe. I sat down stiffly, as if there really was a needle threatening to paralyze my back.

Keeping my chin high, I peered over my nose at Kanyn. When he lifted his eyes from his notebook, I asked, "Did Amaris write me up?"

As if I'd asked a dumb question, he let out a sigh and continued scribbling. "No, it was Edith."

"You sure Amaris didn't ask her to write me up?"

Kanyn's eyes flashed up at me, then he set his pen down. "Do you think Amaris has something against you?"

"I think he's a bastard with a lot of time," I replied, looking him square in the eyes.

"That's ... Accurate."

A shiver traveled through my right leg at the desire to fidget. I couldn't keep up my edge for long, especially with someone who gave me no antagonism back. "What did she write me up for?"

"Apparently she saw you coming from the kitchen in the middle of the night, which is off limits to you at that time," Kanyn replied. "That's your third shot. Care to explain what you were doing there?"

"Looking around," I replied. I didn't want there to be a moment of hesitation, anything for him to detect my lie. For all I knew however, he could already know what I was really doing there, what I'd taken. But I would lie through my teeth if I had to for this radio, this chance at escape, even if he knew I was. "It gets boring seeing the same halls every day. This is a big building, I wanted to know what else is in it."

He could have pressed me. I knew he had it in him. He could have interrogated me until I broke in pieces to reveal the truth. But instead, all he said was, "Don't you know curiosity killed the cat?"

"I already feel dead here."

Kanyn stared at me, pushing his notebook away from him. I couldn't make out the question in his eyes, like he was asking me why or how I felt dead here. He didn't know that I knew. I was dead here.

I sighed, looking away from his attempt at an empathetic expression. "Is that all?"

"Is that all you'd like to talk about?"

"Yeah."

"You're trying to explore," he pressed. "Haven't noticed anything else worthy of sharing?"

"For as good as an observer as I am, I've kind of got a lot going on right now to be worried about things outside myself."

"Some people would call that being self-centered."

"And some people would call you manipulative."

"How so?"

"You noticed something good about me that you can use to your advantage, and that's what you're trying to do. I doubt you even cared about this shot, you just wanted a reason to talk to me."

Something close to a smile settled on Kanyn's lips as he looked away. "I'm always looking for a reason to talk to you."

My heart attempted to flutter, but I cursed it. "Try something more interesting than a shot."

** **

Kanyn's sentiment didn't unsettle me. His desire to talk to me, whether genuine or driven by his desire for information, wouldn't derail me from the best chance we had at an escape. If Edith wrote me up, I simply wouldn't give her a reason to again, or any other of them for that matter. Although I'd never deny Kanyn's attempts at compassion, it didn't outweigh our lives being on the line. One of them was by no means worth eighteen of us.

We worked quickly and efficiently to supply Nicolas with everything he needed. I did my part with the knife. Chance, Valentina, Jacqueline, and Kaisa were also willing to risk a shot—or worse—to get things. The others were too timid, or the majority of us agreed their level of stealth would do more harm than good.

I took deep breaths through my nose as I walked through the dormitory halls. Carrying such paraphernalia created an unsettling confidence. A feeling that, unchecked, could lead to mistakes, to failure. We had to be above the curve to have even considered the idea of building a radio. We should pride ourselves on that. But could we?

I knocked on one of the doors, and within seconds it opened. Carefully, I passed Nicolas the napkin ball. "Some more nails, complementary of Theo."

"Thanks," he said, quickly taking the ball over to his bed and shoving it between the mattresses.

"How are we looking?"

"Great. We just need a few more things and then we'll be set," he replied, coming back to the door. "And Kaisa found a great spot, like an attic of some sort, that we can keep it."

"That sounds great." I should have added more. Wanted to. But there was only emptiness where there should have been encouragement. My next set of words weren't any better. "You really think this will work?"

"I hope so. Or else ..." His face dropped to the floor as he shifted on his feet.

I didn't know if I hated seeing him uncomfortable or if I just didn't want to hear the other option, but I reached out and gripped his shoulder, causing him to look back up at me. "There is no or else. It's going to work."

He forced a smile, all he could give me, but it was something.

"I'll see you tomorrow," I said, releasing my grip. But I didn't want to move. I could have continued standing there, waiting for him to close the door in my face. He wouldn't, and I forced my feet to move, walking down the hallway. A few steps away I heard the soft click of the door.

A shiver traveled down my arms and legs. I wasn't cold, but the feeling from the last part of my conversation with Nicolas was more ice than emotion. The radio had to work. We risked everything just stealing parts for it. It was our only way out, our only chance.

The smell of tobacco laced its way under my nose, and I followed the scent to find one of my classmates, Garth, leaning against a column in the entryway to the courtyard. His hands were wrapped around his torso, and he moved them sporadically up and down as if he was trying to warm himself, although it wasn't cold enough to be shivering. The cigarette dangled from his mouth.

"You okay, Garth?" I asked.

His head jerked in my direction, eyes like headlights. "Oh. You're in my class, aren't you? Cori, right?"

I nodded as I cautiously approached him. It smelt like tobacco, but maybe that wasn't all there was in his cigarette. "You don't look too good."

He squeezed his eyes shut, and I could see him bite down hard on the cigarette. When he opened his eyes, he said in a low voice, "I've just been thinking a lot."

Thinking or hallucinating, I wanted to ask. He still rubbed at his arms, though less than when I'd first come upon him.

"I can't stand it here. I don't know anything and there seems to be no way to find any answers."

"Join the club," I murmured, leaning beside him.

Garth removed the cigarette from his lips for about two seconds before immediately inserting it again. "I need to know where we are, whether it's an island or some city. It's driving me crazy." He once again removed the cigarette, this time blowing out a long breath of tobacco and nicotine. "I finally figured out how."

My thoughts immediately reverted back to the boy who'd tried to escape a few days ago. The image of him standing, the lance pierced through his spine and gut, made my eyes water. "How?" I asked dryly. Surely Garth remembered the boy's attempt too. Even talking about it sounded foolish.

"The water tower is taller than the walls. If I just climb up there, I'll be able to see."

He said it so simply, like it was the easiest of plans. And in any other situation, it might have been the easiest plan. But here, nothing was easy.

"And how do you expect to get up there?" I asked. "I don't think I've ever seen anyone going anywhere near it."

"Sneak out at night."

Normally, that wouldn't have piqued my interest. But in lieu of all my recent sneaking around, his scheme stirred a new curiosity in me. When I first arrived, everything and anything seemed impossible. Any ideas died seconds after forming. But at this moment, we had pickpocketed almost all the pieces to assemble a radio. We knew more, we were more aware. And better, we were bolder.

"You really think that would work?" I asked, folding my arms across my chest. "That you could do that and not get caught?"

He shrugged, his gaze fixed on the darkening sky. "What else is there to do? And I have to know."

The belief that he could actually pull that off hadn't fully enveloped me, but brazen curiosity had. "Then what time are we doing this?"

Garth's eyes darted over to me. "We?"

I nodded. "You've got me intrigued."

"Uh ..." He suddenly dropped his cigarette, and he crushed the still burning end into the ground. "I guess one would be safe. Yeah, one."

"One it is then."

＊＊

As the hours passed, the excitement in me spiked. Fear became a stranger. The Cori from college never would have taken a chance like this. She didn't like uncertainty. She could talk a big game but couldn't give the same attitude to the action. I liked this new uninhibited Cori, I just hoped she would stay past tonight.

As I walked through the halls to meet Garth, in the still of the night, the solitude of the situation began to weigh on me. I hadn't told anyone about his plan. None of the other Orders knew what I was about to do. None of them could help me should something happen. I'd wanted to tell Meg, but she would worry. I wanted to tell Chance, at least he'd probably encourage me. But I didn't tell anyone. If this worked, we'd have two opportunities of escape instead of one. But if it failed, at least only I would be the one to suffer.

Garth waited for me in same spot I'd found him earlier, almost in the exact same pose. Smoke trailed from the end of his cigarette, but this time he stamped it out the moment he saw me. "You don't have to do this," he said to me.

Of course I didn't have to. I didn't have to do anything, but then all I would be doing was waiting patiently for my death. "I'm already here," was my response.

He nodded once, then started trudging through the grass toward the water tower. I followed a few steps behind, the grass silently squishing under my feet. I couldn't help but look back. No one should be awake to see us, but nothing happened as it should here.

As we got closer, I looked upward at the tower looming above us. If we could make it to the top, we really would be able to see over the wall.

I let in a long breath as a thought that had been trying to settle on me finally did. If we climbed to the top and looked over the wall, and only feet away was a city as bright as New York, I would be sick to my stomach. I would faint, dissipate, all at once. Civilization—rescue—so close and yet so far from all our suffering.

We reached the foot of the tower and Garth asked, "You ever went rock climbing before?"

This was nothing like a rock-climbing wall, but I replied, "Maybe once."

We stood for a moment, gazing up at the obstacle in front of us. There wasn't a real ladder, just footholds all the way up its eight legs until you reached the container. I reached out and locked my hand into one of the rungs. The cold metal pricked against my skin.

Me touching the tower must have given Garth the last push he needed to fully commit. He started climbing, one arm reaching over the other, like a scared monkey.

Surely I didn't look any different, and each time my hand grabbed a new spot, the cold stung it again. And I was out of shape. Those few times I'd visited the gym weren't doing anything for me now. My body sagged as I kept pushing it up, higher and higher.

Looking to my right, my vision was still obstructed by the wall. Even tilting my chin wouldn't allow me to see anything over it. I still had a ways to climb, but there was a smile twitching at my lips. This might actually work. Even if we couldn't get over the wall, seeing over it would be a big accomplishment.

I looked back over my shoulder just once, and that was when I saw him.

He was jogging toward the water tower—toward us—and it would only be a few seconds before he reached us. The grin etched onto Jutas's face as he approached sent chills through my bones.

"Garth," I hissed, and motioned toward the approaching threat.

Garth looked over his shoulder. "Shit," he muttered, but one hand continued to rise above the other.

"What are you doing?"

"Why would I go down where they can catch me?"

My skin was frozen to the metal of the tower. Up, down, neither was a good option. I could climb down and let Jutas get at me first. Maybe he'd have mercy. Unlikely. I could keep climbing, maybe even make it to the top before Jutas got to me, and I'd still have something to share with the others. Unless of course Jutas killed me before I could get a word out.

My feet began backing down the side of the towers before I could make a decision. My arms and legs shook like gelatin. At least if I reached the ground, maybe I could run away and hide.

The tower suddenly rattled under my hold, and when I looked down, my fingernails almost dug into the metal. Jutas shimmied up the side of the water tower, moving swiftly, like he'd done it many times.

I couldn't get myself to move faster, barely able to keep myself moving downwards. My heart rapped against the inside of my chest like it was trying to wake me up from a bad dream.

Jutas climbed on Garth's side, coming up directly underneath him. With every inch Jutas closed in, my breath increased. My breathing was the only thing I could hear, encompassing even my thoughts. I looked down. Still had a few feet to go until my feet touched the ground again.

I looked up again, and my stomach dropped out seeing that in seconds, Jutas had closed the gap between him and Garth. He was right next to Garth.

Horrified, I watched as Jutas leaned over to Garth, bringing his fist down on Garth's left wrist. Garth yelled in pain. Jutas braced one arm against the tower. With his other arm, he yanked Garth to him by his shirt, then shoved him backwards hard. Garth's hands immediately lost their hold on the metal, and his body hurtled to the ground.

I froze, completely unable to get anything to keep moving.

The tower began to rattle even more as Jutas aggressively maneuvered in my direction.

I watched him approach me like watching a truck careen toward me. I wanted to pass through the walls of the tower into the water. I wanted a hole to suddenly burst in front of me, letting the water wash me away. I wanted anything but to be here. Any sense of courage had disappeared.

Jutas was just two arms lengths away, and I made a snap decision. I'd rather take my chances than be shoved off like Garth. I let go.

I expected the ground to smack me the way common sense should have when Garth first introduced his idea to me. It never did, and instead of a paralyzing explosion of pain, I felt pressure just below my shoulders and under my knees.

A squeeze. A tight embrace.

I hadn't realized I closed my eyes, thinking the blackness was just a moment of unconsciousness. Opening my eyes, I saw the underside of Kanyn's chin.

Immediately I wanted him to look down and envelop me in his warm brown eyes, if only to stop the quaking of my bones. But he kept his eyes forward, and slightly turning my head, I saw why.

Jutas approached with wide steps and a full grin. "Want me to spin her head around—"

"I've got it," Kanyn interrupted. "You take care of the body."

Jutas folded his arms across his chest and gazed at Garth's body. I had to strain my neck to see out of Kanyn's hold. Garth lay on the ground, his head lolled to the left, a small trail of blood rivering from the back of his skull. I glanced at Jutas and to my disgust, he looked undoubtedly proud of his work.

I didn't study him for long, because Kanyn started walking away, back toward the building. I wanted to jump out of his arms, but I trembled so furiously I dreaded I'd pass out, my brain surely rattling inside my skull.

He didn't stop walking when he reached the patio, continuing down the hallway, clutching me to his chest.

18

Kanyn carried me all the way to his office, only setting me on my feet when we were beside my usual chair. Trembling less, I still had to ease myself out of his arms and into the seat.

He sat in his chair across from me, but he didn't speak right away. It took me something close to ten minutes to stop shaking, but I'd lost all feeling in my extremities. My mind kept jumping back to the image of Garth falling from the tower to the ground. After rewatching it four times, I scrunched my eyes shut.

"Are you okay?" Kanyn finally asked. "Do you need some water?"

Slowly, I opened my eyes. The longer I'd sat the more intense my anxiety had become, getting myself to the point where I'd almost forgotten there was someone else in the room with me. I shook my head.

His gaze washed over me, then tilted back down to the book in his lap.

Sitting there wasn't doing anything to calm me down. I needed answers, and Kanyn was the only person who could give them to me.

"Why did you save me?" I asked.

"Would you have preferred to die?"

"Did you see what Jutas did? He pushed Garth off. We weren't supposed to be up there, but he didn't have to kill him."

"I agree," Kanyn said. "If I could have stopped Jutas, I would have."

"You don't sound like it."

He looked away from me for a moment, letting out an exhausted exhale. "If I could have stopped him, I would have, and I mean that. But there are some things you can't understand, Cori."

"I could if you told me."

He didn't meet my eyes again, but shook his head a fraction.

I didn't have time for his melodrama. Rolling my eyes, I said, "Just give me my shot so I can go."

He sighed. "You already have three shots."

"So, is this my fourth one?"

He rubbed his eyes, exhaling through his circled lips.

I tried him again. "Would you give me a fourth one?"

He continued to rub his eyes, like if he did so long enough the answer would come to him. Finally he replied, "I think you need to go to bed."

I wasn't going to argue. Truly I knew I'd tried my luck challenging him to a fourth shot. As I stood up, I asked, "What about Garth?"

"I can't do anything for him now," Kanyn said.

"Well, are you going to tell anybody? I mean, people will notice he's gone. And surely you have supervisors or something you have to report to, if Jutas hasn't already done it."

"I'll handle it, it's none of your business."

"None of my business?" I leaned over on Kanyn's desk, and I was sure when he looked up, he could see directly into my cleavage. "I saw Jutas push Garth off that water tower to his death."

"Which neither of you should have been on in the first place."

"You can't tell me that what we did equated to one of us dying."

Kanyn didn't break eye contact with me for what felt like several minutes, although surely it was only seconds. He looked back onto the papers in front of him. "I'll handle it. You can return to your room."

I wanted to say more, but I knew I was pushing it, I had seen it in his eyes. I turned and headed toward the door, refusing to look back because if I did, I knew words would escape my lips.

As I reached the door, Kanyn added, "I suggest you actually return to your room and avoid any more deviancy."

✳ ✳

Although I hadn't smacked into the ground, my nerves had. They were shot, and I fought the urge to continuously tremble throughout the day.

I didn't tell anyone about my daring escapade, especially now that I thought of it as a stupidly daring escapade. Every so often the sight of Garth falling from the tower flashed across my vision, followed by an arrow of guilt. Jutas could have picked either of us to go after first, and he chose Garth. It wasn't my fault, I wanted to scream it from the rooftops. It wouldn't matter, no one knew, and no one would do anything about it if they did.

By the time I made it to free period, my lungs hurt from using the same amount of air to internally scream. Although I might have been better off sitting alone in a corner, I opted to try for the comfort of a group setting, settling in with Sherman, Darcy, and Olivia.

"Damn, this place just doesn't change does it," Olivia said.

"Neither do the people," Darcy said, looking around. "Everyone reeks of either fear or complacency."

I fought the urge to sniff myself. All day I'd been feeling neither of the two, so what did I smell like?

"Something bothering you, Sherman?" I heard Darcy ask, but didn't look up to be a part of their conversation. Wasn't something wrong with each of us? And more and more each day? I already felt like I was carrying a mountain, I didn't need to know about anyone else's.

"There's a kid in my class. He wasn't there today."

Our eyes—even mine—immediately jumped to him. Without really knowing anything, we knew what that meant.

"Who was he?" Darcy asked.

Sherman shrugged, tugging at his fingers. "I don't know. I never talked to him, just noticed him. Smelled him really, he reeked."

My body stiffened. "Like cigarettes?" I asked.

Sherman nodded, beginning to tug harder on his fingers. "Yeah. It was weird, that's how I first knew he wasn't there. I didn't smell him."

"Maybe he didn't feel well today," Darcy said.

Sherman shook his head, pulling his fingers quicker. "I don't think so. I really don't think so. He was perfectly fine yesterday. I don't think he's sick."

I wanted to seal my lips with glue, but I couldn't stop myself from prying. "What do you think happened to him then? If he's not sick."

"I don't know. Whatever happens to all the others who don't come back," Sherman said.

"They go home," Olivia said.

"They don't go home," Sherman said quickly.

For the first time in days, I flashed back to the stack of bodies in that basement room. A shiver rocked my torso as I quickly cleared the image from my mind and focused on Sherman. He couldn't risk telling Darcy and Olivia what we knew.

"How do you know they don't go home?" Olivia asked.

Sherman looked around nervously, slipping in a quick glance at me, then whispered, "I've seen people."

"Where?" Darcy asked.

"Just in my head," he replied. "I've seen images of people. I don't know who they are, but they're young, just like us."

"And?"

Sherman shook his head, hugging himself. "I don't know where they are. But they don't look good. Some are just dead, but some ..." He paused, shutting his eyes and biting down hard on his lip. "Some are mutilated."

I should have reached out to him, touched him in some way to offer comfort. But I didn't and I couldn't. I was frozen standing next to him, not even my lips could tremble. He hadn't been with us that night, so how he'd seen the bodies himself I wasn't sure. Was he really seeing visions in his head? Possibly, Zahir had heard voices. But the ability to see dead people hadn't been in the book we read on Orders.

I wanted to ask him how long he'd been having these visions. They clearly had taken their toll on him. My stiff bones finally moved as I noticed Sherman step away from me, one hand clutching his stomach, the other on his head.

Darcy and Olivia's attention moved back to him, Darcy immediately coming to Sherman's side. "Sherman, what's wrong?"

"We shouldn't be here," he sputtered, shaking his head. His body visibly trembled. "None of us should be here." The hand on his head dropped to his stomach and he doubled over, squeezing his eyes shut. "I feel like I'm going to throw up."

"It's alright, just calm down," Darcy said softly, gently rubbing his back. "You're really worked up right now, take a deep breath."

At first he acted like he didn't even feel her, holding in his crouched position, shaking and clutching his stomach. I finally forced my legs to work, moving closer to him just in time to hear Sherman murmur, "No, guys, I really feel sick." He suddenly stood up, his chest visibly pounding in and out. "I'm going to throw up."

Darcy, Olivia, and I immediately jumped back away from him, seconds before Sherman bent over and released a thin stream of bile from his mouth. He wiped any residue away from his mouth, then hugged his quaking body. His eyes, although pointed at the floor, were misty.

By now other kids were watching, uncertainty and hesitation flashing across each of their faces. They edged closer. My face matched theirs, I was sure of it. The only person who looked an ounce confident was Darcy, hovering close to Sherman and whispering to him.

The crowd of kids separated as Provos walked up. He stopped right in front of Sherman, bending at the waist and gripping Sherman's face in his hands.

"He's having a seizure," Darcy told him. "He's epileptic."

"Everyone back up," Provos instructed. He kept his hands on Sherman's face and squinted to look into his eyes. "Do you have a time on this seizure? Has he had them before?"

Darcy nodded, rubbing her hands together. "He's had one before in his room, but it only lasted about two minutes. I don't know how long it's been."

Although he was looking directly at Provos, the glaze still covered Sherman's eyes.

"Can you still hear me?" Provos asked him.

I hadn't backed up with the other kids to create a perfect ring of space around Sherman. I was close enough I could reach out and touch him, close enough to hear him whisper to Provos, "W-We shouldn't be here. You're bad people. You're hurting us."

I half expected Provos to snap his neck or slit his throat right then, but in truth, the little I knew about him proved quick violence wasn't part of his temperament. I noticed him flinch, but he didn't let go of Sherman's face. If anything, his hold relaxed.

Sherman on the other hand was nothing near relaxed, in fact his words had set him off again, quivering worse than before. He looked like the opposite of a bobble head, a bobble body with his body trembling but his head still in Provos's hands. And then he started screaming. A loud blood curdling scream that could only come straight from the depths of his body, from the pit of his horror. His eyes were whiter than his skin, and I could only imagine he was reliving all the dead and mutilated bodies he'd seen. By now everyone was watching the screaming, spasming boy.

"Sherman, you have to calm down," Provos said, his tone sharper but with a tinge of desperation.

"Please, Sherman," Darcy begged, her hands clasped together. "Just calm down."

Trainus plowed through the crowd, coming over to Provos's side. "Let him go, Provos," he instructed, setting a hand on Provos's shoulder.

Provos hesitated, then stepped back from Sherman. "It's been longer than the recommended time. He needs serious help."

The synapses in my brain began firing. Sherman needed real help, more than what they could offer him here. That meant this was his chance. They would have to send him outside this place. He would get out, he could get us help. I'd stepped so far inside myself I didn't even notice Amaris join the group until I heard him asking, "What's going on?"

"He's having a seizure," Darcy replied without taking her eyes off Sherman. "We need to get him help."

"I got it," Amaris said, stepping directly in front of Sherman.

Darcy's voice rose as she became more frantic. "He just needs to ride it out—"

Before anyone could utter a word, Amaris slid his hands around Sherman's head and jerked it sideways. The spasming limbs instantly ceased and Sherman's body crumpled out of Amaris's hands to the floor.

The floor tilted as I stared down at Sherman's lifeless body. Just seconds ago, it'd been writhing, squirming like it was trying to get away from itself. Now it was perfectly still.

"All better," Amaris purred as he began walking away.

"Why did you do that!" Darcy yelled at him. He stopped and turned his face to look back at her. "You bastard! He was having a seizure, he would have been fine in a few minutes!"

Amaris shrugged. "I didn't know that. He was causing a scene."

"You're a monster!" Darcy yelled. Although there was too much space between them to make for a good attack, she lunged at him. Two others caught her just in time to keep her from getting any closer to Amaris. Not that he was bothered by any of it, he watched with amused eyes, a grin tugging at the edge of his lips. Darcy continued to yell profanities, and after a few seconds, Amaris walked away, leaving her to only yell in his wake.

I looked at Trainus and Provos and found myself surprised at their expression. It was nothing short of their normal apathetic expression, but in their eyes and the rigidity of their body there was uncertainty. Provos's gaze flickered down to the dead boy, and he stepped back.

I wished I could take a picture of his face, to keep that look on his face forever. He'd tried to help, no one could deny it. But his companion had mercilessly killed, and for the first time, one of them looked like they couldn't stand to stand by their comrade.

None of them tried to silence Darcy, only her two friends who still held her whispered warnings in her ears.

I dared to look again at Sherman's body lying on the ground. His eyes were still open, his head turned at a sickening, unnatural degree.

The urge to run after Amaris, to confront him on his actions, coursed through my veins, but I held myself in place. I couldn't risk getting in trouble again, not for me and not for the rest of us who were still alive.

Closing my eyes, I turned away.

They hadn't even known—they couldn't have—and yet they'd succeeded in killing another Order. We didn't have much time.

✳ ✳

I carried weights in the heels of my shoes for the rest of the day. The visual of Garth falling from the water tower had been replaced by Amaris breaking Sherman's neck.

The rest of free period had continued in an uncomfortable silence, the loudest sound being Darcy's uncontrollable sobs. That stayed with me too. Her wails played between my ears like a soundtrack.

I caught myself for just a moment wondering about Provos. I'd heard what Sherman said to him, and I'd seen him flinch at his words. Provos had to have known that Sherman knew about them, and yet he continued to try and help him. But why?

I only mulled over that for a few minutes, because the fact of the matter was that regardless of Provos's actions in that moment, he was still one of them. And they wanted us dead.

When I returned to my room that evening, stomach moaning since I'd barely eaten anything at dinner, I stopped just inside the door, noticing the smallest scrap of paper sitting by the corner.

Picking it up, the letters N I I D E F H S had been scribbled in even smaller handwriting, with the N underlined. I held the paper to my nose as I sat down on my bed. It took less than two minutes for the meaning to come to me, and I immediately stood up, ripping the paper into shreds.

FINISHED.

Nicolas had mentioned when he was ready, he'd let us know with some kind of code. I'd expected it to be something more complex than just a scrambled word, but it did the trick.

I was almost to Nicolas's room when I bumped into Chance.

"Coincidence?" he asked.

"I doubt it," I replied.

"Then you got a little note too," he said with a chuckle. "Man, I'm happy he chose something simple like that. When he said he would let us know by code, I thought it was going to be something hard. The kid's too smart for his own good."

I smiled. Maybe, but he had figured out how to build a radio out of random parts, and I certainly couldn't do that. We needed smart.

We arrived at Nicolas's door, and just as Chance raised his hand to knock, the door swung open, and Nicolas was walking out before we could even react.

"Were you watching for us?" Chance asked as Nicolas closed the door behind him.

He nodded but raised a finger to his lips. Then he motioned for us to follow him. We walked in silence out of the dormitory halls, weaving through halls I hadn't dared to venture down. Our trek led us to a solitary door, which when opened revealed dusty, rising stairs. At the top was an attic of sorts, loosely filled with taped up cardboard boxes and wooden shelves.

Nicolas shifted a few boxes away from a corner and slid out the jumbled mess of what I assumed to be the radio.

"That's it?" Chance asked, and Nicolas snapped around to shush him. Chance lowered his voice and repeated, "That's it?"

"What were you expecting?" Nicolas replied as he settled onto his knees to work. His fingers began moving over the wires and random metal items, assembling the final pieces.

Chance had already said what I was thinking. It really didn't look like much, more like a kindergarten art project, but with metals. My lips moved to ask a more clarifying, less degrading, question, but Chance again beat me to it.

"So, Nicolas, buddy," he said. "You too must think that looks like just a mess of metal, right?"

Nicolas didn't look up, but he did nod his head.

"Will it work?" I asked.

Nicolas didn't reply for a few more minutes as his fingers worked to connect wires and press small pieces into others. Finally, he straightened up on his knees and let out a deep breath. "Here goes nothing."

Here goes something, I wanted to correct him. It certainly hadn't been nothing with all we'd risked building this tiny bit of machinery. And it certainly wouldn't be nothing if this was our saving grace. It had to work.

For Sherman.

The room was silent, and for a moment the three of us simply stared at the hunk of junk. Then, even though Nicolas held the earbud to his ear, I heard the spark of static. My eyes met Nicolas's.

"It works," he breathed.

"It works?" Chance parroted.

Nicolas stuck a thumbs up practically in Chance's face. "It works!"

Chance clapped his hands together, a smile spreading so big it was barely contained by his face. "Find someone! Find a music station, anything!"

"It's only outbound remember," Nicolas said, but his tone held the same joy Chance's face did.

"Then put out a message," I said.

"Okay, okay." Nicolas let out two quick breaths before jumping into his message. "This is an SOS to anyone who receives this message. A distress signal. My name is Nicolas and I'm being held on an island, possibly off the coast of Greece, along with almost a hundred other young adults both male and female. We have been taken from our homes, stripped of our belongings, and kept here against our will by threat of death. If anyone hears this, please send help immediately. This is an SOS, a distress signal, a call for help." He repeated the message in full three times.

As he removed the earbud from his ear, I realized I'd been holding my breath the entire time. "Do you think anyone will get it?" I asked.

"We can only hope," he replied.

Chance let out a groan, and both our eyes jumped to him in question. "We won't know if they get it right? Because this thing only works one way, only sends a signal out. Right? We can't get a message in?"

Nicolas nodded.

Chance crossed his arms and looked away.

"It's better than nothing," I reminded him. "And like Nicolas said, hopefully someone hears our message and sends help. Greece at least."

"If we really are off the coast of Greece," Chance muttered.

I wanted to say more, but I figured Chance was already thinking himself deeper into skepticism, and there was no point. I looked at Nicolas.

He moved the radio back into the corner and put the sheet over it. "We'll just have to wait and see."

19

Waiting had a weight to it. Like someone sitting on your shoulders, or if a sack of potatoes hung around your shoulders like a shawl. That was the weight of waiting. I felt it, and I was pretty sure everyone else did too.

Uncertainty had its own weight, but that was like if the person sitting on your shoulders was also holding a five-gallon jug of water. I didn't really feel it, but it added extra load.

I came across Chance sitting an awkward few feet away from Kaisa on the patio. They weren't speaking, and at first I reconsidered if I should join their silence. I did though, plopping down between the two of them.

Chance broke the silence, and in a low voice he said, "It's been two days."

I nodded at him, lacing my fingers together in front of my folded knees.

"And nothing," he continued.

"At least the radio worked."

"Did it work? We've gotten nothing back."

"It's a one-way radio, we won't get something back."

Chance ran his hand over the front of his hair, smoothing it against his face. "I know. I guess I just thought ..."

"You thought we'd be rescued within the hour?"

He glanced at me for a moment before returning his gaze to the ground. "Hoped."

I pushed a breath out through my lips. I didn't want to let on, but I too had thought something might happen. I didn't know what, but just something, and the lack of anything had certainly lowered my spirits.

Chance suddenly nudged me, and I looked over at him. He nodded toward Kaisa. "She's been watching those two boys throw that ball back and forth for like five minutes."

I looked over at her. Sure enough, she was turned all the way around, and I followed her gaze to the two boys her eyes were glued to.

A smile tugged at my lips. Props to her for being so brazen upon seeing a cute guy. Leaning into Chance, I whispered, "Which one do you think she's looking at?"

"Oh, for sure the guy on the left," he replied. "Look at those arms."

I tossed a quick glare at Chance to make him wipe the grin off his face.

"Is there a reason why you're watching those two?" Chance asked Kaisa.

Without taking her attention off them, she replied, "I thought I felt something from the two of them."

The grin on Chance's face immediately vanished. "Like Order stuff?"

She nodded. "But maybe I'm wrong. I haven't seen anything out of the ordinary."

"Maybe you're not going to see anything just watching them," I suggested. As soon as the words were out of my mouth, it happened.

The boy to the left, with a neat buzz cut and wide shoulders threw the ball much harder than he had before, and it flew over the blond boy's head. Without even taking a step toward it, the blond stretched out his hand and the ball flew back toward it. At the last second, the blond clicked his wrist and the ball zoomed toward the first boy. The first boy opened his mouth to shout, thrown off guard by how fast his friend had returned the ball, and put his hand up, even though it was clear the ball would sail over his outstretched hand. To my surprise, it didn't. The ball neatly stopped midair right above the first boy's fingertips.

My jaw dropped. Looking at Chance, he was just as surprised.

A smile spread on Kaisa's lips. "Did you see that?"

"I did." But I barely believed I had.

"They're definitely Orders," she said.

"They can't just do that in front of people," Chance hissed.

"We have to tell them," I said.

"Chance, go tell them," Kaisa instructed.

"What, why me?"

"You're a guy."

"That's your argument?" he asked. He looked at the two boys. I didn't understand why he was nervous. They looked like pretty approachable guys. Still, I wouldn't want to be the one having to try and explain some weird stuff like this.

"Go," Kaisa said, pushing his shoulder.

He stood up and brushed off his pants, stalling. Then, he strolled over to the guys, waving as he approached. They stopped their game when they noticed him, neither looking annoyed at being interrupted.

"What do you think he's going to say?" I asked.

Kaisa shrugged. "Probably something stupid. Then we'll have to step in."

"Then why did you send him?"

She shrugged again and looked over toward where the three boys were chatting. I watched too, trying to pick out the mood of the situation from so far away. They were in conversation, and from my vantage point, the boys didn't look too standoffish.

"Counting them, we then have—"

"Twenty," Kaisa finished for me. "Twenty Orders."

Twenty. Had it not been for Sherman, there'd be twenty-one. Still, we'd gone from such a small, frightened group to twenty strong.

A sickening feeling settled in my gut. There were over one hundred kids here, and twenty of us had created a safeguard. Just because they weren't like us, did that mean we should leave them out?

The feeling muted itself as Chance strolled back over to us.

"Well?" Kaisa asked.

"Yeah, they think I'm crazy."

She raised her eyebrows. "They're passing a ball between them without touching it, and they think you're crazy?"

He threw up his hands. "You can try if you think you can do better."

"Well, someone has to make them understand," she said as she stood up, also brushing any dirt off her pants.

Chance took his seat beside me, and I raised an eyebrow at him. "She's right. They're passing a ball between them without using their hands. What did you say for them to think you're the crazy one?"

He rubbed his hands together. "I probably just didn't say the right thing. Kaisa is better at explaining all this anyway."

Looking over my shoulder, I saw she was fully enveloped in conversation with the two boys.

"Do you think we're doing them a disservice?"

I looked back at Chance, feeling both my eyebrows lift. "What do you mean?"

"By telling them," he replied. "Not just these two, but everyone we've told. I don't know, sometimes I think we shouldn't have told people. I feel like we've given them more to fear, or worse."

"What's worse than fear?"

He met my eyes. "False hope."

✳ ✳

I never got a chance to officially meet the new Orders from yesterday. Kaisa told me their names—Filip and Luc—and explained to me the next morning that she'd persuaded them to at least talk more with her, being that neither of them could deny their inhuman abilities. She met with them later that night with Killian, and from there was able to fully explain the situation.

As I walked into the room for free period, taking a seat against the wall to read, I pondered over our current situation.

Twenty of us, one radio, one chance at escape.

Chance's comment from yesterday entered my thoughts. Were we doing the other Orders a disservice? We told them so they'd know who they were to these murders, that they were the targets, so that they could then protect themselves better. But by revealing their identity to them, had we put them in more danger? We'd made them more aware, and therefore caused them to lose all naivete to the plight around them.

And to add to that, we gave them comfort in knowing there were more like them, more Orders, but was it all false considering we had no idea how to save ourselves.

As I opened my book, I tried to clear my head of my worries. We'd already succeeded in something unimaginable. We'd built a device to communicate with the outside world. I wanted to hold on to the hope that our efforts wouldn't go to waste. We'd escape, it would just take patience.

I looked up from my book at the exact moment to catch Kanyn looking over at me. His sparkling eyes sent a warm tingle through my body. Despite myself, I flashed him a soft smile.

No, not despite myself. I could smile at him. He was the only decent one of them. He'd saved me and not even given me a shot, and unbeknownst to him, we had a working radio to get messages out for help. For once I could smile.

He didn't return my smile, but I thought for a second I saw the expression on his face soften before he looked away.

I couldn't remove the smile from my face, even as I looked back down at my book. If I could stand outside myself and look at myself, I would have thought myself an idiot, smiling because of one of them. I told myself I was smiling more because we had a working radio than anything Kanyn had ever done.

After a few minutes reading, I looked up again, this time the smile gone from my face. Where was Nicolas? He hadn't met me in the hallway like he usually did, and it was odd for him to be here in free period and not hanging out with me. He could have gone to the library or something, but usually we went places together, or at least let each other know. I did a once around the room with my eyes, but I couldn't spot the blond-haired genius. Assuming he'd show up whenever he wanted to, I lowered my eyes back to my book.

It was about ten minutes before movement at the top of my vision, just past the tip of my book, caught my attention. I looked up to see Nicolas approaching, just two steps away. He seemed hurried, even as he sat down next to me and immediately began pawing through his backpack.

"Hey, where have you—"

"Don't look at me," he hissed. "Act like I've been here the whole time."

I made a conscious effort not to look up from my book at him. "What are you talking about? Where were you?"

"I went to go check on the radio," he replied.

"And?"

Although I couldn't look at him, I could hear his hesitation. "I ran into some trouble."

"What happened?"

"I left my last class early so I could go check on the radio and make it back for this period," he explained. "When I got there, I found two of them in the room. They know about the radio."

I had to clench my entire body to keep from looking at him. "Did they see you?"

"I don't know," he replied. "I almost walked in, but I don't think they did. But one of them—I don't know his name, he has light blond hair—he thought he heard something at the door and he came out as I was walking away. I tried to ditch him in the hallways, but I don't know, I'm hoping ..." His words trailed off.

"What is it?" I asked.

"He just walked in."

I looked up from my book to see Astaroth standing just inside the doorway, scanning the room. Not finding what he was looking for, he went over to Amaris, his lips moving quickly for whatever he was saying.

Amaris's lips spread into a thin cruel smile, and he nodded at the end of their conversation. He must have sent a message telepathically to Tolison and Kanyn because when he looked at either of them, their eyes met in an unspoken understanding. He turned his attention to the room, and in a loud voice announced, "Alright you worms. Shut up, we have a situation."

The room immediately dropped into silence. Teachers across the world would be put to shame by Amaris. However, most if not all of us also knew he had murdered someone, so no one dared to cross him.

"Crap," Nicolas groaned beside me. I felt him quietly move away from me.

"It seems that someone in this room, some little bright-eyed genius, has built himself a radio," Amaris said. He slowly paced through the room as he spoke. "A radio as I see it is a communication device, a device for communicating. A device that can be used to communicate with the outside world. And as I remember, one of the rules is absolutely no communication with the outside world."

I couldn't look at Nicolas, but I wanted to if only to keep him from doing anything rash.

"But which one of you thought he was smart enough to build one?" Amaris swiveled on his heel as he looked at everyone in the room. "I know it was one of you. All you have to do is step forward, it makes everything easier. Because if you don't, I will do anything to get it out of you."

Out of the corner of my vision, I noticed Tolison's eyes flicker to Nicolas.

Amaris was serious, and to prove his point, he walked up to a boy with thick glasses hiding dark under-eye bags and shoved his face into the boy's. "Was it you?"

The boy shook his head, though it was almost indistinguishable from the rest of his quaking body.

Amaris sneered. "No, with those jitters you wouldn't have the nerve to hide something so unpermitted." He moved away from him, his eyes searching for his next victim.

I ached to look over at Nicolas. I didn't want him to turn himself in. But several thoughts were whirling around in my head. What if Nicolas gave in? Or what if we hadn't been as careful as we thought, and someone else turned us in? Or what if Amaris just kept up this malicious interrogation.

I flinched as Amaris hopped in front of a girl with blond hair braided into thin pigtails down her back. "How about you?" he sneered.

The girl shook her head, and tears immediately started falling down her face.

I looked over at Kanyn to see his reaction to this means of torture. At least he looked unhappy with Amaris too.

Amaris walked in a wide circle, his eyes seemingly falling on every single person in the room. "Doing this would take forever," he said. "Thank goodness we don't have to. I already know who it is."

If I was standing outside my own body, I would have called his bluff. But to my horror, he turned and looked straight at Nicolas.

Now I looked over at him. The color had completely drained from his face.

Amaris took a step toward him and before I could catch myself, I stepped forward.

"I built the radio."

Everyone's attention turned to me, including Nicolas.

"I mean," I continued quickly. "I made Nicolas build the radio. I couldn't do it by myself. And I asked him to go check it for me." I expected Kanyn to step forward to discipline me, but my blood turned cold when Amaris stepped up to me first. I rubbed my hands together in a feeble attempt to get my blood circulating.

His eyes bored right through me, burning me. I tried to hold his gaze but could only for a few seconds at a time. "You?" he asked.

I nodded.

"Number Five Hundred and Seven," Amaris purred. "That was a bold move."

I didn't know what he wanted me to say, but I could feel my level of insolence rising in response to his tone.

"Did you really think you wouldn't get caught?" he asked. "Or that you could hide behind one of your fellow peons?"

More rising, harder to hold my tongue.

"It must suck to be so stupid, to incredibly underestimate us and overestimate yourself," Amaris went on. "How embarrassing. I don't even know that you deserve punishment because of how stupid—"

"It wasn't stupid." For a brief second it was an out of body experience, and I was standing across the room, watching myself talk back to him.

"I'm sorry, what?"

I met his eyes. "It wasn't stupid. Can you build a radio? If you were in our shoes, could you scavenge for parts and build a whole radio? You wouldn't last a minute in our position." I should have stopped but I couldn't control my mouth. "And if anything is embarrassing, it's that it took you this long to find out about our radio. A simple radio. Who knows what other things are going on under your nose that you have no idea about."

Something snapped behind Amaris's eyes, and in a blinding second, he reached for my neck. It was only my instinctual step back that allowed him to only grip the collar of my shirt and not my throat. Gasps erupted around the room at his lunge.

Would he kill me like he had that boy? Right here in front of everyone? Clearly, he was capable. My blood wasn't cold anymore, instead it moved like lava through my veins. If he wanted to kill me, he sure as hell could because he would only serve to spur the others.

To my surprise, both Tolison and Kanyn stepped forward.

"Amaris, I understand your frustration, but this is not the way to handle this," Tolison said. "Number Five Hundred and Seven is under Kanyn's supervision and therefore it is up to him to deal with her."

A part of me hated Kanyn for not speaking up on my behalf, but that same part of me knew him saying anything to defend me would only provoke Amaris more.

Amaris glared at me, then at his two companions, before releasing me.

"Number Five Hundred and Seven, you may go with Kanyn," Tolison said.

I looked over at Kanyn, who was already heading toward the door. Assuming he wanted me to follow, I fell into step behind him. Before leaving the room, I managed a quick glance at Nicolas. The guy couldn't get any paler as he watched me. Hopefully knowing I was with Kanyn and not at Amaris's mercy would calm his nerves at least a little. And hopefully since I'd so brazenly took the blame, no one would look toward him again.

I stared straight ahead as I walked behind Kanyn. I knew exactly where we were going, and anyone who saw us probably did too. By the time we got to his office, the nerves from earlier had completely disappeared, replaced with an apathetic curiosity as to what he would say.

As per usual, he sat opposite me scribbling notes. If this was another situation, I'd be really interested to read all the notes he had on me. Maybe I'd learn something about myself. After a few minutes, he put down his pencil and leaned back in his chair, his brown eyes doing a complete sweep of me.

"Yes?" I asked, with less respect than I should have had.

"How long are you going to keep up that ridiculous story?"

"Excuse me?"

"You didn't build the radio, nor did you ask Number Four Hundred and Twenty-Six to do so," Kanyn replied. "He's your companion and you're covering for him."

Of course he'd seen right through me. Still, I tried to play the fool. "Why would you think I would cover for anyone?"

He rested his cheek on his fist. "Because your sense of loyalty is high."

"The idea of us against all of you doesn't really seem like loyalty, more like survival."

"So, you lied to elongate the safety of someone on the same side as you," he said. "Isn't that loyalty?"

Leaning back in my chair and crossing my arms, I didn't bother to argue. He knew the truth no matter what I said, and I didn't really feel like exerting the energy to try to convince him otherwise.

"You're right, I guess," he continued. "It's really just stupidity."

My face stung with anger. "Are you really insulting me?"

"You lie to keep another person safe which only puts you in trouble," he said. "Which is logically ridiculous because between you and Number Four Hundred and Twenty-Six, you've been disciplined more times, meaning you put yourself in more trouble than he would have received. It doesn't balance out, which is what makes it such an absurd decision."

"It was my decision. And I made it based on how I felt, not the mathematical outcome."

"You can't be so rash like that."

The tips of my ears started to burn. "Now you're telling me what decisions I can and can't make for myself?"

"It's not about that."

"Then what is it?"

Kanyn took a deep breath and pressed his fingers into his temple. "You have to be careful, Cori."

"Why?"

"Because they'll find you."

His comment hit me like a slap in the face. "They'll find me?"

Kanyn sighed. "I told you about The Order. You know they're looking for them." He licked his lower lip before continuing. "Cori, you're one of the Orders."

20

"What?"

"You are an Order."

"How ... Why would you think that?"

"It's very apparent," Kanyn replied.

The muscles in my back locked. How apparent? Apparent enough that he'd noticed it in the others as well? Attempting to keep my nerves at bay, I asked, "How long have you known?"

"From the first day I saw you."

The first day he saw me. A day I didn't know would change my whole life. It felt like a distant memory, when I'd seen Kanyn following Chance at the movies.

"Without getting too deep into it, we also have some abilities. And there is a special connection between us and Orders. Any true Order can see us at any time, even when we're invisible to others. That day I came after that boy, no one else could see me. But you could. I knew right away."

I hardened my face to keep from expressing anything. Had I just ignored the situation with Chance that day, none of my friends nor I would have ever ended up here. I'd made a crucial mistake, and I didn't even know it. Keeping my face still, I asked "Have you figured out others that quickly?"

"It's different for everyone," he replied. "You being able to see me was a very big indicator. Not everyone falls into the same circumstances."

So, there was a possibility for others to be known, and they didn't even know it. The others flipped across my brain like a book. Had any of them made a mistake the way I had? Were any of them in jeopardy?

"What about the people you don't know for sure?" I asked, hearing my voice quiet a decibel. "The people who don't make the same mistakes I did."

Kanyn watched me for a moment, like he was deciding whether he should reveal more to me. "There are a range of characteristics we look for."

I grinded my back teeth together. "I'm an Order, and I haven't been pulled aside yet." More like dragged out of my bed in the middle of the night. "Why is that?"

He didn't answer me right away, fiddling with the pen in his hand. He exhaled through his nose then finally replied, "I haven't told anyone."

"Why not?" I asked. "You said you wanted to find the Orders to protect them. Why would you keep me from the others?" I was testing him. He claimed he was honest—he acted like he wanted to be honest with me. This was his chance.

Kanyn's eyes flickered around the room, and his grip on the pen tightened. "They ... We aren't trying to protect them. If they discover you're an Order, they'll kill you."

The room dropped into complete silence. The world tilted. I already knew all this, but somehow it was different hearing it from him. He was confirming everything we thought. And most importantly, he was being honest with me.

I'd doubted his intentions every moment from the moment I'd met him. I'd been trying to figure him out and anticipate his actions, to stay one step ahead of him so he wouldn't find out my secret before I found out his. I was too careless, too reckless, and I hadn't even realized how obvious I'd been since I stepped onto the grounds. This entire time he'd been the only reason I hadn't been caught.

He cleared his throat. "I can't imagine there's anything you can think of to say after hearing that—"

"Have there been others?"

"What?"

"Other Orders before me. I assume so, and I'm sure there are others here. But have there been others you've found out before me, who you have let the others know about?"

"Yes."

I sucked in a deep breath. We were entering into a conversation I'd only thought about the answers with myself. "How many others?"

"Eight," he replied, then added, "No, nine."

The number was a rock dropping into my stomach. "Nine dead."

He nodded.

A lump began forming in my throat. "All here?"

He shook his head. "No. Only six were here."

"Six!" I covered my mouth to keep from screaming anything else. I hadn't prepared myself for more than half to have been found here.

The questions were snowballing at the tip of my tongue, and I squeezed my eyes shut to hold myself together. I wanted to ask about Sherman, Dara, and Gianni, to know exactly how they'd found out about them, but I didn't want to give away that I knew anything about anyone else being an Order.

I pushed a ball of air out through my nose, then slowly removed my hand from my mouth. "Do you know which ones they were? Out of the thirty-six."

"Numbers seven, three, twenty-two, nineteen, thirty-five, twenty-eight, thirteen, fourteen, and twenty-three."

"You remember all of them."

"I remember what numbers they were," Kanyn replied. "I only met Nineteen, Seven, and Twenty-two." He paused, then added, "I saw Thirteen die."

Out of my options, I picked a random number to start with. "What was Nineteen like?"

"She was ... Sweet."

Sweet. That was the only word he had to describe her. Someone they'd tortured and murdered and all he remembered her as was sweet.

Anger seethed in the pit of my stomach, in fact my belly felt like it had a small fire in it. I let out a low breath and asked, "And the others?"

Kanyn's eyes wandered as he thought. "I honestly don't remember much about them. I believe Thirty-Five lived on a large farm."

"Why do you call them by their numbers?"

"That's how I know them."

"You don't know their names?"

"I don't remember."

"You don't remember any of their names? You killed them and you don't remember their names, not even one of them?"

He shifted in his chair, his gaze still refusing to rest on me. Finally, he said, "Nineteen's name was Meryem."

The floor dropped out from under my chair. I'd wanted to hear him remember someone's name, they were people. But hearing him say her name made me feel nauseous. They'd hunted a girl, someone named Meryem, and killed her. They did it. He did it.

It was my turn to shift uncomfortably in my chair. "Why would you tell me all of this?"

"I just want you to make it as long as you can," he replied. "Stop making such reckless decisions. It only directs their attention to you."

"Maybe I want their attention."

Kanyn leaned back in his chair. "If you want it, trust me, you'll get it soon enough."

For the first time in a long time with Kanyn I was at a loss for words. There was no backhand comment or sarcastic statement waiting at the tip of my tongue, no excuse or lie I felt I had to tell to protect me or anyone else. He knew I was an Order. He knew my secret, and it seemed like there was nothing else I could hide from him.

I'd tried so hard, thought I'd watched my back, my every move—but he still knew. And worse, he knew that the others would know soon too. I wasn't safe. None of us were safe. Our hopes of calling for help had been dashed. We would die here, it was just a matter of time.

✳ ✳

I avoided Kanyn for the next few days. I also did everything I could to keep any attention off me. Kanyn had known right away because I'd seen him, and he'd somehow found it in his heart to tell me such things. But the others weren't like that, so I had no idea what they'd noticed about me.

The past days had been pretty quiet. A kid got in trouble for hoarding food in his room, but that wasn't much cause for commotion. Us Orders stayed low, in fact some of us weren't even speaking. I'd told Kaisa and Chance about my conversation with Kanyn, and they agreed—our escape seemed at a loss for now, but we had to keep watching our backs.

The first day I'd been completely paranoid, looking over my shoulders everywhere I went. I felt like every one of them had eyes on me, like I had a target on my back. As the days went on, my paranoia lessened, as did my hope for anything good.

I was headed to the library to do some studying with Kaisa and Meg. The hallway was unusually empty that afternoon, but it felt normal. It seemed no one really had the spirit to hang around outside their rooms anymore.

As I passed by a storage closet near the end of the hall, its door being slightly ajar caught my eye, just enough to momentarily take my attention off the despondency. It was unusual for anything to be out of order around here, but I figured it was nothing to concern myself with.

I had one foot around the corner when two strong hands wrapped around me, an arm around my torso and a hand slapped across my mouth. My attacker jerked me back around the corner and into the storage closet.

"Don't scream, I'm not going to hurt you."

I had to clench my teeth together to keep any noise from coming out. When I'd satisfied him, he freed me. I twisted around in the dark storage room to see who he was.

Mostly hidden by the darkness, he stood a whole head taller than me. One shade darker than my own, but his skin was smooth like butter and his teeth, perfect, shone like pearls decorating his mouth.

"Who are you?" I demanded.

"My name is Daniel," he said. "I'm number thirty."

"What does that mean?" The realization hit me as the words came out. "You're an Order."

He nodded. "Good, you already know. So are you."

"How do you know that?"

"I can feel it," he replied. "How many others are here? I think I've sensed five others so far."

"There's twenty here," I replied. Then I added, "Alive."

His face fell. "How many dead?"

"Three in my time here," I said. "One of them was number three, and one was fourteen. I don't know the other's number." I paused before adding, "There have been others killed before I got here."

"We imagined," he said.

"We?" I asked. "Are there more of you?"

"There's myself and one other," he replied. "But she isn't here right now. She's coming."

"When? From where?"

"That isn't important," Daniel said. "The when is important, however. She'll be here in two days."

"Two days?" I asked. "And what's supposed to happen then?"

"We free the Orders," he said. "We heard your message, I'm sorry we couldn't get one back. We came as soon as we could."

"It's alright, it's great that you're at least here," I said. My mind was racing. "But two days? All twenty of us are going to escape here in two days? How is that supposed to happen?"

"We'll fly out of here on helicopters," Daniel said.

"There's helicopters coming?"

He nodded. "And armed men. We're getting you all safely out of here."

"What about everyone else?"

"We'd love to help them, but these people are killing Orders—"

"They're killing people who aren't in the Order too," I interrupted. "Everyone dies here. You just have to wait for it."

"Look, I wish there was something we could do, but we only have enough room for the Orders. We'll just have to hope that once all the members of the Order are gone, they don't have a point to kill the others."

I wasn't satisfied with his answer, but who was I to stand in the way of rescuing the Orders? "When is all this supposed to take place?"

"Around twelve at night. You'll know, you'll hear the helicopters. The men have been told to open fire."

"Open fire?" I hissed. "What about the other people here who aren't trying to kill us?"

"They're trained," Daniel replied, not that that was a satisfying answer either. He continued without anything else in regard to that. "On the southwest side of the building, seven o'clock, there's a large field before the wall. That's the pick-up spot. Everyone needs to be there within five minutes of the helicopters landing."

"Five minutes? What if we get, you know, caught sneaking out to a helicopter?"

"There's twenty of you. Watch each other's back, act like a team. Make sure everyone gets where they're supposed to be."

Wiping my palms against my pants, I looked away from Daniel. For all the time I'd been trapped here, all I wanted was some kind of an escape plan. Here one was with helicopters and armed guards, and my stomach was completely liquid. The idea that all twenty of us could escape safely sounded impossible.

And then it would only be twenty. I estimated about a hundred kids here, and only twenty would make it out. Was that fair? They deserved freedom as much as we did. They deserved to live.

"I know how this must sound," he said.

"It sounds like we're being really selfish," I said, hearing my voice ripple.

He let out a short sigh. "We can't get everyone. It's you they want, all twenty." He put a hand on my shoulder. "We'll just have to hope when their objectives are gone, the others will be saved."

What even was hope anymore. Even this moment didn't feel like my prayers were being answered.

Daniel gave me a slight nudge toward the door, and I came back to reality.

Help was on its way, but it hadn't arrived yet.

"Remember, two days," he said as I opened the door.

Stepping out of the closet, closing the door behind me, I felt like I was stepping back into a vacuum, my chest heavy.

Two days. I could make it for two more days.

I took one step away before realizing I'd forgotten to ask one crucial detail. I opened the door again, asking, "Wait, where are you going to—"

The closet was empty. He was gone.

21

I only had to tell three people—Kaisa, Chance, and Valentina—to get the news out to the other Orders. The excitement was palpable, but we knew we had to keep up the downtrodden attitudes everyone else shared.

We had no belongings, so nothing to pack—nothing to waste the time doing except waiting.

Srey suggested sewing little bags for us to take toiletries from the bathroom, but that idea was quickly shot down. We didn't know what they did while we were away in our classes, especially after finding the radio. If they found bags of supplies, they might catch wind someone was planning to escape.

I did however change my diet. I didn't know what was coming, what our escape would entail. I wanted to be as physically ready as I was mentally. And I wasn't the only one.

When the day of departure finally arrived—the longest forty-eight hours of our entire lives—a noticeable confidence also arrived with it. We felt it in each other. Hudson's chest looked two sizes bigger as he paraded around.

Glancing at the clock as I passed it in the hallway, the hands pointed to three fifty-five. Only eight hours left.

I looked over at Theo walking beside me. He'd also looked at the clock when we passed. We were all counting down.

"I am talking to you!"

We directed our attention in front of us, further down the hall.

Valentina was seated on one of the benches, running a file across her nails. Namira, another of our few female captors, stood above her.

"You don't have a reason?" Namira was asking her.

"Nope," Valentina replied, without even looking up at her. She looked more interested in the filing of her nails than the enraged expression painted on Namira's face.

"You just felt like not showing up to your last class."

Valentina held her right hand out in front of her, inspecting her filing job. "That is *correcto*."

I glanced at Theo. We were all doing such a good job in maintaining our hopeless facades. We were almost out.

Theo didn't stop walking, but he slowed his pace. I matched his.

"That's a shot," Namira said. "But I'll be nice and only require you to scrub the floors of all the bathrooms instead."

Finally, Valentina gave her attention to Namira, standing up as she did and sliding her file into her back pocket. "I don't think so."

Namira looked like she'd been hit by a truck, gaping at Valentina. "What did you say?"

Valentina put some space between her and Namira. "I'm not scrubbing the bathroom floors. I'm not scrubbing any floors. You can have someone else do it."

Theo and I exchanged glances, pausing in the hallway. It wasn't new to either of us that Valentina was quite the firecracker, but wasn't she pushing it just a little? At this point, was there even a way for us to step in if we needed to?

A few kids had been watching the confrontation from the beginning, but by then more kids were watching.

Namira's irritation was obvious. She didn't have the same intimidating nature as Amaris did, and she knew it. Her glare intensified. "You either take the punishment, or that'll be two shots Number Four Hundred and Forty-One."

With one perfectly filed red nail, Valentina tapped her chin. "No."

A low murmur escaped the group of spectators.

Before Namira could reply, although the rage in her was near palpable, Valentina added, "I'm not getting a shot. I'm not scrubbing floors. I'm not scared of you. *Eres una bruja*, a witch, and I don't believe in that. You don't own me, and I'm not scared of you or any of your little *compinches*."

"You are out of line," Namira snapped, her voice up by two decibels. "*Tomátela*."

Namira's eyes grew two sizes, and I thought she might have exploded. "That's a shot!" she yelled. I was honestly just surprised in all this time she hadn't attempted to get physically aggressive with Valentina.

Valentina threw her head back and laughed loudly. "*Dámelo*. I'll gladly take it."

Namira made a swipe for Valentina's arm, but she dodged with a grin, then flashed her middle finger before walking down the hall.

I ran my tongue behind my lower row of teeth, just to get an idea of if my jaw was hanging open. I didn't know which I was more amazed at— Valentina's outburst or Namira just letting her walk away.

"She's pushing it," Theo whispered to me.

I nodded, and a smile tried to push onto my lips. It was almost admirable, I wished I had the gall to let loose on these freaks like her. But we were so close to freedom, we couldn't do anything to risk it. "I'll find her later and talk to her," I said.

Not that I even knew what to say. Frankly, as long as she didn't get herself locked up—or killed—she could do whatever she wanted. Tonight was the night.

✳ ✳

Eleven thirty.

I paced the length of the bedroom. Meg sat patiently reading a book on her bed. Our boots waited by the door. Whenever the signal happened, we were ready. It was just a question of when.

I'd been pacing for at least an hour, and Meg finally closed her book in her lap and looked at me with raised eyebrows. "You're going to wear a hole in the floor."

"My mom used to say that," I said without stopping.

"I'm sure it wasn't just to hear herself talk," she said, but her comment didn't have as much bite as it could have.

I slowed my pacing until I finally came to a stop next to my bed. I pulled Mark's hoodie up a little so my nose was buried inside. Sometimes I thought I could still smell him on it. I stared at the floor where I'd been walking, and after a few minutes my brain started to trick me into seeing an actual wear pattern in the floor. Finally, I shifted my gaze over to Meg to find her looking at me. "What?"

"I wish Ben was leaving with us."

I sat down beside her on her bed and gave her a one-armed hug. "I know. Me too."

She was staring at the sheets underneath her bare feet. "And ..."

"And what?"

"Have you thought about, well, if we missed someone?" she asked. "Missed an Order, and now we're going to leave them behind."

I closed my eyes and swallowed. "I have thought about it. Kaisa and I talked about it. The only thing we can do is hope for the best and plan to come back for them when we can."

Meg shook her head. "This place, it's absolutely horrible. But," she looked at me, "do you think anyone will even believe us when we tell them about it?"

"Of course they will," I replied, rubbing her back. "There's over a hundred kids here, all missing from around the world. Someone will listen to us, and then they'll burn this place to the ground."

"I hope so," she said. The bite was there. Her ire and hurt spiraled around her, I could feel it.

That made me uncomfortable, because if the roles were reversed, she'd feel nothing emitting off me.

Her spindles suddenly turned cold at a knock on our door. "Expecting someone?" she asked me.

I shook my head as I stood up. "Probably just someone who's nervous." Opening the door, my stomach dropped to the floor.

Hunter stood outside.

"Hunter, what—"

"Kanyn wants to see you."

He wanted to see me now? In less than thirty minutes, I needed to be on my way to the southwestern side of the building. I didn't have time to have some long conversation with him. But I couldn't risk making him or Hunter suspicious.

"Alright, I can get there myself," I said, sliding into my shoes. "I know the way to his office."

"He's not in his office."

I looked at him. "Then where is he?"

He cleared his throat before replying, "He's in his room. I'll show you to it."

I could feel Meg's gaze on my back. There were so many reasons why this was a bad idea. I didn't have a lot of time left as it was to have a conversation with Kanyn, and now I was going to his room. I didn't even know where their rooms were in relation to everything else. Why did he not want to see me in his office? What could I possibly have done in the past few days?

As I left the room with Hunter, my hairs began to stand on end. What if Kanyn knew? He saw and figured out so many things I never dreamed he would. What if he knew tonight was the night? Would he try and stop us? Or would he just kill me?

Their quarters were located on the complete opposite end of the building, the north side. We passed by rooms and hallways I didn't even know existed. Even if one of us got lost, we'd never find ourselves wandering this way.

Hunter stopped at a door indistinguishable from the rest and knocked lightly on it.

"Do you know why he wants to see me?" I whispered.

Hunter paused, keeping his eyes pointed at the door, and for a second I thought he might give me an answer. All he replied was no.

We waited, and Hunter raised his fist to knock again, but Kanyn opened the door just before he could. He didn't look at me, only Hunter. "Thank you."

Hunter nodded, and without looking at me again, started walking in the opposite direction than we'd come, further down the hallway of doors.

Now Kanyn looked at me, and his expression was something I couldn't figure out. It wasn't his usual stern frown. "Come in."

I stepped around him into the room, trying to hold back how eager I was to see what it looked like.

It matched his office. Brown walls, brown furniture. Another desk with a dim lamp. A long bed with made navy sheets and one tan pillow. Below the window was a three-shelf bookcase, but only the top shelf held books.

"You're not much for decorating," I said.

Then, Kanyn surprised me. He actually did two things that surprised me, one after the other. Firstly, he smiled at me. The ends of his lips fully curved upward. The smile wasn't huge, nothing like a toothy grin, but it was no doubt a smile. Secondly, he walked over to his desk and turned off the light. As he flipped the switch, my stomach lurched in apprehension, but my worries were quickly alleviated.

I expected to be thrown into pitch blackness, but my eye caught something lit above me. Looking up at the ceiling, my breath caught in my throat. Glowing on the ceiling was a painting of a night sky, similar to that of Van Gogh's *Starry Night*, but composed of different brush strokes.

"Did you paint that?" I asked. In the dark I could see Kanyn nod. "It's beautiful."

"No one has ever seen it," he said. "You're the first."

I found myself getting lost in the art, so much so that I backed up into the bed and sat myself on the edge.

He sat beside me, looking up at his masterpiece too.

"Did you ... I mean, where did this come from?" I asked. "Did you see this somewhere or did you just think of it?"

"I saw it, or something close once. A long time ago. I've just always remembered it."

I felt myself sliding back on my hands, fully enveloped in the curves and swirls. I could lie back and stare at it for hours, and still be able to find something I hadn't noticed before.

I stopped my recline with a sudden halt. I couldn't lose my focus. "Did you have something you wanted to talk to me about?" I asked.

"I just wanted you to see this."

I bit the inside of my lip. Any other night I might have been happy he wanted to show me something so special to him. But tonight was too late, the wrong time.

"No, I did want to talk to you," he spoke up.

My stomach flipped.

"You've done a really good job staying out of trouble these past few days," he said.

"Thanks," I muttered.

He paused. "It seems like you've done a really good job of avoiding me as well."

I glanced at him.

"If you're not in trouble, you have no reason to be sent to see me. And although I could ask for you, I wanted to give you space after our last conversation."

I nodded.

"But you ..." He paused again. "You haven't even looked my way since then."

"I was just trying to ... Give you space as well." Not the exact truth, but truth enough.

It had been hard the past few days, forcing myself not to look in his direction. But he had made it very clear that for all the care I thought I had, it hadn't been enough. I couldn't chance outing myself, or more importantly, any of the others.

He had also made something very vague. He told me I was an Order. He warned me. He'd crossed the line. Before, he'd been playing this game, only hinting at things. But by admitting to me what I was and their intentions—I honestly didn't know what it meant. Obviously he didn't expect me to roll over and give up. But that would have to mean that he ...

"Why did you tell me?" I asked.

"That you are an Order?" he asked, and I nodded. "I told you, so you can hide yourself better."

"Have you ever told anybody else?"

"No."

I swallowed. I was getting closer to a truth I wasn't sure I wanted to hear. "Then why me?"

He sighed before starting. "I'm sure you see me as nothing but your enemy. A murderer as well. And I am, at least an accessory. I can't erase that from your mind, although I must admit, I have to hold myself back from trying."

I shivered. Was that another one of their abilities, that they could they take away memories? Could we?

"When you're sitting across from me with that indignant look on your face, I can't help but hope that you're not thinking too badly of me."

I never was. Even though I wanted to, he'd helped me too many times for me to. And I spent most of my time hoping behind his observing eyes, he wasn't piecing together that I craved his attention.

"I've never met someone who afflicts me the way you do."

I stared straight ahead at the wall across from us. What would happen if I looked at him? Would I finally break into a hundred pieces? Would I melt like chocolate left in the sun? I wanted him to stop talking—I couldn't hear this now—but didn't have the heart to tell him.

"I afflict you?" I asked, hoarsely.

"Like a disease," he replied. "You're in my head, almost like you were doing it intentionally. And it's troubling because it doesn't seem I do the same to you."

"You do a pretty good job of being in my head."

From the corners of my vision, I saw him shake his head. "Not in the same way. I see that you see me as a jailer. But other than that, I can't tell anything about you. You surprise me."

I scoffed. "You don't seem very surprised when I'm in trouble."

"I observe you, that's my job. So I make predictions about you and I've happened to not be wrong. But I don't want to predict what you're thinking. I want to know. I want you to tell me."

His words sent shivers down my spine. But nothing he was saying could subdue the anxiety in my stomach from what was coming. I squinted to read the face of the clock in the dark.

11:54.

I was running out of time, and I still had to find my way through this maze of a building to the south side and then somehow find a way outside. If I was late, hopefully Meg would grab my stuff.

I began blinking faster than I normally would as I considered what he was asking. On one hand, it was an absolute no. He was one of them, he didn't deserve to know my thoughts, and to tell him would be a betrayal.

But on the other hand, here I was, alive. He knew what I was from day one and he'd only kept me safe. He'd been the only one to give me answers, even if I didn't always like them. And that night he held me, carrying me away from the water tower. He didn't know I held on to the feeling of being in his arms and used it to sleep every night since.

I clenched one side of my teeth together. It would be so easy to open myself up to him, in more ways than one. But what if it was all a lie? What if he betrayed me, and I ruined it for everyone. "My thoughts really aren't all that interesting," I said, dryly.

Kanyn chuckled. "Then could you at least tell me—honestly—what you think about me? So I don't have to wonder anymore."

In a split second, I went numb. Gone were the anxiety and the shivers. The only thing left, a hollow connection, like a chord that linked Kanyn and I there in the dark.

"I don't know what to think about you," I said. My voice sounded different, like I was outside my body hearing myself talk. "You've been nothing but nice to me since I arrived. And gentle. I admit I don't mind having to deal with you for trouble. But you're one of them, and you can't change that. You—they—are killing Orders. You brought me here to kill me, even if you haven't done it yet. You already did it to others. You said I was loyal. If I'm an Order, then they are my duty. But ..."

The last words caught in my throat. I'd thought about it before, but always obliterated those thoughts because I had to put the Order first. The words wanted to come out now, they deserved to. I'd done everything for the Order, to the point where we would all be escaping within a few minutes. "... You act like you care about me."

Hot tears welled up in my eyes as soon as the words were out. How dare I say that, how dare I believe that he cared about me. I was an Order, and because of him nine other Orders were dead. How was that caring? If he cared he would help us go free, not keep us locked up here waiting to slaughter us. I waited for him to say something back. I hoped it would be something to give me a reason to hate him.

My eyes flashed over to the clock. 12 on the dot.

And then Kanyn chose to speak. "It's not an act. I do care about you. And I would do anything within my means to protect you."

I'd guessed. Hoped. Wanted. But hearing him actually say it, I faltered. A disturbing happiness welled up inside of me, but I couldn't entertain it. I had to go, unless I wanted to stay here with my murderous jailer and his people. And I almost did.

But this hellhole was too much. I deserved better. The Orders deserved better. I had to go, I had to rip myself away from the moment. I had to break his heart as he would mine. Gently.

I kissed him. More forceful than I'd planned, mainly from the momentum of me thrusting myself forward. I locked my lips on his bottom lip, and he didn't fight me. I only touched him through his lips, but even still I felt his entire body surrender. I could have enveloped myself further in that kiss, could have stayed there with him for hours.

But I ended it. I pulled away, completely separating myself from him. In one fluid motion, I stood up and ran out the door. I was aroused, I was confused, and I was late. My face was hot as I ran, the blood not yet returning to my other extremities. I still tasted him on my lips. And now there was a whirring in my ears.

No, not in my ears. The sound seemed to come from above the building, but also from everywhere at once.

The helicopters were here. And if I heard them, everyone heard them.

22

It took me forever to get my bearings and find myself near the library, and I still had ground to cover. I didn't have time to go back to my room, I could only hope Meg grabbed my things on her way out. Hopefully the others were all there by now.

I heard the footsteps as soon as I turned the corner but didn't have time to stop myself.

Edrick, Tolison, and Namira were running down the hall the way I needed to go.

Edrick looked back and saw me. He immediately broke from the other two and started barreling toward me.

Nearly tripping over myself, I started back the way I came. I refused to look behind me, fearing I'd see him so close that he could bite my collar. My footsteps echoed inside my head, competing against the thumping of my thoughts. I was trying to figure out a route, trying to keep track of time, straining to keep the helicopters close.

I couldn't outrun him. I couldn't outfight him. To think I could outsmart him seemed preposterous, but it could just work. I could hide.

I turned another corner and saw what I was looking for, a broom closet. Even better, three closets. I jumped into the first one, silently closing the door behind me and scooting to the very back of the closet.

For a second, the hall was pin drop quiet. Then I heard him, turning that same corner I had. I heard his footsteps travel right past my closet, but a lump formed in my throat as his footsteps slowed not too far past.

I should have known I couldn't outsmart him. Of course he'd figure out I was hiding. I'd shrunk myself into the corner of the closet, but I suddenly felt like a giant trying to fit in a mouse hole.

His footsteps drew closer, and I held my breath. I almost shrieked hearing one of the closet doors open. Clapping my hand over my mouth, I waited. He was going to find me. And even if I burst out of this closet, he'd catch me and skin me alive.

Suddenly another set of footsteps entered the hallway, lighter than Edrick's had been.

"What are you doing?" the newcomer, a female, asked.

"I—"

"Never mind it, Edrick," the woman interrupted. "We need you outside. Come on." Two sets of footsteps hurried down the hallway until I couldn't hear them anymore.

I let out a sigh, slowly unfolding myself out of the corner. My heart thumped so loudly I thought it would draw attention to me. I wanted to stay here, catch my breath, but I didn't have time. That woman had wanted Edrick outside. They wanted to stop us, which meant we needed to leave now.

The sound of the helicopters was still my only guide, and I ran faster than I'd ever run in that direction, along the way trying to prepare myself in case I ran into another one of them on their way out.

Prepare myself, I thought bitterly. I'd needed some kind of something just a moment ago, and all I'd experienced was three types of panic. I was an Order, and that book said I was supposed to have special abilities. Jacqueline, Filip, Luc—they got to play around with magical abilities. Why couldn't I do anything? In the fissures of my brain, the folds of my heart, the bowels of my being, why couldn't I find any special ability I was supposed to have? This was the time for it.

I was lost, completely surrounded on a side of the compound I'd never been in. Halls multiplied into more halls, stretching into an endless maze.

Finally, I found a door to the outside, and breaking free of my prison, my jaw dropped at what lay before me.

Helicopters rotating in the air low to the ground, search lights sweeping the grassy field in front of me, people running in all directions, gunshots, screaming. I'd entered a battlefield. I couldn't tell Order from monster from the other detainees. And I didn't see Meg anywhere.

By chance I caught sight of Kaisa's blond hair, seeing her making a beeline toward a landed helicopter. Chance ran in front of her, and I had to squint to make out the girl waiting beside the helicopter. Srey.

It was the closest to me, but still several yards away. I'd have to run for my freedom. And I did.

Fortunately, I had a rather clear path, most of the fighting going on to my adjacent left, and there wasn't a single one of my captors in front of me. The screaming and the gunfire sent continuous shivers down my spine.

Were we all here, headed for the choppers? Had all twenty of us made it? I prayed Meg was sitting inside one of them, her journey easy.

Srey's scream shattered my thoughts, and I looked behind me.

Two cars' length away from me, Hunter barreled after me.

Out of fatigue or resignation, my sprint slowed until my steps felt like horse clomps, and I turned around to watch him approach me. I couldn't outdo anything against him on a flat plane, and I preferred to have it end quick. If I was lucky, he'd run me through as he reached me.

At half a car's length, my heart beat so vigorously my body convulsed. A beam of light from a helicopter glossed over his face, igniting my fright into an inferno. I didn't want to die.

I didn't have time to think, just act. I summoned anything, pulled something, then threw what felt like an invisible pulse of energy at Hunter. What I threw felt like a spinning ball, as if for a moment I'd held a hurricane in my hands. A millisecond after it left my hands, the same energy rebounded and slammed into me, so hard it knocked me on my back. The last thing I saw before my eyes closed was Hunter standing absolutely still steps away from me.

When I opened my eyes again, I was surrounded by blackness. Not black, a shade darker than black. My body and the air around me hung with frost. I shivered violently, hugging myself as tightly as I could. My breath turned to white puffs in front of me.

Everyone had disappeared, along with the helicopters, the building, even the field. Had I died? This couldn't be death. I was far from perfect, but still, I didn't expect this to be what met me in the afterlife. I heard something behind me, a noise like water trickling against a tile floor. Turning to see what it was, I stumbled backwards in fright.

Hunter. He stood with his back to me, his hair in its usual tight ponytail fashion. He wore black sweatpants, but other than that, he was naked. A bare torso save for the bandages wrapped around his upper arms, and exposed feet. Although the floor was solid ground, water pooled around his feet as if he stood in a puddle. He didn't move. I didn't know if he knew I was there.

"Hunter," I said softly.

He started to move, but not toward me. He began unwrapping the bandages on his right arm.

I took a step forward and tried again. "Hunter?"

He still didn't acknowledge me, and I was starting to wonder whether this was a dream or not. Maybe I was unconscious right now in the middle of the field.

He finished unwrapping his right arm, letting the bandages drop to the ground at his feet, then started on his left arm.

I squinted to make out the marks on his right arm, continuously stepping forward. When I was about two feet from him, I gasped, able to see the marks clearly.

More than ten deep gashes carved his skin, some scarred over and some freshly done. Looking to his left arm where he'd just finished unwrapping it, I saw the same slices. My hands went to my mouth, and my eyes stung from the tears that rushed to them. Who did this to him? This couldn't have been a battle, some were too fresh, and they were too concentrated.

"Hunter," I said through my fingers.

He took something out of the front of his pants, and I saw the flash of his knife. Although I was still behind him, I was close enough to see his face now. His eyes stared only at the knife as he gripped the knife in his right hand. Before I could react, he took the knife and sliced the skin of his left upper arm.

"Hunter!" I exclaimed, finally taking my hands from my mouth. I saw him wince at the pain, but his grip on the blade only tightened, and he ripped open another line on his arm.

I couldn't watch this anymore. No matter what he was, he didn't deserve to self-harm himself like this.

I reached for him, but the minute my fingers brushed against his skin, they went through it, and the image of Hunter exploded into white particles.

He hadn't really been here. This was a dream. But why would I be dreaming this?

The darkness around me began to shift, bending and twisting, erupting with more colors. I was nauseous watching it all. When the scene settled, I stood in one of the hallways.

Panic gripped me. How did I get back here? Did one of them catch me and bring me here?

I heard footsteps at the end of the hallway. There was no way I could make it to the other end without being seen, so I braced myself and watched to see who would turn the corner.

A wiry girl with low dark bangs turned the corner. She walked quickly, periodically looking behind her to see if someone was following. She walked past me—in fact she walked through me—without even noticing.

This had to be part of the dream too. But I'd never seen that girl before. I looked back at the corner she'd come from and noticed a dark figure watching her from around the corner. The farther the girl went down the hallway, the more the figure came out from the corner until I could see him clearly.

Hunter.

He was following her. No doubt observing her to figure out if she was an Order. He must have already assumed she was if he was full on stalking her.

The world around me began to warp again, and I felt the dizziness again from the swirl of colors. When everything settled, I was in one of the dormitory hallways. From the window and lack of activity in the hall I could tell it was the middle of night. A door opened, and the same girl from before slipped out. She checked the hallway, still blind to me, and scurried into the bathroom.

She may not have been able to see me, but that just meant clearly I wasn't the one who she was worried about. I hurried after her into the bathroom. She didn't even notice me enter.

She stood at the sink, staring at herself in the mirror, a mix of anguish and sorrow across her face. I noticed the scalpel like item balanced on the sink the same time she reached to pick it up. With her other hand, she turned on the water full blast. Tears began to stream down her face, and just as I'd witnessed Hunter slice at his skin, I watched the girl slowly make an incision below her wrist.

I didn't know what to do. Clearly this was a dream or a hallucination. I couldn't interfere.

The door to the bathroom opened, and Hunter walked in.

The girl dropped the scalpel in the sink and backed away from him as he approached, red spilling down her arm and dripping to the floor.

Hunter stopped a few feet from her, scanning the scene he'd walked into.

I watched in horror, my heart threatening to leap out my chest. What was he going to do to her?

To my surprise, he turned off the water, then bent to one knee in front of her. He held out his hand for her wrist, and she gave it to him. He took out a roll of gauze from an inside pocket in his robe and began to wrap her wrist. "So," he said gently, "this is why you're so secretive."

The girl looked as surprised as I did and bobbed her head up and down.

"You're fighting some demon too, and you think this is the way to deal with it." He looked up at her. "It's not." When he finished wrapping her wrist, he stood up and slid his robe down so it hung at his waist. Then he unwrapped the bandages on his left arm, showing them to the girl.

The girl's mouth gaped open, probably in shock at the sheer number of slashes on his arm. "You ... I ..."

"I know what you're going through," he said. "Trust me. What you're doing isn't the answer." He tossed the bandages in the trash, then put his robe back on properly. "You shouldn't be up this time of night. Go back to your room." He didn't even wait for her to move, and instead left the bathroom, taking the scalpel with him.

I watched the girl's reaction for as long as the dream would let me. She shrank to the ground, buried her head in her hands, and cried. The world changed for the fourth time, and this time I was in a room I'd never seen.

Hunter, Astaroth, and three of them I'd only heard their names briefly—Zeno, Cyrillion, and Brunhild—all stood around conversating. From the grave looks on their faces, it was something serious.

"The girl with the bangs, what's her name? Whatever. I don't think she's an Order."

"I agree with you, Zeno, and I've heard a couple of the others expressing the same thing," Cyrillion said. "It seems that her secretiveness is more shyness than sneakiness."

"She's just taking up space then," Astaroth said.

I noticed Hunter wasn't saying anything, and instead staring at the ground just in front of his feet.

"I agree, brother. We've spent too much time looking into her, time we could have spent on others." Cyrillion shifted his gaze directly to Hunter. "Hunter, you will take care of it."

A flash of emotion sparked across his face, then he looked up, only showing his usual stoic expression. "What do you mean?"

"You will see to it that she is taken care of," Cyrillion said.

"Meaning?" Hunter asked.

My stomach dropped the same time Cyrillion said the words, "You kill her."

I wanted to vomit, lie down, disappear. Hunter actually tried to be nice to that girl. He could have gotten her in trouble when he'd found her, but instead he chose to connect with her on a level I didn't think was even possible for him. Now Cyrillion was asking her to kill her. Surely this hurt Hunter as much as it hurt me to watch it.

Surely, he wouldn't do it. Hunter was smart—deadly, but smart. Surely, he could find a way around it.

The world shifted, screeching to a new scene so fast I thought I would tumble backwards from vertigo.

It was early morning. The sky was bright blue, but the sun couldn't be seen yet. The girl sat cross-legged outside in the grass, her hands on either of her legs, meditating perhaps.

Hunter walked out, dressed in his normal robes, and the same stoic expression on his face.

The girl heard him approaching, and turned her face to him, a bright smile on her face. Obviously the two of them got along well—not many people smiled at Hunter.

He didn't return her smile, which I take it was odd of him from the girl's reaction of her smile dropping. "What's wrong?" she asked.

He didn't speak, and when he was a foot away, motioned for her to stand up.

She slowly got to her feet, still trying to read his emotions.

I could see the mix of emotions on his face. I swear I saw his face twitching to hold the emotionless expression. I knew what was coming, and couldn't do anything about it. As nice as Hunter wanted to be, he couldn't defy what he was. I turned away, but still heard the girl scream, then everything went quiet.

I couldn't get myself to turn back around.

Hunter walked around me, his blade gripped so tightly in his hand his fingers were white.

Everything inside of me went cold, and I couldn't even feel my own heartbeat. Something in my brain allowed me to kickstart my muscles enough to run after him.

He walked quickly, just short of a sprint. I had to jog to keep up with him. He turned a corner, then opened a door to a supply closet. I managed to squeeze inside just before he shut the door with a thud just short of a slam. His breathing had become heavy, almost to the level of concerning. He plopped down on an upside-down bucket, closing his eyes and clenching his fists so tightly he drew blood. I wanted to reach out and comfort him, but I'd accepted by now that this was a hallucination, a memory more than likely.

The air started to change, and my throat suddenly closed up, as if someone had reached out from behind and wrapped their fingers around it. I gasped for breath and the scene around me swirled into blackness. My eyes closed and I felt weightless. My feet weren't touching the ground anymore, I couldn't tell which way was up or down.

"Cori!"

My throat opened and a burst of air rushed into my lungs. My eyes popped open next, and I saw myself gripping at grass around me. A loud incessant whirring filled my ears, dominating over any other sounds.

"Cori! Cori, get up! Can you hear me?"

My eyes darted around to find where the voice was coming from. They landed on the person still standing a few yards away from me.

Hunter stood perfectly still, an astounded expression frozen on his face as he stared straight ahead. Then he blinked, and seemed to come back from whatever trance he'd been in.

Hands fell upon my shoulders and yanked me upward onto my feet, turning me about face.

Chance stood directly in front of me, him being the one supporting me, and Kaisa stood a few feet behind him. "Come on, we have to go!" he yelled above the loud whirring, which coming back into the situation I understood was the helicopter waiting for us.

I still couldn't process everything happening around me—or that had just happened—but I let Chance guide me to the hovering helicopter.

Srey helped us in, helping Kaisa first, then me, then Chance. As soon as he was in, throwing himself onto his back on the floor of the chopper, we began to slowly rise into the sky.

My eyes landed on the pilot, who was turned around in his seat surveying us. He turned back around, lifting his radio and mouthing words that couldn't be heard over the rotors.

I dared to look back at the scene we were leaving.

They filled the yard, battling other kids and keeping them from making it to the helicopters. I felt a sharp prick in my bottom lip and realized I'd clamped down on it.

All those kids we were leaving behind, possibly even other Orders. They didn't understand why we had to go. But we'd be back for them. That's what I tried to tell myself.

As I scanned the battlefield, my gaze landed on the spot I'd almost died.

Still standing there, like he was frozen in time, stood Hunter, watching the helicopter climb higher into the air.

I squinted, trying to make out the expression on his shrinking face.

The door to the helicopter suddenly slammed closed. I hadn't seen Chance get up to do so, but he slumped back down onto the floor, resting his back against the door.

I looked around the helicopter. Srey and Kaisa had managed to pull themselves into chairs, both of their chests quickly rising and falling. Srey's tan knuckles were white where she clutched the arms of her chair, like we could fall out of the sky at any time.

The pilot stared straight ahead, focused on the path before him.

How many of us made it to the helicopters? Hopefully they wouldn't have taken off without us all secured, but then with that fighting quickly moving toward the helicopters ...

Kaisa tapped me on the shoulder. "What happened to you back there?" she asked. "You just ... Collapsed or something."

I couldn't tell her even if I wanted to. "I tripped."

She rolled her eyes and looked away. "Great timing for that," she muttered.

I didn't know what happened. I didn't fully understand many of the things that had happened in that place. I didn't understand Hunter, I didn't understand Kanyn, I didn't understand them.

I let out a shaky breath as I closed my eyes.

None of what I didn't understand mattered. I didn't need to understand. I was leaving all that behind.

We all were.

About the Author

Birdy Browne is a new and upcoming author from Atlanta, where she's been churning out compelling stories since the day she learned to write. Although her education took her in the direction of public libraries and psychology, Browne has always had a love for writing. Browne's goal is to create new and unexpected fantasy novels full of complex emotions and morally gray characters.

9 789898 900551 2